BITTERSWEET WORDS

What was he doing in the garden with his wife? He had responded instinctively to the seductive softness in her large brown eyes. He had never before or since his marriage had a lover who could excite him as Emily always had in their years together. Was it simply desire, then, that coursed through his veins? Could it be sated by possessing her body again or was there more than mere lust at work?

"Emily, I . . ." This was not going to be easy. She looked up at him, her eyes full of questions. "Emily, I owe you an apology. A long overdue apology."

"For what?"

She could ask that? Did she really not know?

"I wronged you in many ways and I am sorry. Even if we had fallen out of love, I should never have treated you the way I did."

Emily flinched as if he had struck her. Fallen out of love. He spoke of falling out of love as if it were a mutual thing, but it wasn't. Only he had fallen out of love. Her heart ached with a queer, pulling pain.

"I guess that is the penalty for a marriage such as ours," he continued. "In our parents' day we would not have been allowed to marry for love. Maybe that is wiser after all."

He looked sad, she thought, longing to stroke his face and ease away the lines that time and trouble had placed on his brow. Still so handsome! Still the man who made her heart beat faster and her body ache with longing. . . .

BOOK YOUR PLACE ON OUR WEBSITE AND MAKE THE READING CONNECTION!

We've created a customized website just for our very special readers, where you can get the inside scoop on everything that's going on with Zebra, Pinnacle and Kensington books.

When you come online, you'll have the exciting opportunity to:

- View covers of upcoming books
- Read sample chapters
- Learn about our future publishing schedule (listed by publication month *and author*)
- Find out when your favorite authors will be visiting a city near you
- Search for and order backlist books from our online catalog
- Check out author bios and background information
- Send e-mail to your favorite authors
- Meet the Kensington staff online
- Join us in weekly chats with authors, readers and other guests
- Get writing guidelines
- AND MUCH MORE!

Visit our website at
http://www.zebrabooks.com

LADY DELAFONT'S DILEMMA

Donna Simpson

Zebra Books
Kensington Publishing Corp.

http://www.zebrabooks.com

ZEBRA BOOKS are published by

Kensington Publishing Corp.
850 Third Avenue
New York, NY 10022

First Zebra Printing: August, 2000
10 9 8 7 6 5 4 3 2 1

Printed in the United States of America

For Mick, who dreamed bigger dreams than I ever thought were possible and helped to make them reality.
Thank you for that and so much more!

Books by Donna Simpson

LORD ST. CLAIRE'S ANGEL

LADY DELAFONT'S DILEMMA

Published by Zebra Books

One

"My lady has grown *fat!*"

The words were spat from the lips of a long, lean man, a quizzing glass held to his eye.

"I suppose that explains Prinny's newfound passion for her."

The tall man's companion, a small, elegantly dressed gentleman, sat languidly tapping his fan against the edge of the opera box. The first man whirled to gaze down at him, forgetting the supposed need for the eyeglass.

"Lessington, do you mean to say my lady wife has captured Florrie's wandering eye?" His dark eyebrows raised over equally dark eyes. He had been called saturnine, satanic, and even Luciferian in recent years owing to his dark complexion, black eyes and hair, and his penchant for all black clothing, but mostly for his uncertain temper.

All was not black on Baxter Delafont, Marquess of Sedgely, though. The dark wings of hair at his temples were streaked with silver, and the dour temperament was not always evident. He had been known to soften in the presence of his mistress, Annabelle Gudge, better known by her stage name of Belle Gallant. Intimate friends had noted that at times he treated the sylphlike beauty with an almost paternal affection. At that moment, though, his expression was one of disbelief as he stared at his friend Sylvester Lessington.

That man, at least ten years Delafont's junior, fanned

himself delicately with a chicken-skin fan and replied, "Oh, yes. Prinny is devoted to the marchioness and pays her the most extravagant compliments. Sends her gifts, it is rumored! It is whispered that he has even taken to writing verse—econiums to her grace, beauty and charm."

Delafont raised his eyeglass again and gazed across the heated, noisy opera house at the box occupied by his wife, Emily, his aunt—who was also his wife's companion, he had heard—and their escorts. Good Lord, it was Fawley she was with! That windy sop!

As he watched his wife intently, her head turned, and he could see her gaze off into the distance. For that moment, he knew from experience, she was gone from the crowd. She had always had the ability to leave a crowded place when the heat and noise became too much for her and wander in her mind the lonely hills and moors of her native Yorkshire.

For an instant he, too, was transported back to that moment more than fifteen years ago when he had first seen her. He was on his way to visit distant relatives on a repairing lease. Riding along a country road on a lovely, late-spring day in Yorkshire, he came to a spot where the bridge was washed out and stopped to watch in amusement as a girl he took for a village maiden led a broken-down hack through the stream. She was shoeless, hatless and had her old gown pulled up to reveal dainty ankles and a shapely calf—a dairymaid perhaps or barmaid.

He was not in such a hurry that he minded in the least stopping to flirt with a buxom, pretty maiden, and Emily was pretty, with rosebud lips and big brown eyes. She had been shy but not timid, and the encounter had ended with a stolen kiss, the sweetness of which still lingered on his lips all these years later.

Oh, yes, he could still remember the heavy fullness of her lovely breasts pressed against his waistcoat and the silky feel of her hair as his hand caressed it. His attentions had been teasing until that point, but he recognized in that moment the full urgency of his ardor. She had been naive and sweet, and her innocent passion had sent his pulse racing. He had left her after that blissful interlude determined to seek her out and press his suit once he was settled in his temporary home.

But then it turned out she was a poor but genteel relative of his—a cousin, many times removed—and resided as a kind of companion to his aunt at the house he was visiting. Attracted first by her beauty, he was utterly enslaved by her gentle sweetness and modesty. There was no question of merely tumbling her in the nearest bed or convenient corner; she was of good family, a lady. Wedded bliss was the only way to sample her charms to the full extent that he desired, and since he had fallen deeply in love with her, he needed only to follow his inclinations. Their marriage less than a year later had been the talk of the *ton*.

Though he was not yet the marquess, he was still a viscount with a fat purse and an even more elevated future title as his father's heir. He could have looked much higher for a wife, and indeed his mother was bitterly disappointed in him, but he only wanted Emily. She was, he said, the love of his life.

A tap on his elbow brought him back. "I say, Del, you've gone away on me!" Lessington said peevishly. "You've been staring at your wife in the most vulgar way imaginable, old man. Simply not done! 'Specially when you're separated!"

"Thank you, Less," Del said, caustically. "God knows I would not want to offend your delicate sensibilities."

His biting remark set the other man to laughing, a hearty sound unlike his usual refined titter.

"That's right, think of me, old man. Look, concentrate on your lovely lady bird; the lights are going down and this is her dramatic entrance. She begged me for this part, and as she is your protégé, I gave her a shot. She has not disappointed. Half of London is mad for her already. The male half, anyway."

Delafont, called Del most often by his friends and Baxter only by his wife, settled into his chair and watched Belle Gallant float onto the stage, her tiny, perfect figure swathed in delicate, diaphanous draperies. She was a fairy in *A Midsummer Night's Dream* and had chattered about nothing else when he saw her the previous night. He faced the stage and ostensibly paid sufficient attention to his little lady bird, but his mind stubbornly returned to his glimpse of Emily. He had not seen her for . . . how long? More than a year, more like two, actually. He had been traveling the Continent, which was where he had found the entrancing Belle. Emily, he knew, had been keeping to her lonely Yorkshire estate, but she must have decided this year to brave the London season. Would she be staying all through the spring?

When had she gotten fat, he wondered. She had always been pleasantly rounded, but his glimpse of her had revealed a much fuller bosom, rounder arms and the hint of a double chin. And so Prinny was chasing after her now, eh? She was younger than his usual flirts, being . . . hmmm, thirty-six, he decided. She would be thirty-seven on June fourth, three months away.

And he was forty-two. And Belle Gallant was twenty-one, half his age. And what in God's name was this morbid obsession with numbers? The lights brightened again and Lessington rose.

"End of the last act, old man. Unless you mean to stay for the farce?"

"What? Oh, no, of course not." Del smiled up at his friend. Less was a fribble, to be sure, but an entertaining one. As well as being a successful theater owner twice over, he wrote the most comic and vitriolic verse about the Prince Regent, risking royal censure and imprisonment did he but reveal his true name. But he wrote under the nom de plume of Geste Royale. More than that, though, he was a loyal and good friend, one of the few people Delafont knew he could trust with his life, if need be.

"I thought not," Less said. "It is my theater but even

I cannot abide the farce. It is a necessity, though, or the patrons in the pit will riot. I thought perhaps we would go and get a bite to eat, and you could tell me all your adventures these last two years."

Delafont stood, straightening his pantaloons and coat. "I would like nothing better, Less, but I must look in on the Groveson frolic."

Less made a face.

"Promised Lady Groveson—bosom bow of m'mother. Don't dare put her off."

"What a bore!" Less pouted. His narrow, clever face and mobile mouth made him unusually expressive. His parents had been actors, but despite having a distinct dramatic flair, he had neither the desire nor the temperament to be an actor. With patronage from the elite such as the marquess, he had instead become a theater owner and entitled to entrée into society. He had never been able to assume the correct bored expression of a true dilettante for longer than a few minutes, though, unless he was consciously acting a part, which it must be said he was a great deal of the time. A sparkle of mischief came into his light-gray eyes.

"I have an invitation, believe it or not. Lady Groveson, a high stickler if ever I have seen one, has decided I am amusing. I think I shall attend—I want to be there in case you decide to dance with your lady wife!"

Del shuddered. "I'd sooner waltz with Prinny himself!"

"Don't think you're his type!" Less quipped. "You're not even *my* type. Much too tall."

"Thank you, Bev," Emily Delafont said, smiling up at her escort Lord Fawley as he draped her silk shawl over her bare arms. She turned to make sure her aunt by marriage was following them out of the box.

Dearest Dodo, she thought, as she watched her elderly companion pick up her reticule. It was a treat to be able to accompany her to the theater, something the woman enjoyed above all else. They had been rusticating in York-shire for so long they had had to spend a week when they arrived in London three weeks before just attiring themselves in the new styles so they wouldn't look a quiz as they joined society.

Even before engaging a modiste, though, Emily had sent out a footman to rent boxes at the theater and the opera. If they were going to reenter London society, they must see and be seen at all the most desirable events. Sylvester Lessington's theater had become eminently fash-ionable recently. She hoped she would see dear Less, a friend to both her and her husband, sometime soon.

This spring she had felt, finally, like crawling out of the hole of self-recrimination and anger she had been thrown into by her husband's desertion. Her beloved niece, Celestine Simons—Lady St. Claire now—was newly married, and somehow, seeing new love burgeon like that, she had felt impatient with herself for hiding from life for so long. Dear Celestine was now in Italy on an extended wedding tour that would hopefully, with the heat and dryness of the warmer climes, heal the latest outburst of her arthritis.

And Emily had decided to come to London. She and her husband, Baxter Delafont, the Marquess of Sedgely, had lived separately for nearly five years now, and they should be able to inhabit the same city with impunity. Not that Baxter—most of his friends called him Del, but she preferred his given name—was in London, or even likely to come.

She had heard, through the rumor mill, that he was still gallivanting the Continent, so at least she didn't have to worry about running into him just yet. Worry, she chided herself, as she waited for Dodo. Why should she worry about seeing him? There was no feeling left be-tween them, and it would be the merest awkward moment when they met, and then it would be over.

Fawley took her arm as they descended the stairs to-ward the front doors and their waiting carriage. Lady Dianne Delafont, known as Dodo to her intimates, followed with Major Carson, her escort and fervent admirer.

It was so wonderful to have dear Dodo's support, Emily thought with gratitude, even more so now that she had reentered society. She was Baxter's aunt and the only one in the family who didn't blame her for her husband's desertion. "They," mostly her mother-in-law and everyone within her influence, blamed her even more for not presenting him with an heir before the break, as if it were not what she prayed and wished for and desired above all else.

She hadn't pushed Baxter away—not really. Surely he must have seen how desperately she loved him, how much she had needed his support and approval! She had made no effort to hide that from him. Couldn't he see how she was hurting? It was he who had grown distant and cold, finally putting into words what they had both known for a long time, that their marriage was over in all but name.

He would not divorce her unless *she* desired it, he said, but he would have his freedom. She had been deeply hurt but had not said a word to keep him. After all, if he did not love her enough to work through their problems, then she would not beg. And so a legal bill of separation had been drawn up, and they parted formally. Since they had not been together in the marriage bed for two years, it was a formality only—they were already separated in everything but the legal definition.

But darling Dodo, his father's younger sister, was steadfast in her loyalty and two years ago, when Emily was forced to retreat to Yorkshire, asked to come to Emily as her companion. The good Lord knew she had no need of a home, as she was wealthy in her own right, but she was a wonderful friend and Emily had gratefully accepted.

But Dodo had not been happy in Yorkshire. She hated nature and the harsh, wild clime of Yorkshire and thrived on the theater and people and the kind of crowd that visited literary salons and the opera and crowded routs. She had been ecstatic at the idea of coming back to London.

"Shall we go to the Groveson ball, Dodo?" she asked over her shoulder, as they reached a landing where the stairs turned.

Dianne 'Dodo' Delafont, sixty-three years of age and a spinster, gazed down at her niece. Her dark eyes sparkled and a girlish expression lit her narrow, long-jawed face. "Could we? I would love it above all things, if you desire it, Em."

"Then let us be dissipated and drink champagne and waltz until dawn!" Emily laughed. "And maybe you will be surrounded by beaux and dance every dance."

The elderly spinster's expression became arch. "Perhaps, if the major will dance . . . ."

Major Carson, a bluff, upright, rigorously martial man, turned from berating the couple in front of them, who dawdled on the stairs, blocking their progress, and said, "What? Dance? I don't dance—never have!"

Lord Fawley, ever polite, stepped into the breech. "If Lady Dianne would honor me, I would be proud to bespeak the first dance on her card."

Emily squeezed his arm affectionately. Beverley Fawley, Viscount Sumter, was the sweetest man in London, a city not known for good people. He was sweet and sane and trustworthy. She never had to worry about his motives in escorting her, no matter how much people gossiped, because she knew he was not interested in a dalliance. She had a feeling that there was a tragic romance in his past or even unrequited love in his present, but she never pressed him about it. Maybe that delicacy was why he clung to her in the swirl of bitter gossip that was London society. She turned back to descend the rest of the stairs, as the blockage seemed to have eased. She glanced down to the bottom, where a chandelier brightly lit the foyer and gasped, stumbling and only kept from falling by Fawley's grip.

"Em, whatever is wrong, dear girl?" he asked, setting her to rights.

She was speechless, staring down into a pair of cold, black eyes. Her knees weakened, but she resolutely clung to her escort. Baxter Delafont in London! She would *not* let her long-absent husband see how much the first sight of him in two years had affected her. But if she could have sunk into a hole that very second, she would gladly have done so.

Delafont House, an elegant town home in Mayfair, presented a tidy, calmly decorous face to the square within which it was situated. A fenced park was across the cobbled street from it, a small green patch of peace and prosperity in which the neighborhood dogs were exercised and nannies took their tiny charges for daily airing.

The house itself was high and narrow, one of the middle in a block of four—one was vacant, one dwelt in year-round by a rich, retired surgeon and one rented out to a bumptious country squire and his noisy brood of children. He had brought them and his tired wife to fire off his eldest daughter on the marriage mart.

The squire and his lady had called that morning in early March and sat in the parlor sipping tea with Emily. She listened patiently while the squire, a Mr. Duff, expounded on how little he liked to take his attention away from his farms and crops, but his duty to his daughter, a taking little thing, he said, was more important. She had a chance at a title, it was said, and he wasn't going to stand in his little girl's way.

Emily appeared to listen and even responded on occasion, but she contemplated with most of her mind the previous evening's sighting of her estranged husband. How handsome he looked, she thought sadly. And how supercilious his expression as he gazed up at her, clutching onto Fawley's arm like a fainthearted widgeon. Baxter had said nothing to her, but then, he didn't need to. His look said everything.

She spread her hands out on her lap as she nodded politely to Squire Duff. She glanced down at her wedding ring, her only adornment. It was an oval-cut ruby of unusually deep color and impeccable cut. She had been a girl of twenty-one when she had accepted it—a girl who looked forward to a life of bliss with the man she loved deeply and completely.

How time had changed all. Now she lived alone with a companion, like a dowager, though her husband was still vibrantly alive and handsomer than ever.

What errant nonsense, she thought, bringing herself up sharply. Baxter Delafont was a cold, emotionally stunted villain and the fact that he was still the handsomest man she had ever seen had nothing to do with anything. It was not his looks she had fallen in love with, it was who she had thought he was—a warm, giving, tender man. She was wrong.

The last time she had seen him was two years ago when he called on her to suggest—nay, *order*—her retirement to the Yorkshire house, which he deeded to her clear and free. She was entitled to stay at the Delafont seat, Brockwith Manor in Surrey, but the dowager lived there and she and Emily had never gotten along. So she had gone to Yorkshire, and had not been back to London since, feeling too humiliated by her banishment to hold her head up among the *ton*. It was with a broken spirit and wounded soul that she crawled away to the north country.

What had changed? Why had she, one cold, bleak January morning, awoken to the clear knowledge that she was missing life and must go to London? She had grown restless, she thought, since her Christmas visit to Cumbria, where she witnessed her niece, a governess to good friends of hers, fall in love and marry a young man of rakish leanings who had, surprisingly, fallen deeply in love with her.

But that could not be the only explanation. Perhaps it

had just been the impetus that had led her to explore her life and find it sadly wanting. There were many changes in her, she thought. She had gained weight over the last couple of years, at least two or three stone, and knew she presented a sadly different appearance to friends with whom she had become reacquainted. She saw it in their eyes as they greeted her—heard it in their pause before they assured her she was looking marvelous. Baxter was as lean and handsome as ever and she was as round as a pudding. How apt were culinary metaphors, she thought wryly. Food was important in Yorkshire through the long dreary winter.

Rare roast beef with suet pudding, scones with fresh butter, cook's famous Banbury cakes—all those homely delights whiled away dark winter evenings by the fire as she and Dodo played piquet. And all the while Baxter was traveling in sunny Italy and the Greek Isles.

But she had found a measure of serenity in the last two years, too, as some of the splintered pieces of her heart fused. It might not be whole again, but it beat stronger and steadier for two years of contemplation. She had felt ready to take on society once more, daunting as it could sometimes be to someone who preferred the country. And although that new serenity had been shaken by the sight of her husband and the knowledge that he, too, was in London, it would not send her scurrying back to the safety of Yorkshire.

Emily was awoken from her daydreams by the stir of her guests. The tired-looking wife of the loquacious squire was examining her kindly and saying, "I'm sure you must have been wishing for us to go this age, my lady, and so we will take our leave. If we might beg your indulgence, could we bring our daughter, Eudora, to meet you sometime?"

Emily, afraid she had been intolerably rude while lost in thought, found herself agreeing with more enthusiasm than she would have thought possible. "Oh, please do, for it is such a treat to have visitors!"

When they were gone, she rang for more tea and was joined by Dodo. The older woman gazed at her over her spectacles, shrewdly assessing her hag-ridden face and tired eyes.

"My dear, why do you not go back to bed? I am sure you must not have slept a wink all night."

"As bad as that?" Emily laughed, putting her hands to her cheeks. "I cannot imagine how I would look if we *had* gone to the Groveson ball last night after all. I must increase my stamina to enjoy all the delights of the season."

"My poor child, do not try to fool me. I was an aging spinster before you were born. That encounter with Del was a shock to you, yes?"

Ruefully realizing that she could not evade this particular inquisition, she nodded. "I do not know why, Dodo dear, unless it was just so unexpected. Baxter is nothing to me, nor I to him! But to see him so suddenly . . . ."

Dodo compressed her thin lips until they were a straight line. She shook her head and sighed. "Two foolish children," she murmured.

Emily bristled. "I am not the foolish one. I never asked for this separation, and Baxter could very well . . . ."

Trumble, the butler, swept the door open at that moment and announced, "Her ladyship, the Dowager Marchioness of Sedgely."

Emily gasped and flushed, standing hurriedly as her mother-in-law swept into the room in a swirl of ermine and velvet, swathed to the chin despite the moderating temperatures outside. Dodo rolled her eyes but approached her sister-in-law and dutifully kissed the faintly lined and powdered cheek.

"Don't stand there gawping, girl," the dowager said to Emily. "Pour me some tea. It is perishing cold outside, as my driver would say." Lady Marie shrugged out of her fur-trimmed pelisse, rightly judging that a footman would be there to catch it before it ever fell to the floor.

"Cold it is not, Marie," Dodo pronounced, giving

Emily time to come to her senses. "After you have experienced a few winters in Yorkshire, nothing will ever feel cold to you again. It is positively warm out there."

Emily hurriedly poured a steaming cup of tea from the tray that had just been delivered by swift, efficient hands, and gave it to her now-seated mother-in-law.

"What . . . what a pleasant surprise to see you, Mother," Emily stuttered.

"Nonsense. You're not pleased at all. In fact you are horrified," Lady Delafont announced, with some satisfaction. "I am a little horrified myself to be here, if you must know. I was pried from my comfortable Bath existence by a very disturbing letter I had from a dear friend, Lady Shelburne."

Emily and Dodo exchanged looks. Bath? So after prying Emily out of Brockwith Manor, Marie had not even stayed there but had retreated to her home in Bath. Emily had suspected from the beginning that her mother-in-law only stayed at Brockwith out of some perverse desire to annoy her son's wife.

"By the way, Emily," the dowager said, glaring at her, "you are much changed. Whatever do you mean by getting so fat? How can you win back my son when you look like a pudding bag with eyes?"

Dodo's mouth took on that grim, compressed look again, and she said, "Now look here, Marie, I know you were wont to badger the poor child in past days but—"

"Dodo, it is not necessary to engage in my fight." Emily smiled at her companion, then turned to her mother-in-law. She took a deep breath and stiffened her spine. "I have no desire to win back your wretched son, my lady. It was not I who created the rift, and so it is not up to me to heal it. Not that it ever could be healed. He said the most unspeakable things to me when last we spoke—at your behest, I might add—and I have no desire to ever see him again."

Lady Marie Delafont's pale-blue eyes narrowed. She gazed steadily at her daughter-in-law, looking her up and down with a fishy stare. "Ain't increasing with some other man's brat, are you?"

Emily gasped and in quivering outrage, stood, sweeping back the skirt of her dress and holding her head high. "I think you have said everything you possibly can to insult and defame me, ma'am. I suggest you leave."

The woman took a sip of tea. "Do not fly up into the boughs, Emily. I was merely asking. You have become notorious now that the Regent has written a poem calling you his . . . what was it . . . his 'darling dumpling'?"

Emily flushed in anger and plunked down on the sofa, unaware that she had caused Dodo to spill tea over the rug. "I cannot believe that rubbish made it all the way to Bath! Of course, with gabblemongers like Lady Shelburne around, it is no wonder. His Highness has been very kind to me on the two or three occasions when we have met, and simply because some odious verse merchant put the Prince's name to a scurrilous piece of nonsense . . . ."

"You mean the Prince did not write it?" The dowager's gaze was direct and challenging.

"Of course not! Do you think the Prince's superb artistic sense would produce such execrable drivel, not to mention the fact that his Highness's honor would never allow him to compromise a lady in such a way. And how did that miserable publisher get a copy of a piece produced by our Regent?"

"If what you say is true, my dear, we must set about immediately to refute it."

Emily sighed impatiently. "Surely, my lady, you know that to even acknowledge the existence of such rubbish and deny it is to give it credibility. And there is no way to deny it without impugning the honor of his Highness. It is a pickle, but there is no way out."

"Nonsense," Lady Delafont said briskly. "There is always a way. Then we can set about making you presentable again and get you back with my son so you can produce an heir before you are too old, if you haven't dried up already."

Emily felt like shrieking with frustration but held back, only pointing a cold stare at her mother-in-law as she stood to face her. "My lady," she said, her voice dripping ice, "nothing on this earth, and only God himself in heaven, could send me back to that coldhearted beast you call son. We are through forever and for all time. My dislike for him is only exceeded by his distaste for me. And I do *not* care to lose weight!"

On that note Emily turned and with graceful dignity left the room, spoiling the exit utterly by tripping on the carpet.

Two

Belle squealed in pleasure and whirled around her dressing room—little more than a closet she shared with three other girls—in a youthful display of high spirits. Mocking her, Baxter Delafont covered his ears and groaned.

"Please, Belle! With that caterwauling I can't tell if my little trinket pleases you or not!"

The girl, slim and supple as a willow sapling, whirled again past her casually abandoned dresses and shifts discarded over a nearby chair, landing inelegantly in the marquess's lap. He expelled a lungful of air in a *whoof.*

"I love it, Del! You know I do!" Lolling on his lap, clad only in her shift and stockings, she held the diamond and sapphire collar up to the candlelight. She threw her arms around his neck and squeezed. "You are too good to me, luvey!"

Delafont grimly reflected that if she wanted to return the favor she would get off his trick knee, which was aching abominably. He couldn't resist the girl's joy, though. He remembered her as he had first found her with a barbaric Cockney accent, tawdry finery and an ugly bruiser of an employer-protector. She had been traveling the Continent with the lowest type of acting troupe, which performed bawdy and salacious skits for any and all who would pay tuppence.

Del had been traveling as a way to escape the tedium of home, or at least that was what he told himself and anyone else who asked. As a diversion, he and a couple of friends had attended the tent show when they stopped temporarily near Milan to rest their horses. The show had been almost obscene, some of the performances bordering on representations of sexual acts, and Baxter had been on the point of leaving. In fact, he had already left the tent when he heard a commotion near a cart that served as the show's headquarters.

Belle, or Annabelle Gudge as she had been christened, was being abused by her foul employer. The man was battering her around the head while she screeched out vituperation at him, kicking and scratching like a tiny tiger. At first he had not been sure if the slender figure was a child or an adult, but in either case he was bound by his own code to intervene on behalf of a party so much the weaker. He waded into the fray, got a bloody nose but thankfully nothing worse, and pulled Belle away from the man, a huge behemoth with fists like hams.

When the fellow saw the way things were, and perhaps the quality of Del's jacket, he retreated. Belle was fired immediately, and Del was saddled with a pathetically grateful but very common little wench. She couldn't have been more than eighteen or nineteen at the time, though it was hard to tell, she was so skinny and dirty.

She absolutely refused to leave his side. He had offered her money, thinking at least to keep her from her present life for a while, but she looked at him with a wounded expression that surprised him. She might not know much, she said, in a barely understandable street accent, but she knew enough to know that she owed him, not the other way around, and she was going to find some way to repay him for rescuing her. Giving in to the inevitable he hired a tutor to restrain the worst of her accent, and she surprised everyone by blossoming quickly into a very comely, enthusiastic young woman. It was touching how grateful she was.

But then she started pleading to become his mistress, convinced it was the only way she could repay him. He had said no, had been adamant. But she cried and stormed and wheedled, and finally got him drunk and seduced him. It was no excuse. He hadn't wanted her so much as he was lonely and had not been with a woman for too long. And she seemed to want him so very badly; perhaps that had been the charm. He had never needed a boost to his opinion of himself, but Emily's rejection of him had left him shaken.

He would never forget the last time he had bedded his previously passionate wife. Things had been deteriorating between them for a year or more, but at least they always had their passion for each other. But that last time she had lain in his arms like a fence post, neither giving nor apparently receiving any pleasure from the act.

And so Belle's obvious desire for him was a powerful aphrodisiac. Maybe he had used his intoxication to rationalize the deed, but the end result was that he bedded her, and after that there was no retreating; she would not allow it.

She was no ingenuous virgin. Though she didn't speak of it much, he gathered that she had been sleeping with men for years, for the first time when she was perhaps as young as ten. It was a miracle she didn't have syphilis or a couple of bastards following her about. He suspected from hints she had dropped that she had miscarried a couple of times, though it was something of which she had never spoken.

Her life had been unbelievably brutal, and he felt sorry for her. She expressed an interest in being an actress, and so after a time together traveling Europe, he sent her ahead to London with a letter of introduction to Sylvester Lessington, one of London's premier theater owners and an old and valued friend, and she had started her illustrious career as Belle Gallant, opera dancer extraordinaire.

By the time he got back to London, her career was in full swing, and he assumed that their brief affair was over, but no, she was still grateful and still determined to be his mistress, she had told him the night before. It was not as if she didn't have other offers. There were several young bucks desperate to take her under their protection. She treated them all with an airy disdain, according to Less, that drove them all mad with frustration.

She was no longer the ragtag little waif he had first taken under his wing but had blossomed into a lithe, pretty butterfly. Her golden hair was soft and glinted in the stage lights and her skin had the dewy perfection of youth, a very fetching bundle indeed, and a very loyal one.

This night was his second back in town, the night after seeing his wife and having the dubious satisfaction of seeing her quail under his gaze. His first order of business had been buying the trinket for Belle, but now he had real business to attend to. Gently, he disengaged her arms from around his neck and pushed her off his lap.

He stood, wincing at the pain in his knee, which creaked as he moved, and said, "I must be going, my dear. There is a man awaiting me."

"Wouldn't you rather I come back to your town house with you," she purred, rubbing her sinuous body against his in a display of erotic abandon he had at first found enchantingly provocative.

Unfortunately, Belle was a one-note symphony where lovemaking was concerned—all youthful eagerness and demanding energy. Del suspected that she would cheerfully do it anywhere, even on the floor in her dressing room. His tastes were more sophisticated, and he longed for the more drawn out eroticism of an older woman, one more willing to put off immediate gratification for the gradual banking of the fires of passion, leading to a taste of heaven at the end of hours of love play.

He sighed.

"Belle, I really must go. Are your accommodations to your liking?" He placed his hands gently on her shoulders and put her firmly from him.

Her tiny mouth drew down in a pout that might have

been charmingly childlike, if Del had cared for that sort of thing. All her childishness did for him was make him feel like an aging satyr. She turned away, caressing the jeweled collar he had just given her.

"I suppose," she answered. "But I don't see why I cannot live with you."

"Belle, I have explained before. It just cannot be. This is London, not the Continent, and things are very different here. I have a reputation to uphold." He suppressed another spurt of irritation at her importunity. He leaned over and kissed her brow. "Good night, my dear. Tomorrow night I will come to you, I promise."

Her voice tight with pique, she said, "Good night, Del."

Surely it wasn't relief he felt, the marquess wondered, as he left the side entrance of the theater. What was wrong with him that he did not really feel up to bedding that adorable creature? He realized the feeling had been coming on for quite a while. He felt, in some absurd way, paternal toward Belle. She was, after all, his creation.

She had been a vulgar little guttersnipe when she had attached herself to him with limpetlike firmness. Unable to bear her as she was, he had made her over, and then she had become his mistress. Would he have chosen her out of that night's theater cast for seduction it there were no other history between them?

No. In all honesty he was more attracted to the leading lady, Felice DeMornay, a woman of mature attraction and sophistication. He strode down the dark street, the nip of spring air a welcome tonic for his exhaustion. There were no two ways about it, he was going to have to let Belle go as his mistress. But she seemed sincerely attached to him, so how to do it without breaking the poor young thing's heart? It was a puzzle he would have to solve before long.

Emily drifted from the refreshment room into the main ballroom of the Jersey mansion. Sally Jersey was always an amusing hostess, but for some reason this evening's entertainment felt flat. She glanced across the ballroom with some amusement at her companion.

Dodo had quite her own court of aging military gents crowding her. Though she had never complained in the two years they had lived at Emily's home in Yorkshire, she really did not like the long, cold winter nights, nor the wild hills and sometimes dreary countryside. She belonged in London amid the social hurricane of gossip and parties and balls. Her advanced years did not change that fact.

A touch of Emily's elbow made her whirl around.

"Mr. Lessington!" she cried, seeing that the small, elegantly dressed gentleman was the one who had accosted her.

Lessington made a graceful leg. "Your servant, my lady, though I am hurt that you no longer feel free to call me Less, as you used to do. What a delight to see you gracing the salons and ballrooms of London again. I heard weeks ago that you had come home, but we have not yet chanced to be at the same frivolity. Whatever made you decide to join the land of the living for the season?"

At first Emily had been rather pleased to see the man in front of her, but she abruptly remembered that Lessington and her husband were intimate friends, and that Baxter might be anywhere. Her eyes darted around the room in sudden nervousness.

"Del is not here . . . yet," Lessington said, with the hint of an amused smile on his narrow face.

"I—I was not . . ." A rueful smile crossed Emily's normally placid face. "You know me too well, Less. How I have missed you these past few years." She took his offered arm, their heights matching so well that their shoulders rubbed companionably, and they strolled around the crowded ballroom, chatting desultorily about absent friends and present enemies—all the tittle-tattle of London life. At least some of the windows had been opened, so the room was not so stifling hot as it might have been.

But still, the mingled scent of hundreds of people—their body odor and their perfumes—was overpowering.

Emily squeezed the man's arm as they paused near a window, and she drank greedily of the fresh air that puffed in past the heavy draperies. Lessington had been a good friend during the worst of her and Baxter's breakup, and yet he had managed to stay close to her husband as well.

He was an unlikely friend for Baxter Delafont, many said. Delafont was lean and saturnine, dark of visage and mind. Lessington was a good-natured fribble, with a rapier-sharp wit and a light, breezy nature. Yet behind his scathing tongue and brilliant eye lay a man of intense human compassion. He understood pain more deeply than others and offered just the right blend of sympathy, bracing good sense and humor. Few had had the opportunity to catch sight of that side of him, but he had been a friend to Emily, and she had once ruined one of his best coats crying on his shoulder over her breakup with her husband.

Tonight his sartorial splendor stretched to pale-blue breeches, lemon yellow waistcoat and a peacock-blue cutaway coat, nipped in at the waist and shot with silver threads that glittered in the shimmering light from the chandeliers and wall sconces. He looked the perfect elegant peacock, with a variety of quizzing glasses and fobs attached to his waistcoat. Emily looked into his intelligent, light-gray eyes.

"How is he, Less?"

He gazed over at her with a quizzical smile. He did not need to ask of whom she inquired. "And why would you want to know that? Do you care?"

"Of . . . of course not, but I may still inquire, may I not? We are still married." Her voice was low and quiet, barely carrying over the orchestra and chatter of the crowd.

"Of course, my dear," he said, patting her hand where it lay on his arm. "Del is . . . hardened. Embittered. He has come back from abroad even more cynical and jaded than when he left."

Emily sighed. "Why am I not all amazement at that news? Rumor has stated that he has a child mistress."

Lessington shuddered. "Annabelle Gudge," he said darkly, his pale brows drawn down over his gray eyes. "She has been 'reborn in the person of Belle Gallant."

"But 'twas she in the play the other night at your theater, was it not? She was the wood sprite that caught everyone's attention so. She is lovely. Why the shudder?" Emily slanted a curious gaze over at her companion, then hastily nodded her recognition to a couple who were passing. It would not do to offend anyone, now that she was back among the *ton*.

"My dear, she is a complete little primitive. She is pretty in a very common way, but she is a tart, and she has no conversation!"

That last indictment was Lessington's most severe condemnation. Conversation, and not always just gossip, was his lifeblood. Emily felt that there was much more there, but did not want to probe for fear of seeming too curious. And really, what did it matter to her whom Baxter took into his bed? A small frisson of pain shot through her heart, and she reluctantly admitted to herself that perhaps it did matter, just the tiniest bit.

She supposed it was partly jealousy that Baxter could expend his sexual energy on someone else, and Emily had never been with anyone but him. She could have had affairs, perhaps, but she still felt very married. She meant the nuptial vows when she spoke them, and only death could end that. She had been such a green girl when she and Baxter had fallen in love and married. He had introduced her to the world of sensual love, and she would never forget those nights when they were first wed.

She had matured, and was now a sophisticated society matron, but at heart she was very much still that same naive Yorkshire country girl. Taking a lover would require a level of sophistication and worldliness that she could not even pretend to. It just wasn't in her, she thought. She allowed other men to escort her places, for after all, one could not remain in seclusion if one came to London for the season. Lord Fawley was always available to take her anywhere and was an undemanding companion for an evening. But she still had no desire to take someone to bed.

Or so she told herself. If there were nights when a longing to be held and made love to overwhelmed her, she could ignore it in the daytime. Years of tamping down her sexuality had left her with a great deal of control, and sometimes she wondered if the passionate young woman she had once been was now just a memory. Certainly the bitterness between her and Baxter in the latter years of their lives together had put an effective damper on desire. She had felt nothing the last time they made love, though she remembered it well for the sadness she had felt after, and for the tears that flowed all night after he left her bed to return to his own, something he had never done before.

But it would not do to get maudlin now! She was in London, and she had recovered from her depression, and she was with a good and valued friend. She remembered her mother-in-law's visit of the day before. Less would appreciate the true hideousness of that little contretemps, and so she told him the story as they continued on their slow perambulation of the ballroom. Less laughed in all the right places as Emily described the dowager's critical eyeing of her figure, question about her increasing and pronouncement that she must get back together with Baxter and produce an heir.

They stood and watched the figures of a country dance for a few minutes, the girls in their white gowns floating like young fairies, the men in their sober hues joining and parting from the ladies. Less glanced over at her again.

He cleared his throat. "My dear, you have gained a little weight, you know."

Miserably, Emily glanced down at her rounded figure and then back up at her friend. "You think I don't know that?" she asked, with a hint of frost in her voice.

Less squeezed her arm. "It was not meant as a criticism, my dear. Just concern that you are unhappy and are taking out your worries at the dinner table."

Emily smiled, the quick flare of anger dissipated. She was too happy to see Less again to stay angry at him when she knew he did not mean to interfere or criticize. "Perhaps I am. Food is soothing sometimes. But I have found peace in these last two years, my friend. I have learned who I am inside and found that I am a good person who didn't deserve what Baxter did to me—the way he discarded me like an old newspaper."

She saw her friend's mobile face shutter and hurriedly said, "I am not going to criticize him to you. I know how you feel about him, and I would never place you in the middle of us. Remember, I didn't, even when the break was new and raw. I certainly am not going to start now that it is old and healed."

Lessington sighed. "I only wish Del had half your philosophy. If you have found peace, I am glad, but I wish you could impart the secret to your husband. He is bitter, Em, to the core. He conceals it well but . . . ."

"Well, what do I see here?"

A familiar drawl that sent shivers up her spine and made Lessington's head whip around interrupted their talk. It was Delafont, standing before them in his crisp, elegant black evening wear. Emily felt the blood drain from her face. There would be no escaping as there had been the night at the theater, no hasty brushing past with down-turned eyes. Perhaps this was inevitable, but that did not make it any easier.

"Del!" Lessington recovered first and greeted his friend more heartily than was his wont.

"Less," Del said evenly. He turned to his wife. "Emily, how are you?"

"Baxter. I . . . I am well."

"You look in exceedingly good health."

Emily reflected bitterly that that was Baxter's way of saying she was fat. "I am," she said, a trifle too loudly. "I am in perfect health thanks to the bracing Yorkshire air."

A couple beside them watched avidly. All society was aware that the Marquess of Sedgely and his wife lived apart, and so they watched to catch any scandalous tidbits of acrimony to spread among society.

Del's gaze sharpened at her words. "You must be careful, or you will have all of society trooping to Yorkshire to test the air as a curative. And would that not disturb the quietude that you so enjoy?"

"There is little threat of that, my lord, as the cure is not for physical ailments but for those of the mind only."

"There are enough ailments of the mind in the upper ten thousand to fill the Yorkshire countryside, you may be sure."

Emily had not another word to offer. She had thought her heart proof against her husband, but she found being in his company hideous torture. What was it about his voice, his eyes, his presence, that caused emotion and pain to thrum through her sensation-deadened body?

He was a handsome man, granted. He was lean and dark and compelling, and when dressed all in black evening dress, he caused the strangest sensations in her stomach. Unbidden, pictures of their nights together tormented her. She knew every inch of his glorious, lean body, and her own started a strange vibrating chorus of desires, her breasts tingling, her hands unconsciously clenching and unclenching, and her most secret, inner spots growing amorous at the thought of the fulfillment his body had given hers in other times. She thought that she was past any passionate response to him or any man, but it seemed that she was not. He still affected her.

Aware that he was watching her, waiting for her next verbal parry, she turned to Less. She could not speak. It was so lowering to find that after all this time her husband still affected her senses, sending them reeling with desire, that she was stunned into silence and her normal composure was absent. Less gazed into her eyes, saw the mute appeal in them perhaps and rushed to speech.

"Del, I did not think you meant to come to the ball until later. Much later. Did you not have some business to take care of?"

As the two friends chatted, without the need for Emily's attention, she strove to regain control of her unruly responses to her husband's mere presence. She would not have him know her feelings; it was too humiliating. It was easier to calm herself once she thought again of their last meeting. It had been at Brockwith Manor as he requested that she leave, so his mother could live there in peace. As it there was not enough room in that huge Palladian pile for them both to exist without even seeing each other for months at a time!

They had, as always, fallen into an argument, and Baxter had said, out of the blue, "Perhaps you should sleep in some other man's bed, Emily. Then if you don't get with child, you will know to stop blaming me for our inability to conceive!"

His voice had been icy, and Emily had been totally at sea as to how that old wound had been reopened when they had not even been speaking of children. Of course she had reacted with anger. How dare he suggest she was at fault for their brangling? Their argument had become even more vicious, then, and had ended in a screaming match. She had fled to her room, and he had been gone when next she descended, leaving only a note of instructions and the information that in future he would deal with her through his solicitor. That was two years ago now. She had packed up her belongings within weeks and departed for Yorkshire, to be joined shortly afterward by her aunt by marriage, Dodo Delafont.

She became aware that Less was addressing her again and smiled at him.

"He is gone, my dear. You may emerge from your brown study and tell me where you have been."

Emily gave a rueful laugh. "Is it that obvious when I do that?"

"Only to those who know you. What were you thinking? I thought I saw anger on your pretty face."

Rather than reveal her thoughts, she said, "Pretty? Oh, Less! Don't flatter me, I know I am sadly changed."

He sighed. "Emily, my dear heart—"

"No!" Emily put up one hand. "It is really not something that concerns me. I have changed outside and in. But I know what others see. I know what Baxter sees. His own mother called me . . . what was it? Something like 'a pudding with eyes.'"

Lessington did not respond with one of his usual bright sallies. He turned to her and said, "My dear, you are still so beautiful, if you could only see yourself as others see you. And that is not empty ballroom flattery, but God's own truth. And you have not gained so very much weight, my dear."

He held her at arm's length and looked her over critically, his eyes traveling down her body with an assessing gleam. "Not even two stone. I'll warrant some would say the bounty of your décolletage alone is worth it."

She flushed and he chuckled, but fell to silence as he glanced across the room. "Oh, Lord, that bore Fawley is coming this way, and there is more yet that I want to say to you. May I call on you, dear heart? I have something of importance to discuss with you, something that requires privacy"

"What is wrong, Less?" Emily saw the tightening of the man's jaw and the worried look that marred his normally pleasant expression. "Is it something about your family? Or are you sick?"

"No. It is not myself about whom I would speak with you. It's Delafont. Emily, I must talk to you about Delafont. I am frightened for him, for his life, and I think you are the only who can help him."

Three

For just that barest moment, Delafont thought, as he walked away from Less and his wife, he had seen her—the girl he had married. When Emily first looked at him, her eyes had widened into those twin, pansy brown pools, her dewy, rosy lips had parted and she had stared at him with something that dressed in a semblance of the desire he had once awakened in her luscious, innocent body.

And his own traitorous body had responded instinctively, sending that unmistakable, urgent summons trilling through his bloodstream, heeding the siren call of the prey leading the hunter on with smoldering glances and delicious tremors of need. At one time Emily could glance at him from across a crowded ballroom, her unspoken "I want you" darting through the heaviest crowd, and he would feel a surge of lust pounding through his veins in answer as he watched her slip away.

He would make some excuse to their hosts and follow her, whispering in her ear what he planned to do to her when he got her alone. They were barely able to contain themselves, sometimes, until they got into the carriage before flinging themselves at each other. On occasion they had not even waited to get home before coupling in frantic need in the dim interior of his sumptuous carriage, only to repeat the experience more leisurely once in the safe haven of his room. The memory of that halcyon period lingered within him still as the happiest years of his life.

When had that changed? How had something so powerful died?

It had not been sudden. There had been no unforgivable deed or horrible occurrence to separate them. Through the years a word here, a look there, a pointed criticism, a barbed comment—all had conspired to lower the temperature between them until it got frosty, like early autumn descending in August. Lust had cooled; sexual encounters had become infrequent and less heated.

Others had helped in the disenchantment—his mother and father, well-meaning friends and relatives—somehow it had all combined to finally end in rows and vituperative recriminations. And so their marriage had died, on the rack of anger and bitterness.

Delafont left the Jersey ball and strolled back toward his town house through the odorous city streets. In those first few seconds he had seen all of the embittered detachment fall away from Emily like petals from a flower. Her face had been naked in its emotional response to his presence, a response compounded, maybe, of old desire and leftover love. And then he had seen her go off in one of her trances, and the familiar bitterness had marred her expression, lining her formerly smooth brow and darkening her eyes. He had taken his leave of Less, then, and strolled on, a dull ache in his chest.

What did he want of Emily? Did he approach her to torture her? It must be that, for he could think of no other reason why he gravitated to her side when they clearly couldn't stand the sight of each other. He wanted her to share his own pain, the unhealed wound of their failed marriage that still scarred his soul, as they had shared love and passion at one time.

Lost in his thoughts he did not hear the footsteps behind him. But he felt the cosh as it slugged into his neck at the base of his skull, and he felt the ground as he crashed to it, his trick knee folding under him like a rotten tree limb.

And then he didn't feel anything.

* * *

Even if there had been no other reason to choose the sitting room of Delafont House to occupy on a spring morning, the brilliant sunshine that streamed through the window and the fact that it faced the park opposite would have been enough. But the sitting room was lovely, too, decorated in cream and ivory, with accents in pale blue and rose. It was Emily's favorite room in the house, and the one where she sat even when alone. But Less had said he would call.

He had been annoyingly obscure the night before, not willing to elaborate on his dramatic statement. She had not believed he was serious at first, but a restless night of thought had convinced her that her old friend surely would not frighten her for nothing. But was this supposed threat literal or figurative? One could not always tell with Less.

Trumble came to the door of the sitting room. "Mr. Lessington," he announced.

Emily looked up in pleasure from her embroidery. "Less, how nice to see you!"

"I told you I would come and here I am, early for me."

Trumble closed the door and Lessington came to sit beside Emily, admiring her needlework with a critical eye.

"Very nice design, my dear," he said. "Very Oriental, in the current style. What was your inspiration, for I believe I espy one of your own designs?"

"You are right. How good of you to remember my passion for creating my own work. It is my depiction of a seraglio, or will be when it is done. Unfit subject for a lady, no doubt, but the one that appeals to me at the moment. I designed it to while away a long winter in Yorkshire but have had little time for it since we arrived in London." She laid her work aside and took her friend's hands. She chafed them between her own.

"It must be cold out," she commented, looking out

the window at the bright spring sunshine. "Your hands are freezing."

"You know me. I am seldom warm enough." He shivered.

They spoke on neutral topics for a few minutes, but then a silence fell between them, and Emily waited patiently for Less to bring the reason for his visit. His words the previous night seemed dramatic and overstated in the daylight, but he must have something to say. Why he would think she could or would help her husband was beyond her, but she would hear him out at the very least before sending him on his way with a flea in his ear.

Finally he cleared his throat and glanced up with a frankly assessing expression on his mobile face. "I need to know your true feelings about Del, my dear, with no anger or bitterness, no remembered hate. Just the plain mutton with no sauce."

Her first instincts were to pour out all of her feelings about his treatment of her and how they could not be together anymore without acrimony, but that was not what he was asking for. She drew her eyebrows together and looked down at her plain rose muslin gown.

What did she feel for her husband? She still desired him, and that was maddening in the extreme, humiliating, in fact, when she knew that he didn't—*couldn't*—share her feelings. She was angry with him. She hated him . . . no. No, that wasn't true.

Delicately she probed around the edges of her emotion, as if it were a bruise to be hesitantly tested until she learned just how much it was going to hurt. When Less said Baxter was in danger, her first thought had been a jolt of fear. Her husband, in danger? What could she do, how could she help him, protect him, keep him from harm?

She would lay down her life to save his, if it was necessary.

How mortifying. She still loved him, after everything. Even pain had not been able to eradicate the fervent, deep attachment she felt for him. Did that indicate a lack of respect for herself, that she should love him still after the things he had said to her? She hoped not—didn't really think so. After all, if she had no self-respect she would have thrown herself at his feet the moment she saw him again and begged him to make love to her. But she did still love him. She looked up into Less's kind gray eyes.

He smiled over at her. "I thought so. Good."

"Good?" she said, rising from the sofa and pacing the length of the room, not surprised that he could divine what she felt. He had ever had the unnerving ability to look into her eyes and understand her feelings. "It most assuredly is not good. I love him, Less. I still love him, after all these years, just as if we had never been apart."

She went to the window and gazed out at the park across the street. A black-clad nanny wheeled a pram through the gate and headed through the park with her charge. Green, tender leaves unfurled in the trees, filtering the harsh sunlight into lacy patterns on the gravel walk. It was a scene of hope and rebirth, the new season eradicating the signs of a dirty winter in the city, but she could not feel that bud of hope and renewal. She crossed her arms and hugged herself.

"I don't know if my love is just the remains of what we had, or if it still exists for the man as he now is. He hates me, Less, and I don't know what I ever did to him. He can't even look at me without that supercilious sneer on his face. When he sees me . . . ." Her words trailed off as a couple of hot tears welled up and rolled silently down her cheeks.

Less came up behind her and put his gentle hands on her shoulders as they shook with sobs. "Please, Em, don't cry! I did not come here to make you cry! I love you, you silly girl, and I hate to see you unhappy."

When she half turned, startled, he said, "Not like that, widgeon! I love you in the same way I love Del. He is my dearest friend, and he is driving me to distraction!"

Her tears forgotten, Emily turned and took Less's hands in her own, chafing them again. They started to warm under her plump, pink hands.

"How the *ton* would stare to hear you speak like that! They all think you are a heartless dilettante, like Brummel. But what are you talking about, Less? What's wrong with Baxter?"

"Two things. He is deeply unhappy, my dear; I think he still loves you."

"You start to sound like the dowager. Only she doesn't speak of love, just the succession," she said, pulling her hands away.

"No, you promised to hear me out. That is just one thing." He took her hands back, trapping them between his own.

The warm beams of sunshine streaming through the window picked out threads of silver in Less's hair, and Emily thought irrelevantly that her friend was terribly young to be turning gray. And yet he often spoke as if he were her senior, not a few years her junior. Perhaps he was an old soul.

"I will hear you out," she agreed, speaking softly.

Less stared out the window as a carriage clattered past on the cobblestones. It pulled up in front of the home next to them and disgorged a tumultuous family: a rotund country squire, his tired wife, a girl who appeared to be their daughter and a host of other children. A small sweeper boy begged pennies from the groom in exchange for cleaning the gutter where the family had stepped down.

"Del is in danger," he finally said, through tightened lips. "He won't tell me what he is up to or what he has been doing, but it is dangerous. I feel it in my bones!"

"You sound like my superstitious Tante Hélêne," Emily joked. Then she saw the serious expression on Less's face.

"You really are afraid for him!" she exclaimed. "You should know that Baxter can look after himself, whatever he is involved in. I never knew a more capable man, nor a smarter, more judicious one. What could he possibly be doing that would bring him danger?"

"I don't know," Lessington said, his face haggard in the harsh light. His eyes narrowed and his lips pursed, as he stared grimly out at the innocuous scene.

"Less, you're scaring me! What are you talking about? Tell me everything." She led him back over to the couch and they sat together.

Trumble opened the door again and Emily feared another visitor, but it was just the footman bringing tea. As he set the tray down, Emily said, "Please, Trumble, I am not at home this morning, if anyone else calls. And no interruptions, please."

"Very good, my lady," he said and withdrew, closing the door discreetly behind him.

"Now, what are you talking about?" She noted dispassionately that her hands were shaking and made the conscious effort to still them. To distract herself she poured tea, leaving the cream pitcher and sugar in front of Less as she sipped her own black.

She had never seen Less so serious. Even when she was crying on his shoulder he had been breezy, predicting that she would get over Baxter and take a lover. He had forced her to stop looking at things with such a bleak outlook and hope for healing in the future. And healing had come—or so she thought, anyway. Now that he had forced her to admit she still loved her husband, the ache seemed to be back.

"This is not widely known, and Del would *kill* me if he knew I was telling you, but someone tried to murder him a month ago."

"But I thought he was still on the Continent a month ago." Emily paled visibly. Her cup rattled against its saucer.

"He was. It was there the attempt was made."

Emily breathed a sigh of relief, wondering at her own spurt of fear for her husband. Was she destined always to be tied to him, to his fate, worrying over him as if their lives and future were still intertwined? "Well, then, the danger is left behind. What was it, brigands out for his purse?"

"No, Em. Another attempt was made last night."

Emily gasped. "When? How? Is he going to be all right? But, how could it have happened last night? I saw him at the ball, and he never said anything . . . ."

"It happened on his way home from the ball. *After* I told you I was worried about him. This is the third such incident that I know about! Someone tried to do him in on the packet from Calais, as well; that was just last week. I saw him this morning, and he will survive with nothing more than a knot the size of an egg on his skull. Luckily a Good Samaritan found him before the blackguard could finish him off."

Lessington's face was gray. He sipped his tea.

Emily tried to absorb this news. What a concerted effort to kill him, that three tries had been made in a short period of time! A shiver coursed down her spine and trilled out into her limbs. Baxter in danger! She felt an almost unconquerable urge to fly to his side, to nurse him as she had during their marriage when he hurt his knee in a fall from a horse and when he had suffered a bout with fever.

"What is he into? Why is someone trying to kill him?"

"He won't tell me."

"Why are you telling me all of this?"

"Because you love him. And because you might be able to help."

"How?" Emily traced the outline of the handle of her teacup. "How can I help him when he can barely stand the sight of me? When we fall to quarreling whenever we're near? And even if we were close as we once were, what could I do to stop some bloodthirsty murderer from getting his hands on him?"

"The main problem, as I see it, is that Del does not have anything to live for."

"Oh, fustian!" exclaimed Emily, looking up at Less with

her wide brown eyes trained on his face, looking for signs that he was cozening her. "Nothing to live for? The man is gorgeous, well to grass and has a beautiful mistress! What more does a man need?"

"His wife!" Less's expressive voice throbbed with intensity. He set his cup down on the table with a jarring clank. "He needs his wife, whom, though he will not admit it, he still loves desperately!"

Again, tears! And she was not a teary-eyed female, had always prided herself as being made of sterner stuff. She shook her head. "Oh, my dear friend, if I could believe you for a second . . . but I don't. You didn't see him that time at Brockwith. There was pure, raw venom in his eyes when he looked at me. My love for him is for what was, not for what is. And his love for me is . . . gone."

Less's face sagged in desolation. "I thought you would want to help."

"If I could, I would . . . but how? What can I do?"

"Del is involved in something. When he was on the Continent, the government was using him as a courier or something like that. Nothing formal, I believe, which is all the more dangerous for him."

"What do you mean?"

"I think the very informality of the arrangement allows the government to give him much riskier assignments, for if he is killed, no blame will be attached to them as there is no way to tie him in with the work."

"How do you know all of this? Or are you guessing?"

"Some of it is conjecture," Less admitted. "But some of it is based on . . . I have a close, personal friend in the government. Very highly placed. And he would not confirm it but hinted that I was right."

"You still haven't said what I can really do to help."

"As I said, Del doesn't seem to care if he lives or dies. He is liable to take more risks if he doesn't care. I know he cannot quit what he is doing for the country, but I am convinced he could be doing it more carefully. Somehow, he has exposed himself, or there would not be assassins after him."

Emily tried to take it all in. Baxter in danger! And Less, convinced she was the only one who could convince him to take more care. She turned back to her friend.

"Why don't you go to his mistress, Less? Surely she can charm Baxter into being more careful." The hint of ice in her voice betrayed her own feelings on the subject of the mistress, but with Less she did not worry about the naked nature of her pain. He would understand.

Less shook his head. "She is a child, Emily, without the worth of your little finger. Del doesn't care about her; she is just a pretty toy. He picked her up on the Continent, and with his overdeveloped feeling of responsibility, cannot shake her from his side now. Please, say you will think about it."

Emily paused.

What could she do? It seemed to her that Less was mistaken in his reading of Baxter's feelings toward her, but was that any reason to deny her help if it would make a difference? She did not know. "Before I make up my mind, I need to see him again," she said. Unless they could get past the bitterness and come to some kind of understanding, there was no point in even thinking about trying to help. "Take me to him, Less. Take me to my husband."

Four

His face a perfect mask of indifference, Delafont's butler announced, "Lady Delafont, Marchioness of Sedgely, and Mr. Sylvester Lessington." He then bowed and departed.

Emily nervously smoothed the rose muslin down over her hips and entered the room on Less's arm. She was surprised to find three faces turned in their direction. Of course Baxter was there, but there was also a young man of startling beauty and impeccable tailoring, and a lovely girl of not more than twenty, a vision in white silk and silver lace, a dress wholly unsuited to afternoon visiting.

The young man stood as they entered the room, but Baxter remained seated, his foot up on a stool, where the girl sat.

"Less!" Del said. "How nice of you to join us. Emily, I really didn't expect the pleasure of a visit from you." His voice was as urbane and smooth as ever.

Only by inflection could Emily catch his meaning. He was not pleased to see her.

"When I told Emily about your little . . . accident, she would not be kept from your side." Less quirked a cocky smile at his friend, as though daring him to scold for bringing Emily.

Del nodded. "Excuse me for not getting up. I seem to have twisted my ankle in last evening's little set-to, as well as getting a bump on the head. Emily, Less, this is my rescuer from last night, Vicomte Etienne Marchant, and this charming young lady is London's newest rage, the actress and dancer Belle Gallant.''

Emily felt her welcoming smile freeze on her lips. Baxter's mistress, brazenly visiting his house as if she had just as much right as anyone else! She felt Less stir at her side and heard his whisper; "I didn't know she would be here. My apologies, dear heart."

The girl had bounced to her feet and stood staring at her lover's wife with a saucy grin on her face. But the young French nobleman, sweeping back his thick, chestnut hair, advanced first, hand outstretched. He shook hands with Less, but when he took Emily's gloved hand, he bent low over it and pressed a kiss to the silk.

"Enchanté, madame." His eyes were deep, soulful brown, and as he gazed into Emily's, they lit with the golden fire of admiration. "Pardon, but are you . . ." He hesitated and glanced back at Del. "The butler, he say you are the marchioness, no?"

"Yes," Emily said, her voice low and trembling. "I am the marquess's wife."

The air in the room became charged with a current, as the air before a lightning strike. The vicomte still held her hand with his own, and he led her to a seat on the same divan as he himself had been seated upon. Less, a look of unholy glee on his expressive face, took a seat where he could observe everything.

Belle, her movements exaggeratedly flirtatious, moved to stand in front of Emily. Her face had a hard expression of brittle dislike as she stuck out her hand. "As the vee-compt has monopolized you, I'll have to force the introduction. As Del said, I am Belle Gallant."

Emily took her hand, and with a smile, shook it. Never had her innate composure been more needed than at that moment, to keep her grip light and her voice steady. A surge of jealousy pounded through her veins, but she suppressed it and smiled. "I must say, reports don't begin to do you justice, Miss Gallant. I have only seen you from my box at the theater, and that is too far to judge, but now I can see that you are even more beautiful than they say."

Belle's smile became hesitant, and she glanced over at her lover before giving a little curtsey and saying, "Thank you, my lady." She retreated to her stool, where she sat by Del's propped-up foot like a chastened child.

Del had regained his own composure and with a significant look at Less, said, "The vicomte was just telling us how he happens to be in London. You are visiting some English friends, I believe, now that the war is over and things begin to return to normal?"

The young man's smooth brow furrowed. "Normal?" he said. "Things will not be normal for a great while to come. The madman's rage through Europe has left my own poor country as an orphan—alone, unwanted, unloved. The rich are now poor, and the poor are destitute. The countryside stinks of death and destruction, and the madman is alive, though in exile, on Saint Helena. I hope he dies a wretched and tortured death."

The pain in the young man's voice touched Emily deeply, and on impulse, she laid her hand over his where it clutched the seat of the divan. He glanced up at her and his expression slowly dissolved from desolation to dawning devotion.

Del watched the interchange with an uneasy feeling in the pit of his stomach. Emily slid her hand over the Frenchman's, and the damned puppy got a completely silly look of love on his damnably handsome face. How could she encourage him like that? He was ten years her junior if he was a day, and she was a married woman, damn her eyes!

Belle tugged at his sleeve.

"What is it?" he said, his voice harsh.

She made a moue of distaste. "Well, if you're going to shout at me . . . ."

He passed one long-fingered hand over his face and took a moment to settle himself. He could consign Less to hell at that moment, and very cheerfully, for bringing

Emily with him. What was he about? Del glanced down at Belle.

"I'm sorry, my dear," he said, under cover of the chatter that filled the room between Emily and the vicomte.

"That is your wife?" she asked, hooking one thumb over her shoulder.

He grabbed her hand. "Please, do not do that, it is vulgar. Yes, that is my wife, Emily."

"I thought she'd be beautiful!" the girl stated, with some satisfaction. "But she's a podgy old gal!"

Del glanced back over at Emily. She had withdrawn her hand, but the Frenchman had moved over until his thigh was resting against hers on the divan. She was pink-cheeked and embarrassed about whatever it was the young man was murmuring. Belle was right; Emily was plump. Her cheeks no longer sloped to hollows under her cheekbones, and a slight doubling of her chin spoiled the once-perfect shape of her face. Her arms above the gloves were quite round.

Of course, the added weight, two stone, perhaps, maybe a little less—certainly less than he had at first estimated—had served to make her already voluptuous bosom even more bountiful. The fullness could not be disguised even by her day gown of soft rose muslin, accented with forest-green velvet ribbons. He remembered from the theater and the ball the night before that the skin of her bosom was still as delicate and perfect as always.

She was still a beautiful woman and sumptuously curvaceous, even if she no longer had a girlish figure. The Frenchman seemed taken with her. He stared at her adoringly like a half-wit moonling, the elegance of his lightly accented voice tripping over compliments to her that were making her blush.

Belle broke into his thoughts, her voice pettish and petulant, her gutter accent coming back as it always did when she was agitated.

"You'd think 'e never saw a woman before! It's positively disgusting, an' with 'er husband sitting right here the whole while! And her so old and fat, besides."

"Belle!" Del said with a warning in his voice. Her tones were shrill and carrying, and he did not want his wife to hear her vulgar comments. He would protect Belle from Emily's disdain. Or Emily from Belle's contempt.

Belle silenced and stared avidly at Emily and the young Frenchman. "P'raps it's just her manner," the girl said, thoughtfully.

Curious, Del glanced over at her. "What do you mean?"

Belle struggled to put into words what was in her mind. Finally, not used to deciphering her own feelings, she shrugged. "I don't know, she just seems . . . she is just . . . a lady." The last word was said wistfully.

Del sighed. It was true. Although a Yorkshire girl more used to country than London ways, Emily carried with her an ineffably regal serenity that was the pattern card of perfect manners. Her voice was well modulated, her walk a glide and her carriage upright and straight-backed.

She even parried the Frenchman's abundant praise with a light laugh and graceful delicacy. And it would always be the same, even if she took the young man as her lover . . . .

Her lover? Where did that thought come from? Del stared at the couple with narrowed eyes. But yes, his regard confirmed his unconscious observation. The young man would eagerly move to make her his mistress if she showed the slightest hint of encouragement. Would she? Would she make an assignation to meet him secretly, that very night, perhaps?

Del scowled and turned his gaze away from them, only to encounter Less's amused eyes. His friend smiled and looked at the pair significantly, as if sharing Del's thoughts.

Del turned back to Belle, who was working herself up into a huff of indignation over being ignored. Before he could say a word to her she had flounced to her feet. "I simply must be on my way!" she announced to the room at large. "I think I shall go shopping!"

Marchant had jumped to his feet at the same moment, his cheeks reddening. "I . . . I fear, Milord Delafont, that I have long overstayed my welcome."

Belle swayed over to his side and gave him a long look up through her lashes. "Then perhaps you can go shopping with me, monsoor?"

He looked startled at her forward behavior. But his elegant manners would not let him ignore such a hint from a lady, or even from a woman he perhaps suspected was *not* a lady. "Of . . . of course, mademoiselle. I should be 'appy to accompany you." With one regretful look down at Emily, he made his bow to Delafont. "Milord, if you will allow it, I will visit again to inquire after your health. Monsieur Lessington."

He turned back to Emily. "Milady, may I beg of you permission to pay my respects to you in person some afternoon?" His tone was lower as he spoke to her.

She blushed becomingly and brought a card from her reticule. "How could I refuse such a lovely request? My card, Monsieur Le Vicomte." She held out her hand once again.

"Enchanté, encore." He bowed low and kissed her gloved hand once again, lingering just a fraction of a second too long for Del's taste.

Belle, her lovely face frozen in an expression of distaste, said good-bye to Emily and Lessington. Then she turned to Del. "Are you sure there is nothing I can do to make you feel better? Nothing at all?"

Just the way she said it implied lewd and lascivious activities unrelated to nursing. Del glanced over at Emily, who tactfully kept her eyes down on her entwined fingers.

"No, Belle. Run along, there's a good girl." He didn't know what possessed him to treat her as if she were a niece, but it was out before he could stop it. Emily could hardly help but know that the girl was his mistress, but it was indecent to have them both in his parlor at once, and it made him feel as awkward as a colt at his first fence. Damn Less!

She pouted and wheeled around on her heel, joining Marchant at the door. They made a handsome couple as she threaded her arm through his.

"Then I will see you another time, Del." Head held high she marched from the room, tugging the reluctant Frenchman with her.

"Whew!" Less uttered, when the door was safely shut behind the retreating guests.

Del sent a cross look his way and glanced pointedly over at Emily. "So, what brings you two out today?"

"Oh, Baxter," Emily said. She rose and crossed the room to him and sank down gracefully on the low stool. Del watched her suspiciously. What had changed her defensiveness since the night before?

"Tell me how it happened." Delicately she touched his ankle and he flinched. Pressing her lips together, she gently massaged the swollen ankle.

At first he groaned in pain, but soon he relaxed, wondering at the sensation of warmth and comfort that came from her touch. He leaned his head back against the chair and closed his eyes. She had always had the natural instincts of a healer, now that he thought about it. It was his injury, not himself, that brought her to him.

He sighed and began his story. "I was on my way home from Lady Jersey's last night. I didn't bring my carriage; you know how I despise waiting and detest being driven. I don't know where my mind was. If I had been paying attention . . . ." He shook his head, a look of chagrin on his face.

She made a sympathetic sound in her throat and massaged his ankle.

It felt so good that despite his efforts to maintain his posture, he found himself relaxing in the chair, slumping against the back. "Anyway," he continued, "before I was aware, someone had socked me in the back of the head with something heavy. I stumbled sideways and my damned trick knee gave out on me and I went crashing down like a great, stupid lump! I was only unconscious for a second, but I knew that my assailant was still there and was about to finish me off, maybe, when out of nowhere came this lad. He decked the villain, who then turned tail and ran. Needless to say, it was the young vicomte who was so handy with his fives, to use boxing cant."

Emily's kneading hand moved up to his knee and he gave another groan, but this was of gratitude as she eased the tight, throbbing pain. He had twisted the damn knee too, as he went down. It made him feel damnably old, going down like that and having a young sprig come to his rescue.

Marchant had called him 'sir' as he helped him up and shouted for aid from the watch. The lad had gazed at him with obvious compassion in his eyes, barely visible in the darkness of that damp alley.

Del opened his eyes to see the pursed, rosy lips and concentration on Emily's smooth face as she kneaded and massaged his sore knee. She had taken his leg across her lap, and he thought how shocked society would be to see him in such close proximity to his wife again, the wife from whom everyone knew he was separated. There was a domestic intimacy in their position that reminded him of days gone by—happy days, contented days, irrecoverable days.

And yet he had no desire to draw away from her. He had long regretted the animosity between them, though he admitted his own part in keeping it going. Maybe this was an opportunity to establish a more mature footing to their separation. He was ready for that if she was.

Suddenly her bare hands—she had stripped off her gloves once Marchant and Belle had departed—on his leg seemed highly improper. He watched in fascination as her delicate, fine-boned hands moved up and down, her thumbs pressing into the muscle and joint of his knee. Occasionally they would stray up his thigh and massage the muscles that had taken a beating from the strain on his knee. She had the touch of an angel, and as the warmth of her hands penetrated through his breeches, he felt the first unmistakable pulse of arousal, as his loins tightened in response to her gentle touch. He badly wanted to surrender to the heat of desire, but common sense doused him with cold reality. This would not do!

"That's enough," he said, jerking his leg away from her and testing his foot on the floor.

Less was staring at him with amusement in his half-closed eyes. So nice that his friend was enjoying his obvious discomfort, he thought, but then he caught Emily's expression, a quickly masked hurt at his abruptness. Damn! He hadn't intended to hurt her feelings, hadn't really thought he still could!

"That . . . that seems much better," Del said. "Thank you, Emily. I had forgotten how efficacious your touch is." He tried a smile and directed it at her.

An answering smile lit up her brown eyes. Their gazes locked for a few moments. Unspoken, they both felt a shaky truce had been effected. It was time, Del thought, and he was glad, especially since they would likely be meeting often since their social circles overlapped. There was nothing left between them now, but perhaps they could manage friendship. If only they had tried to heal their rift years ago.

Less broke into the silence. "Now tell her about the other attempts on your life, Del."

The marquess cast a glowering look at him. "You have not been telling stories to Emily, have you?"

"Just the truth. Come, Del, it *is* the truth."

"Random chance," he said, airily.

"Random chance, three times." Less snorted.

Emily smiled up at her husband from her perch, where Belle had sat just minutes before. "You forget how well I know you, Baxter," she said, laying one hand on his knee. "You are hiding something from us."

Del stared down at her. For a moment he felt married

again; he felt that bond that went beyond sexual intercourse, beyond mere companionship, to a meeting of the
souls. It was what he and Emily had shared from the beginning, that feeling that their hearts were bound together by ties that went so deep that to sunder them
would be death.

But they hadn't died when they separated. Or at least
not outwardly. She had retreated to Yorkshire, at his insistence, he remembered with some shame, and he had
gone traveling.

None of that would have been necessary if they hadn't
drawn apart to the point that their marriage was a farce.
What had changed her? She had gone from the sweet,
carefree Yorkshire girl he had married, to a solemn,
brooding, unhappy woman. Had she fallen out of love
with him? That is what he had believed in his anger, and
she had given him no reason to think otherwise.

And yet here she was, sitting at his knee, begging him
to tell her if he was in danger. He was—mortal danger.
But it was no different than it had been for years, ever
since he had taken on a certain job. She must never know
about that, though, for to know would be to enter peril
herself, and he had sworn never to endanger another
person, least of all someone he had loved so very much.

"Less is a clucking mother hen, Em, and I am sorry if
he has worried you unnecessarily." Too late he realized
he had fallen back into the easy manner of address toward her. He had always called her Em or simply "my
love." He glanced down at her, the cupid's bow of her
pursed lips, wondering if she would object to the familiarity.

"I don't think it is so unnecessary," Emily said with a
worried frown. She sighed and shook her head. Why was
she worried about him? God only knew how she had
dreaded seeing him again when she returned to town.
She could admit that to herself now, as it seemed there
was to be a truce, and the horrible words and recriminations between them at their last meeting a thing of the

past and not to be referred to, though she would never forget them, not if she lived another fifty years.

But why this feeling of responsibility to him? She had no ties with him other than in name. They had agreed to a separation and abided by it for years. And now, simply because she had returned to London, his mother had decided they were to get back together and Less was making her a party to his worries for his friend. But although she wished Baxter well, there was nothing between them anymore, no matter how much she wished it were otherwise. Less was engaging in wishful thinking to believe that Baxter still loved her.

She looked up at her husband. His narrow, aristocratic face, Roman nose and dark, curled locks made him a handsome man, but that was not the only, or even the primary, reason she had fallen in love with him. She had never forgotten the moment they met and the kiss he had stolen as he swept her up and out of the stream she had been wading through.

In that single moment she had known what it was to love, and in the weeks that followed, fell more deeply until she was consumed with the emotion. Her gratitude to Baxter when he professed to love her, too, was almost overwhelming. She had foreseen a long, loving life together, with babies and a country estate to look after.

Instead, her husband had preferred the city, and they had been unable to conceive, though their sexual fervor at first was unquenchable. Was that when he began to fall out of love with her? When she could not give him the son he needed and a nursery full of other children?

She had deeply felt the shame, that what was so easy for other women was impossible for her. But what had hurt more was when she felt Baxter's withdrawal from her, his emotional distance, which seemed to increase with each passing day. With shame she looked back and remembered times when she had relieved her anger with spiteful little comments and barbed observations. But he had deserved some of them! Even if she had not managed to do her duty in regard to providing an heir for the Sedgely line, she still did not deserve the ill will of his mother. He had never once shielded her from the dowager's maliciousness, and she had felt too deeply the justice of the woman's comments to defend herself.

Emily glanced over at Less, who appeared to be almost asleep, with his head back against the cushions of the sofa. She pulled her skirts close to her and rose, picking up her discarded gloves. If Baxter would not speak to them about who was trying to kill him and why, then it was time they left.

It was time anyway; they should have left before this. She would not reflect on how comfortable and right it felt to be touching Baxter again and how even that nearness left her feeling a little breathless. Her corset was too tight, that was all, and it made it difficult to sit on the low stool.

If touching him again had been an unalloyed pleasure, no one else needed to know that or how tempted she had been to touch him in other wifely ways. Wouldn't he have been shocked if she had followed her instincts and let her hand move up his thigh? Her magnetic attraction to him had not diminished over the years it seemed, despite the vitriol between them. It was one thing she would have to learn to ignore.

"Less, we must be going. Baxter has business to attend to, no doubt."

Lessington opened one eye, then sighed and stood. He clucked his tongue, as if over two fractious children, but straightened his cuffs and bowed to his friend.

"Do not get up, Del, old man. I hope your ankle and knee are *not* feeling better soon, as they will keep you safely inside a carriage for some time. Come, my dear. Perhaps his mistress can talk some sense into him if his wife cannot!"

Five

What am I to do? Emily thought, as she strolled the confines of the small, fenced park across from the town house. Her maid sat a discreet distance away, knowing herself to be not needed for the moment. The glittering green of an early-spring day was advancing toward evening, with the slanting sun lighting newly leafed trees with a verdant glow. A light breeze riffled through a sapling sending the new fronds dancing.

Emily sighed and paced. It was not Yorkshire, she thought—not the long, wild walks of springtimes past, when new life after a long, hard winter seemed like a miracle—but it was the best London had to offer, and earlier than the northern counties. It was barely March, and already flowers bloomed. A garden of spring bulbs in a neglected corner caught her attention and she strolled over to it. She bent down to brush some wet, dead leaves from the previous autumn away from the green buds pushing up through the damp earth.

So should I have tended my marriage, she thought, with gentleness and care instead of hurt and withdrawal. Seeing Baxter had been the catalyst of a bout of introspection that was now bearing fruit of a rich and strange sort. Had she ever stopped loving him? No. She had been angry at times. She had hated the sight of him occasionally. But she had never stopped loving him and had never stopped wishing he would come back to her.

A stiffening breeze tugged at her elegant bonnet and

swirled the skirt of her light pelisse, but still she wandered along the meandering pathways. The sky darkened, the breeze chilled, but she paced on.

He was older, there was no disguising that. There were lines under his eyes and beside his mouth, and the slight slackening of the skin under his chin betrayed the passing years. But gazing at him was more precious for that. How could they have let so much time go past and not healed the rift between them? And now it was too late. Too much time had passed. Baxter was polite but distant and was clearly not in love with her anymore. He had moved on to a young mistress, a girl half his age. She was the one who touched him, aroused him, fulfilled him. She was the lucky one who slept in his arms, safe from all the world of troubles.

Baxter was set in his ways and she in hers, and the best she could hope for was the truce they had silently agreed to today. It was good to speak with him and to touch him. It was always good to touch him. If only they had done more of that—more touching and much more talking— during the long years while their marriage dwindled to cool civility and distant courtesy. Or even if they had raged at each other about the things that were really bothering them. Instead they had been oh, so polite, with occasional retreats into distant bitterness, until finally there was nothing left but coldness. Except for that final blaze of anger and the hurtful words he had said to her as he virtually ordered her to leave Brockwith Manor and hie herself to Yorkshire.

She shook her head. He was in danger. Less had not been exaggerating that merely to get the two of them together, as she had at first suspected. But Baxter would not tell either of them why. How strange that he would not even confide in Less, his best friend.

"My lady, it gets late, and you have an engagement after dinner," the maid ventured, coming up behind her on quiet feet.

Emily turned and smiled at the girl, noting for the first

time the twilight sky. "You're right, Agnes. We shall turn back now. Dodo will be wondering what has become of me."

Dianne Delafont—Dodo to those who loved her, and, for the crusty spinster she considered herself to be, there were a surprising number of those—watched out the parlor window as Emily ambled back across the cobbled street, her maid trailing behind. Agnes handed a tip to the little sweeper boy who doffed his ragged hat and gazed after Emily with undisguised admiration. He was a young lad, young enough to be Emily's son, and Dodo wondered if the sight of Emily made him think of warm fires and good food and a blessed refuge from work and worry. She had that effect on people, Dodo thought. Emily had an ability to offer comfort with her words, her sympathy, her presence.

Emily had no idea that what she gave Dodo was a feeling of home and purpose, two ideals she had lacked before becoming Emily's companion. She had never been able to tell her that, and sometimes she worried, because she knew that Emily felt herself to be the one beholden to Dodo, felt that she was the only receiver of benefit from their relationship. Lady Dianne Delafont, confirmed spinster, was not a talker though, and didn't think she could express her feelings in any way that would not seem maudlin and, well, spinsterish.

Anyway, she refused to worry about that. Instead, she would worry over Emily, like she always did. Emily had been to see Baxter, that much she knew. But her niece by marriage had said little beyond that, cloaking herself in that calm reticence that had become her armor over the years.

What had she and Baxter to say to one another after all these years? She had known Baxter since he was born—had seen him grow from a squawking infant, to an impudent boy to a reckless man. Then she had seen the transforming force of love in his life when he and Emily had met and married. It was the making of him in her opinion. But then, over the years Emily and Baxter had seemed to just grow apart, and then came the break. She was not privy to all of the details, nor would she want to be, but Emily had spoken about the final bitter argument that sent her to Yorkshire, and Dodo would never forgive her nephew for his behavior. Men! Once again she was glad that she had withstood the few demands made on her when a girl and had decided never to marry.

Emily climbed the outside steps and Trumble opened the door for her as her maid relieved her of her pelisse and headed for the stairs to the second floor. In moments her niece had joined Dianne.

"How marvelous you look, Dodo!" she exclaimed.

Dianne smiled and preened in front of a mirror over the fireplace. "Thank you, my dear. And thank you for lending me that new dresser, Sylvie. The woman is a marvel!" Her silver hair was swept up in an elegant style that took years off her age, or so the dresser insisted. And she wore a royal-blue silk gown with silver and white lace edging the neck and sleeves.

They ate supper quickly, and then headed out to a musicale at Lady O'Donnell's, a scandalous Irish widow who, though not exactly tip of the *ton,* did have an ear for very good music. Her salons always attracted the best of the new musicians.

As Emily and Dodo walked up the steps, they could hear the light female laughter and low buzz of male voices even before they entered. The windows of the elegant town house were ablaze with sparkling candlelight, and as the butler opened the door for them, they felt the rush of heat from the already packed rooms.

Emily smiled to herself. This was what she had missed in Yorkshire. Not that they never had any company, but they were certainly more isolated, which was what she had liked the place for at first, nursing her wounded heart in solitude.

But now she craved company and music and light, frivolous talk—dancing and laughter and gossip. She was still young; she wanted to *live!* She now appreciated all of the things she had at first despised London for, recognizing her past dislike as fear of the unknown. She squeezed Dodo's arm and they entered together Lady O'Donnell's musical salon.

They chatted with acquaintances, renewed friendships, and then sat together listening to a soprano soloist, an Italian woman whose voice soared and dipped like a swallow in flight. Emily was mesmerized and hardly noticed when Dodo murmured something about retiring to the ladies' withdrawing room for a few moments.

Her eyes closed, Emily listened, translating in her head the woeful tale of a woman betrayed and scorned by the only man she had ever loved. She followed as the woman fled to the edge of a cliff, and with a final farewell flung to the four winds, leaped to her death.

"Chérie, you look most impassioned," a voice whispered in her ear.

Emily's eyes flew open and one hand fluttered to her breast. She glanced quickly to her right to find Vicomte Marchant in Dodo's chair.

"Ah, Monsieur Le Vicomte!" Her heart was pounding and she realized how completely she had been taken away by the soloist's story. She had not even heard or noticed the young man take the chair beside her. How cheeky of him to call her his darling on such a slight acquaintance, even if it was in French!

"I startled you!" the young man exclaimed, his dark, soulful brown eyes fixed on her face. *"Mille pardons,* madame. I saw you so enraptured, and I say to myself, there, *there* is a woman with the soul of an artiste!"

"No, merely with the wit to appreciate an artiste. Madame Fabia is splendid." Emily smiled at him, blushing a little at the admiration she saw in his eyes. So, she had not imagined the undercurrents between them at Baxter's house; he did admire her. How novel a feeling that was, to know herself to be admired by a handsome young man! She had forgotten the tingle of pleasure, the elevated confidence that accompanied such admiration.

The assembled guests were retiring in groups to the refreshment room. Marchant stood and offered his arm, and Emily slid her gloved hand through it. He was just a little taller than she—not a big man like her husband, but with a suggestion of coiled power in his lithe figure. He was most elegant in all black with a Gallic flair all his own. His dark hair curled in a Brutus cut and he smelled faintly of some spicy mixture no doubt concocted by his valet.

Emily found it pleasant to be squired by someone other than Lord Fawley, who, though polite, had a coolness that left her feeling untouched, as though his very arm was wintry. Marchant was anything but cold. He was full of life and warmth, nodding pleasantly to others, but keeping Emily's arm tucked close to his body as he maneuvered them through the crush and found a table a little apart from the others.

Emily sat down and he stood in front of her.

"May I bring you something to eat and drink, my lady?"

She nodded, located Dodo in the crowd and motioned toward her. "Could you also tell my aunt where I am?"

Marchant glanced at the older woman and nodded. "I will ask her to join us," he said and made his way through the crowd.

Emily could not help but admire the fluid grace of his movement, like that of a wildcat through the thick growth of the jungle. She had a cousin who had been to India and when he came back, he had described the tigers—how graceful their movements, how beautiful their appearance, yet how deadly their ferocity. She laughed to herself to think that she was comparing Marchant to one of those dangerous animals.

"So that is Baxter's young rescuer?" Dodo said, as she

came to join Emily at the table. Her niece had told her all about Baxter's mishap as they ate dinner.

"Yes."

"You didn't mention what a breathtaking young man he is," she said, her eyebrows raised in query.

"Is he?" Emily replied, coolly. "I hadn't noticed."

Dodo gave a quick bark of laughter. "Then I should start ordering my mourning clothes, for you are half dead, my dear. Every woman in the room is aware of that exquisite young man."

Emily followed her gaze, and saw that her aunt was correct. Many ladies in the room were casting surreptitious glances his way, and there was a subtle preening in his presence. Women stood taller, threw their breasts out slightly, brushed against him "by accident." He must be used to so much attention, because he knew just how to handle it, how to smile and nod and yet evade collisions with those who would interfere with his objective.

"Well, maybe I did notice," Emily admitted.

Dodo gave a little wave to a friend, and then took a seat. "Good. Then, I know you are still alive. I am old enough to be his mother, if not his grandmother, and I noticed him."

Emily glanced over at her aunt with affection. Dodo made her bow to society long before Emily was even born, and yet she still seemed as fresh as that green girl, knowledgeable but not jaded somehow. "Perhaps he can be the one to finally persuade you to give up your single state?"

It was a long-standing joke between them and Dodo chuckled. "With every woman in London ready to cast out lures in his way? I would stand as much chance as I would of singing like Madame Fabia!"

Marchant came back at that moment with plates for both ladies and disappeared again in search of liquid refreshment and a plate for himself. He returned and sat down with them, entertaining them with some light stories of his adventures during the war years.

"But you are so young!" Dodo said at one point. "Why, the war must be all you can remember."

A shadow of bitterness cast a pall over his lively features for a moment, but then a wry smile twisted his well-shaped lips. "Let me say that I try not to remember. At least, not the most terrible parts."

Emily put her hand over his on the table. He turned his hand and captured hers in his grasp, squeezing it. Dodo watched the interplay with interest, one eyebrow cocked in surprise. In all the years since her separation, Emily had shown interest in no man. But between the young Frenchman and her there seemed to be a sympathy, a meeting of the minds.

And there was no doubt the young man admired her, too. Emily had gained weight over the years in Yorkshire, but then, some men admired that in a woman, Dodo knew. Emily had never been thin, but now she was plump and sleek, like a well-fed house cat, and tonight she was in looks, her golden brown hair dressed high with long tendrils curling around her neck, over her smooth, honey-colored skin. She wore an emerald-green dress of gold-shot silk, the plunging neckline emphasizing her bountiful bosom. An emerald pendant nestled in her cleavage, and Marchant's gaze was often on the necklace—or something in that area.

Would she take him as a lover? Dodo had very little use for her nephew, Emily's husband, having decided that any man mad or stupid enough to let Emily go deserved no consideration. Baxter was too much like his father—her older brother—she thought, too much a Delafont man, arrogant, strong-willed and supercilious.

Emily deserved a little happiness, and if this young man could give that to her, she would wish them joy. But Em had a puritanical streak, and Dodo doubted whether, even if she did take a lover, she would ever allow herself to enjoy the affair. She sighed and finished her lobster patties, drank her ratafia and pushed her plate away.

"May I bring you ladies a cake or other confection?" Marchant asked, springing to his feet.

Dodo eyed him speculatively. "Perhaps you can. Not cakes though. Lemon ice if they have it, any other flavor if they do not," she ordered.

He bowed and, his gaze softening, turned to Emily. "And you, my lady? What sweetness may I bring you?"

I . . . I don't think I want anything," Emily said, confused as much by his intimate tone as his odd word usage.

Marchant protested, but she stood firm. He disappeared into the crowd. Many of the guests were now standing and visiting each other's tables.

"You snap your fingers and that young man will jump directly into your bed," Dodo said, with an amused glance at her niece by marriage.

As she expected, Emily colored, the blush spreading even down her neck and across her décolletage. "Dodo! Really!"

"It's true! He's a handsome sprig, and I have heard tell that Frenchmen are the best lovers. Never had the opportunity to test that. He'd warm your bed for you, and don't tell me you haven't thought of it."

Emily turned her face away to hide her confusion. Dodo had all the bluntness of a past generation, and she had unfortunately hit on the truth. Emily had thought of it. The young man's subtle masculinity and obvious admiration for her had sparked something she thought was long dead.

But she was married! That didn't seem to matter to some women of her acquaintance, she knew. A girl she had gone to school with was now the acknowledged mistress of a well-known speaker in the House of Lords. She dined out on political gossip that everyone knew was pillow talk.

But Emily had never even considered it before. Should she? Knowing that she still loved her husband but that love was futile? It had been so long since she had made love; it had been more than five years since a man had held her in his arms, whispering endearments and teasing her responsive flesh to ecstasy. Her breath came a little faster as she remembered the way Baxter had always approached her, lusty gleam in his eye, and she had known no matter where they were that he wanted her.

He would whisper an invitation to her, and they would disappear like discreet lovers, hardly able to wait until they were out of sight before ripping at each other's clothes in a frenzy of need. Emily sighed. Baxter's merest glance was like a touch on her skin. She had been so madly in love with him that she had, on occasion, taken chances that would have caused quite a scandal if they had been caught.

Once they had made love in the gazebo of a country estate they were visiting. The sensation of fresh country air on her naked skin had been erotic beyond belief, so much so that they had occasionally repeated the experiment at Brockwith Manor, in a little folly that Baxter had fitted up just for that purpose. He would lead her there and make thorough love to her over a long summer afternoon.

But to make love with another man? The thought sent a frisson of excitement, or perhaps fear, trilling along her spine. Maybe she owed it to herself. Could she live the rest of her life, knowing she would never make love again? Never experience the ecstatic surrender that was a woman's greatest gift to a man?

No, that was not right. She would *not* shrivel up and die for lack of her husband. If she could never have Baxter again, then she would find at least physical love in the arms of another man. Had not their marriage vows been sundered when her husband took a mistress, or more likely even long before them, when he had had his first extramarital liaison? Maybe she should summon up her courage and let herself live again. She had never met another man who appealed to her the way Baxter did, but Etienne came close. He certainly did come close.

Marchant returned to the table that moment with

Dodo's lemon ice. Emily gazed up at him and, in a soft voice, said, "I thought you had deserted us." She smiled, her full lips parting over even white teeth.

The vicomte stopped, arrested in midmovement by her expression. His voice fervent, he said, "My lady, if I thought for one moment I was missed, I would never leave your side."

Dodo smiled.

Six

A discreet tap on his door awakened Del in the darkness of his room. "What is it," he mumbled, feeling the throbbing in his foot with a groan of pain.

"My lord, there is a person . . . a Miss Gallant . . . she insists on seeing you. What shall I tell her?" Cromby, Del's butler, spoke in a hushed tone.

"Tell her to go away!" Del grumbled, pulling the covers up over his head. He twisted and turned, trying to get comfortable again, but it was as useless then as it had been hours before, when he finally fell asleep out of exhaustion.

"Sir, I have already said that, but she says she will stand outside the house and sing if she is not admitted. I did not think you would appreciate the scurrilous gossip that type of behavior would incur." The butler's voice had a put-upon expression.

"Very well," Del sighed, throwing the covers back. "Send her up here and direct her to my room."

"Yes, my lord."

Del struggled up to a sitting position, trying to ignore the persistent ache in his ankle. While Emily had touched it the pain seemed to go away, and the remedy lasted for a while after she left, but now it was back to aching again.

He heard a bouncing step on the staircase, one that could only belong to Belle, and then his door flew open. She twirled into the room, rushed across the floor and threw herself on the bed. Del gasped in pain.

"My poor dear," she cried. She bounced off the bed, struck a lucifer from the tinderbox on the side table and lit a couple of candles of the branched candelabra. Her high color and youthful good looks were thrown into ghostly relief by the sudden flare of light.

"I've come to make you all better," she said, climbing back up on the bed. She crawled up next to him and began kissing his neck with exuberant smacking noises, rubbing her face against him like a cat and pushing the covers away from him.

"You are as high as a kite," Del exclaimed, trying to push her away. It was impossible; she clung to him like a bosky barnacle.

She giggled and snuggled up even closer to him, resuming her enthusiastic caresses. "Just a little, Delly-welly! Just a few 'ittle drinks! Champagne! Oceans and oceans of it! I was such a success tonight, my Delly-welly would have been so proud!" Her hand disappeared under the covers.

Del gasped as he felt her small, cold hand on his naked skin. "Belle!" he protested. "You are stinking drunk and I am in pain. Desist at once!"

"Desist at once!" she echoed, copying his voice, but ending with a giggle.

"Belle, behave yourself!" he grunted, grasping her hands and pulling them up from under the covers.

Her only answer was a giggle, but she did let go of him and slipped from the bed. He could see in the candlelight as she unbuttoned her pelisse, that she hadn't a single piece of clothing on underneath it—no chemise, nor stockings, nor petticoats. She hopped back up onto the bed. "I am going to make you feel better, you poor baby!"

"Belle . . ." he grunted, his knee throbbing with each bounce of the mattress. "I insist that you . . . ."

He broke off as he realized that a light snore was his only reply. Belle had collapsed and her piquant little face was blissfully relaxed in drunken sleep, her mouth open a little, her breathing deep and even. He shook his head.

He could only be glad that she had passed out. He had not made love to her since coming back to England, and he did not intend to.

Blowing out the candles, he lay back down, trying to ignore the pulsing ache that sent sharp needles of pain through his ankle. Facing toward the open curtains and the black, star studded sky, he settled himself to go back to sleep, if he could. That was it. He had to solve this dilemma. What was he going to do with Belle Gallant?

Sylvester Lessington stared out the open curtains at that same star-spangled sky. He had been thinking all night of his friends Del and Emily. It grieved him that a man and wife so obviously suited for each other could not seem to find a way back to each other, past the anger and recriminations that had embittered them both. He believed they still loved each other. He hoped that if only he could get them to spend enough time in each other's company, they would come to realize it themselves.

They were so lucky, and they didn't even know it. Their love problems were solvable, not impossible like his own. If they only knew what it felt like to love in secret, not allowed to acknowledge openly the sweet gift of love given with an open heart. The knowledge that the world would condemn what it did not understand destroyed every peaceful, beautiful moment and colored his days with sadness and a dread certainty that his time of loving and being loved was limited and precious. He turned over on his side and stroked the smooth skin of his bed companion, who murmured an incoherent question.

"Go back to sleep, my love," Lessington said, kissing one muscular shoulder. "Go back to sleep."

He sighed and wondered what danger Del was in and why he wouldn't tell either his best friend or his wife about it. He feared for him but had done all he could do by bringing the two of them back together. He curled up by his lover and slowly drifted off to sleep.

* * *

Emily sat in her window seat, thinking over the evening and wondering if she had done the right thing. On the impulse of the moment she had sent definite signals to Marchant, signals that she was ready and willing for an affair. The young man had understood, she was sure, but his response was subtle. He had become just a shade more proprietary toward her, solicitous about the small things, like obtaining her a seat when the music was about to start again, letting his warm fingers linger on the soft skin of her upper arm, above her silk glove.

It had felt like a lover's touch, though. That much she understood. He was claiming her with every movement and every caress. Dodo had stated that Frenchmen were renowned as wonderful lovers. Was Emily destined to find out? Would she even recognize skill, with only one man to judge against? Was skill even important? She had no idea. During the intimate moments of her marriage to Baxter, he had seemed supremely able to her. He had certainly never left her unsatisfied, but then she had loved him. Was sexual intercourse without love different? Did it satisfy down to the soul the way the mating of a man and woman who loved each other did?

Or, as she suspected, was it different for men anyway? That raised other painful questions in her mind, but for once she did not flinch from them. Did Baxter love his mistress? She was an attractive little thing, a good three stone or more lighter than her, slimmer than she had ever been, and well-proportioned, graceful of feature and light of step. Word had quickly spread in London of the new actress and opera dancer, and Emily had even seen her and admired her performance before she knew the girl was Baxter's mistress.

Emily gazed out at the dark sky, the pinpoints of light that were stars a dim reminder of the starlit skies out in the country, where she and Baxter would occasionally walk in the evening. He had not seemed to enjoy the

country as she did, one of the first of many differences
that had become sources of argument for them. Not that
they had fought often; if they had they might have been
able to fight about and resolve the things that really were
killing their marriage.

In surprise, she realized for the first time that she
was angry with Baxter—angry that he had taken a lover,
angry that she was such a young and lovely girl, but
most of all angry that he had deserted her without
fighting to keep their relationship alive, as she had
been willing to do.

Or had she? There had come a time when she was so
unsure of herself and her relationship with her husband
that she had been afraid to ask for anything, and even
more afraid to argue about anything, and so she had
backed away from confrontation. The fury had not gone
away, but it had been sublimated into sullen silence instead. What had made her even more enraged was that
Baxter never seemed to notice when she was upset. How
could he not know what was bothering her?

She had given up a little of that anger when she held
his foot on her lap and soothed his pain, but there was
still a core of it somewhere, burning deep in the pit of
her stomach. Was that why she was considering taking a
lover and that the lover she was considering was the very
man who had saved Baxter's life?

She knew him well enough to know that he must hate
his own helplessness, and his gratitude toward young Marchant would be mixed with anger over the younger man's
vigorous health and youth. If Emily took the vicomte as
a lover and Baxter ever found out about their affair, he
would consider it a deliberate insult. Was that what she
wanted?

With a deep sigh, she slipped down from the window
seat and retreated to bed. Even the mindless act of taking
a lover, which other people did without thought, she had
to complicate by her introspection. However, she could

not go further without thinking it out; that much was clear.

Would she or would she not take Etienne to bed? That was her dilemma.

LADY DELACEY'S AIRS

Baxter Delafont glanced across the table, still nonplussed by a sight he had never expected to see. Belle,
far from being hung over from the previous night, had
recovered with the elasticity that only comes from youth.

Seven

Baxter Delafont glanced across the table, still nonplussed by a sight he had never expected to see. Belle,
far from being hung over from the previous night, had
recovered with the elasticity that only comes from youth.
Worse, she had insisted on accompanying him down to
the breakfast table and fussing over him as if he were
some kind of doddering invalid in his dotage. She had
even stirred his coffee and had to be forcibly stopped
from cutting up his ham.

She sat to his left, humming a little tune, eating but-
tered muffins while she beat out time with a knife on the
edge of the polished oak table. A footman, stiff and dis-
approving, stood behind her chair glaring down at the
top of her head. Baxter attempted to read his paper, but
the *tang tang tang* of the knife was driving him to distraction.

"Belle, do you think you could desist from giving me
the rhythm to your humming? Just for a bit, my dear?"

"Certainly, Del." She stopped.

He went back to reading the paper.

"Del?"

With a sigh he put it down. He should have known
that if he stopped her from one thing, she would need
to do something else. Silence was unbearable, it seemed.
"What is it, Belle?"

"That tutor you hired me in Italy—he taught me the
proper way to talk and walk and all, but did he miss some-

thing?" Her narrow, clever face was turned to one side and her small lips were pursed.

"Whatever do you mean?" Baxter smiled over at her, amused in spite of his annoyance. She looked at that moment like a clever little monkey. She was swathed in one of his figured silk dressing gowns, which was absolutely voluminous on her tiny frame, and she sat cross-legged on the chair.

She looked pensive and stared down at her hands. "Did he miss something? I mean, there is something different about me and, say, your wife."

Baxter sighed and sat back in his chair. He took a deep swallow of his coffee. Yes, there was much that was different, but some of it was innate, a part of Emily from birth, and the rest was the result of youthful training, rigid strictures in the school for young ladies she had attended and unalterable rules and expectations she was raised to observe. How could he explain to Belle that there was no way to replace that kind of background with a few lessons?

"My dear, you are perfect just as you are. Don't start thinking there is something wrong with you."

"But there is something different, isn't there?" Her gaze was stiletto sharp.

"Yes, my dear."

"What is it?"

Baxter shook his head. How could he describe something that was indefinable?

"Well? I'm trying to better myself, Del!"

Her voice, usually so well modulated, thanks to the voice teacher he had hired her, sometimes reverted to its natural whininess when she was perturbed.

He gazed at her with fondness and irritation. How could he say that the same things that made her so delightful, were also her downfalls? That her cheerful aggressiveness had gone from a novelty to a wearing fault? That he longed for the quiet elegance of a real lady in his bed and across from him at his table.

If that was true, then he was in for a lifetime of disappointment, because he was married and always would be married. Therefore he could have no other lady across from him at his table, other than a mistress. He could, he supposed, take for a mistress a widow or dissatisfied wife from his own class, but his sense of what was due his position would not allow him to set up housekeeping with her as if they were married. Others may do that, he thought, but not Baxter Delafont. Even this morning tête à tête was highly irregular and would not be repeated. If Belle would just confine herself to the house he had hired for her, instead of invading his own . . . .

What was he going to do with Belle Gallant?

She moved agitatedly. "Del, you are not helping me! What makes me different from your wife? I saw how the veecompt treated me, like I was no better than I should be. But your wife, he knew right away what she was. Why?"

Baxter felt a swell of compassion and exasperation. He had raised her from brutality and squalor to the heights someone like little Annabelle Gudge could expect. But now she was peering over the wall. Some few rare birds of her species had made it, had married into the aristocracy, or at least the ranks of the gentility. But Belle was not destined to do that, he feared.

She did not have that indefinable something that women like Emily had, a grace and inner light that shone through like gold. Even in a country woman's shabby clothes, the way he had first seen her, something in Emily had glowed. It had saved him from going too far, farther than a simple kiss, though from that first moment he had wanted her.

He laid one long-fingered hand over Belle's smaller one. "My dear, don't distress yourself . . . ."

A commotion broke out in the hall, and Baxter could hear Cromby's voice raise above its usual well-bred moderation.

"Ma'am, my lady, please, let me announce you . . . ."

"I don't need to be announced in my own son's

house," came a strident, familiar trumpet, and then the double doors to the dining room burst open, and the Dowager Marchioness stalked in.

Wonderful, thought Baxter. Just perfect. His mother had impeccable timing. But he refused to be cowed by her and jerk his hand away from Belle like some naughty schoolboy. He was the Marquess of Sedgely, and he would do as he pleased. He could make love to Belle right on the dining room table if he wanted, and it would be no one's business but his own. The dowager stalked around the room, surveying her son and his mistress.

Then, in pointed rudeness, she turned to her son, completely ignoring Belle, and said, "How are you Baxter? I must say, it would have been nice if my son had had the decency to come to Bath to see his aging mother after gallivanting the Continent for years, and only a monthly letter to show for it, but what can I expect? The current generation has no consideration for their elders. And now you have forgotten your manners?"

"I am sorry for not rising, Mother, but I have had a mishap and have sprained my ankle. Pardon me. And, of course, my next order of business was to visit you in Bath, but I see that you have forestalled that, er, pleasure." He glanced at Belle and steeled himself. Under normal circumstances he would have thrown himself from a cliff rather than introduce his mother to his mistress, but since he was plagued by women who insisted on invading his home at inopportune moments . . . .

"Mother, this is Belle Gallant, a friend."

The dowager turned her frosty stare on the girl, who shrank down in her chair, for once intimidated. Her basilisk glare froze the poor girl in her seat, and Belle made no sound for the rest of her visit, but a faint squeak that sounded like "Good morning, my lady."

"Cromby, set a place for my mother. Mother, you will stay and breakfast?"

"Just tea," she said regally, and took a seat opposite Belle, on her son's right hand. "And so you are injured?"

"Just a twist, Mother. I am recovering apace."

"I see that," she muttered, glaring at Belle.

"What brings you all the way from Bath? Besides me, of course?"

Cromby and the footman poured tea, offered muffins, and then tactfully vacated the room, closing the big double doors behind them.

The dowager loaded marmalade on a warm muffin and took a huge bite, chewing thoroughly and swallowing before answering. "Your wife brings me to town."

"Emily? Emily asked you?" Baxter's eyebrows shot up. If he had expected anything, it wasn't that. Emily and his mother had never gotten on, even in the first rosy glow of their new marriage. He had always supposed it was some kind of natural animosity between women vying for the affections of a man. As long as it had not troubled him, he had paid it scant attention.

"No, you fool, of course I meant—"

Baxter glared at her, and for once, she stopped in midsentence. It was too much to be called a fool by his mother in his own house in front of his mistress. This was taking on all the qualities of the farce at the end of the play, and the farce was the part he never stayed to see.

"You are looking quite like your father," she said, more quietly. She took a long sip of tea, making a bit of a face. "Your cook needs a word about the proper steeping of tea. Or the proper purchase. Probably rubbishy smouch from a disreputable tea merchant. You need a wife. Which brings me back to my subject. You *have* a wife, Baxter, and she is fast getting past any hope of childbearing."

"Madam, we are separated. Unless you have forgotten the workings of the human body since your own childbearing, I will remind you that we cannot conceive a child if we do not have sexual relations and we cannot have sexual relations when we are seldom in the same room, and when we are, only with other people! They *would* talk if we did the deed in public."

The dowager's face turned frosty again. "If you think to shock me by plain speaking, you are talking to the wrong woman. When I was fourteen, I caught my father mounting the upstairs maid. He only stopped for a moment to tell me to leave the room before resuming his humping. I have had no illusions about men ever since, including your father. Men will always have other women . . . a certain type of other women." She gave a disdainful look at Belle. "Get your wife with child, as is your duty. I know she is fat and unattractive, but she is your wife and you need an heir. Then afterward you can go back to your little pieces on the side. But right now you should not be wasting your seed by spilling it in the wrong vessel."

Baxter glared at his mother. He remembered the acrimony between Emily and her. At the time he was wont to ascribe it to Emily's impertinence toward her, something his mother was always complaining about, but now he wondered. While his father was alive, things were, if not wonderful, at least tolerable. It was after Baxter ascended to the title when they had been married about five years that things started to fall apart. His mother should have moved to the dower house, but she delayed endlessly, ordering a long, drawn-out series of renovations that made her stay at Brockwith Manor a necessity.

"I have seen my wife since being back, and although she has gained a little weight, she is not unattractive." He felt compelled to defend Emily; he knew not why. Their marriage was over in everything but name, but he did hope to conduct the rest of their lives with civility.

"She is fat! I do not know how she can have let herself go like that, after disappearing in the wilds of Yorkshire for years, but she always was inclined to it, it seems to me. It won't matter so much once she is with child, though—"

"She is not going to be with child!" Baxter shouted.

Belle, still and silent in her chair, glanced at him with eyes wide.

"I thought I raised a son who knew his duty," the dowager said with a trembling voice. "No matter how distasteful you find her, you must get her with child and spawn an heir. It is your duty, and I will not let you forget it!"

A pit of anger flared in his bowels, but it was ingrained in him to never be rude to his parent, no matter what the provocation. A memory came back to him just then, of Emily, tears welling up in her beautiful eyes at something his mother had said to her, something intolerably rude and hurtful. His mother had said to his wife that even the dumbest beast in the field could conceive offspring, so why couldn't she?

Emily had looked over to him, and he had said nothing. What was there to say? He could not be rude to his mother, could he? And there was no answer for that that did not entail rudeness. But shouldn't his duty to his wife have superseded the one to his parents? Once he married, was he not supposed to leave his parents and cleave only unto his wife or something like that?

Was that when Emily's depression had begun, making worse what was already beginning to go bad between them? It seemed to him that his mother had never approved of his choice for a wife, and she made certain that everyone knew it, too. His father had liked Emily after his first disapproval—had called her a pretty, comfortable wife for a man, after which he glared at his own wife—but after he died, and his mother still lived with Emily and Baxter in the title house, that was when things got bad.

And then they had separated. Emily had stayed at Brockwith Manor for a couple of years, living in uneasy retirement with his mother. Why had she stayed, even when he and she had agreed that there was no chance to reconcile? Had she hoped? Had there even then been a chance to make their marriage work?

Perhaps if she had not gone off to Yorkshire they might have made another attempt to live as man and wife again. Or maybe not. He remembered with a stab of something like regret the way he had handled his mother's request that she be sent away. At least he had not been so summary, but he had made it clear that his mother could not continue to live at Brockwith with Emily in any peaceful manner. And he had suggested she might like the house in Yorkshire deeded to her outright.

What was it she had said?

Ah, yes. He remembered. Her eyes cast down at her folded hands, she had said, "Is that what you want, Baxter?"

It had made him angry—furious, in fact. What he *wanted?* He *wanted* his wife back again—the one who smiled and laughed and adored him. He wanted Emily, who made his heart sing and his body thrum with pleasure. He wanted back the easy days of their early marriage when every day was a delight and the nights were heaven.

What he did *not* want was the silent stranger she had become—the quiet, downtrodden little doormat. Every time he was in her presence he felt the weight of guilt descend on him, and that was why he had said what he said. He still wasn't quite sure where it came from, but he told her she should sleep with other men. Then if she didn't have a child, maybe she would stop blaming him.

He had known it would hurt her on many levels: the reminder that she was barren, the implication that he could not care less if she bedded down with someone else, the accusation that she blamed him in some way. Why had he even said it? If he had wanted a fight, he had gotten it. After years of quiet depression she had flared up in anger at his cruel words, and they had had a row of enormous proportions. And then he had felt justified in leaving the next morning with just a cold list of written instructions for her.

And he had not seen her again until that night in the opera house.

Despite his first words to Less, he had felt a jolt of pleasure at the sight of Emily. He never—or rarely, anyway—lied to himself, and yes, it was pleasure he had felt

at seeing her. Not unalloyed pleasure. Not pleasure un-
mixed with pain but pleasure nonetheless. So why had
he been so supercilious to her when they met? Sometimes
he did not understand his own responses to his wife, so
layered were they, and complex.

But then she had come to his side when she found out
about the attack. And she had sat at his feet and touched
his leg, giving him more pleasure with that simple touch
than Belle had in all the times she had made love to him.
Emily's hands soothed and yet aroused him—gave him
ease and inflamed him. Why? She was changed; there was
no disputing his mother's words. She had become a little
plump, but she was still his Emily, still his beautiful bride.

And she seemed to have gained back some of what he
had loved her for. That she had needed his absence to
regain her strength and confidence in herself was a painful reminder that neither of them—toward the end, anyway—had brought out the best in each other. She had
become a weepy stranger, and he had become a cold
monster, hating himself every time he turned away from
her.

His mother had been silent all this time as he sat thinking, and he glanced at her curiously. It was she who had
chased Emily away from Brockwith, and yet now she was
demanding that they get together to produce an heir, the
child that had been denied them during years of loving.
But then his mother believed that conception was a matter of determination. She had always blamed Emily for
not wanting a child enough.

Baxter knew otherwise. He had seen his wife with her
cousin's babies and the children of friends. It had almost
killed him to witness the raw longing in her eyes and
know that he could not fulfill it. He was arrested by that
thought. It came to him in that moment that he blamed
himself for their not being able to conceive and that was
why he had said those horrible words to Emily on the
last day he saw her at Brockwith.

He could give her diamonds and emeralds and rubies,

houses and villas and vacations in Greece, if she wanted, but he could not give her a baby. He had been with many women, and none, to his knowledge, had ever conceived a child by him. Surely that was a rather good indication that the problem was his.

He had done Emily a grave injustice in what he had said to her, and it stung even more now that he knew where it had come from. But it was far too late to make amends for the past now. Far too late. No matter what his mother wanted, it was not going to happen. After the other day, he had some hope that he and Emily could learn to be civil to one another. She had a forgiving heart, he believed. Maybe she had forgiven him for his spiteful words.

"You are ignoring me, Baxter, but you should know that I will not just go away. I want you to get back with that wife of yours and have a child."

"It is hardly that easy, Mother."

"Nonsense. I have put it to her as well, and I am sure she will see sense. Once you two do your duty, then you can forget each other and we can raise the next marquess."

Baxter stared at her in unfeigned wonder. Did she really believe it was just that easy—that one made up one's mind to have a child and went about conceiving it? That one could determine the sex of a child just by sheer willpower? He supposed she believed that one knew the moment it had happened, too. Maybe in her own remarkable physiology she had known the moment she had conceived him, Baxter Eggleton Godfrey Delafont. And he supposed after that she saw no reason to go on with the ridiculous business of sharing a bed with her husband. The marquess, his father, had certainly had enough mistresses.

"Do you mean," Baxter said slowly, struck by something she said, "that you went to my wife and told her we needed to get together to create an heir?"

"I did. Why do you think I came to London? Dreadful

city! Even in spring. It stinks and it is dirty." She drained her cup and stood. "I came the moment I heard she was back in town. You do not think I am so deluded that I thought you could conceive an heir by mail, did you?"

"Whyever not, Mother? I'm sure *you* could."

She snorted as she stood and raised herself to her full height, not inconsiderable for a woman. "I will leave you to finish your breakfast, Baxter." She threw a disdainful look at Belle, who remained silent and still in her chair, her eyes unaccustomedly downcast. "I will expect you to dispense with the services of your mistress until you conceive with Emily. No sense in wasting your potential. Of course, I fully understand that you will not be able to do so until your ankle heals, but with your constitution, that should be soon. Good day. I am staying with your Aunt Ophelia while in London. You know where to find me."

She swept from the room.

Eight

"Lady van Hoffen and Lady Grishelda May van Hoffen," Trumble announced, bowing the ladies into Emily's parlor.

"Grishelda! Lady van Hoffen!" Emily said. "How nice to see you both in London! It seems an age since we met in Cumbria at Christmas!" She rose and took Grishelda's hands in her own, noting how the spare young woman seemed to have lost weight and color since their mutual stay with the Marquess and Marchioness of Ladymead. The marquess's younger brother was the very same young man who had married her niece, Celestine Simon. Lady van Hoffen had taken her daughter, Grishelda, there, in the hope that *she* would be his chosen bride.

Lady van Hoffen, a showy redhead of around forty, pasted a fake smile on her round, still-pretty face. "It does seem an age, does it not? I was just saying to Grishelda that to look at her face you would think it had been years, not months, so changed is she!" She cast an unfriendly look at her daughter and took a seat by the tea tray.

Emily pursed her lips and shook her head. She had never been able to manufacture even a slight liking for the mother, but Lady Grishelda was another matter. She was similar to her own niece, which perhaps explained her preference, in that both were thin and serious, and good to the core. But where Celestine had an optimistic outlook on life, despite the severe deprivation she had undergone for much of her existence and the pain and suffering of arthritis, Grishelda seemed to look on the world with unfriendly eyes. In their few conversations it had become clear that she believed the world held little happiness for her, and that she must be content with what good she could do in her life.

She looked like she had been ill. Her pale-blue eyes were dark-rimmed and her cheeks hollow. There was no tactful way to ask if something was wrong, however, so she settled on sitting Grishelda down beside her and plying her with cakes and tea. The girl's abstraction was troubling, though, so when Lady van Hoffen's attention was diverted by Dodo's entrance and subsequent conversation, Emily said, in an undertone, "Pardon me if I am poking my nose in where it does not belong, but are you unhappy, my dear?"

Grishelda stared down at her thin hands, knotting and unknotting the fringe on her Norwich shawl of fine gray silk. "I am wretched, Lady Delafont . . ."

"Emily, dear, call me Emily."

Tears welled in the girl's fine eyes at the sympathy in her hostess's voice. "Oh, Emily, I am wretched. I am being pushed and prodded until I think I will go mad!"

"What is it?" Emily asked, concerned at the sharp hint of desperation in the girl's voice.

"It . . . it is my mother. She has a friend, a Captain Dempster, and he is always visiting . . . even overnight."

It was no surprise that Lady van Hoffen would be so indiscreet. She was a blowsy woman plucked from the stage in her teens by an elderly foreign nobleman who survived the marriage only two years, long enough to see the birth of his daughter and to see that she favored him in looks enough to be sure of her legitimacy. After his death, Lady van Hoffen had set off on a long and scandalous bout of affairs that titillated even the most sophisticated of dilettantes. She was avid in the pursuit of male admirers even twenty years into her widowhood.

"Why is that a problem, my dear? I don't mean to be snide, but has your mother not done that before?"

"Oh, often! I have learned to lock my door and not come out till morning—learned it at a very young age." Her pale blue eyes held a haunted look, as she glanced over at her mother and lowered her voice even more. "But Captain Dempster . . . I am sure he picks my lock. I awoke late one night to find him standing over my bed! I screamed and he put his hand over my mouth. He said I must have failed to lock my door, and he was just checking to make sure I was all right."

Emily sighed and took the girl's hand. Lady van Hoffen glanced over at them suspiciously, but Emily sent her a bright smile and nod, and she rejoined her conversation with Dodo, who sent a significant glance Emily's way.

"You are of age, are you not, my dear?"

Grishelda nodded. "I am soon to be twenty-three."

"Then why do you not simply leave? Go back to your country estate."

The girl glanced over at her mother yet again. "I . . . I thought of that, but when I told my mother, she . . . she did not react well. She intends that I shall marry this season, and she has picked my suitor, an elderly roué named Lord Saunders."

"Saunders! That old lecher? She cannot force you to marry, my dear."

"She controls my fortune until I am twenty-five or until I marry. And she has implied that if I do not go along with her she will have me kidnapped and taken over the border, telling all that I am a runaway bride!"

Grishelda's voice was thin with fear, and so Emily did not give vent to her first instinctive reaction, a loud noise of disbelief. It was her firm opinion that the girl's mother was just trying to lay pressure on her to do what she wanted. After all, this was England, not some colonial backwater where lawlessness was rife. No one could force her to marry! But the girl was obviously worried, so Emily said, "My dear, if ever you need help I am here. Please feel free to come to me any time and for any reason."

Grishelda gratefully sighed and took a proffered cup of tea. "I feel better just for having told someone. I have no friends . . . . I never seemed to have the ability to make friends. At Christmas, though, I felt that with both you and Celestine I could talk openly."

"I am glad you feel that way, my dear. Indeed, you remind me of my niece a great deal. She is a very good woman."

"You don't know me very well, though," Grishelda said, gloomily. She cast a dark look in her mother's direction. "Sometimes I think I am more like my mo—"

Trumble entered. "Mr. Lessington," he said.

"Less! How good to see you." Emily rose and took his hand, pulling him over to meet Grishelda. Out of the corner of her eyes, she could see Lady van Hoffen preening, pushing out her bosom and smirking as an attractive male entered the room. He merely acknowledged the introduction with a bow, made his obeisance to Dodo and joined Emily and Grishelda.

Of course the conversation could not return to the personal matters they had been discussing, but Emily had the satisfaction of seeing Grishelda more relaxed in Less's undemanding company, and when she rose to go at her mother's insistence, the young woman pressed Emily's hand and whispered, "Thank you" in a soft tone. Dodo followed them out.

"I am glad to finally get you alone, my dear!" Less took her arm and led her back to the settee.

"You sound so serious, Less! What is it? Has Baxter . . ." Emily felt her heart constrict. And yet, surely, if Baxter was in trouble, her friend would have said so immediately.

"And you would have me believe you do not love him," Less teased, with a smile.

Emily relaxed. "I believe I admitted that I still do, much to my chagrin."

He patted her hand. "I know, my dear. I will not tease you any longer." He gave her a considering look. "Would you take him back if he came back to you?"

She pulled away from him. Why did he have to ask questions like that now? She had just made the decision to move on with her life; she had made the momentous resolution to take a lover and stop drying up like an old maid. And then Less had to ask if she would take her husband back into her arms and her bed? Hypothetical lovemaking would not keep her warm at night She still loved Baxter, but she saw no possibility that their marriage could ever be reanimated.

Perhaps when they were first separated she should have made more of a push to reawaken the love they had had for each other, but it had been five years since their legal separation, and even before that things had not been good for a long time. How could Less think that after all this time they could heal the rift between them?

"You talk in riddles, Less. What did you really come here to impart? Come, I can see you are bursting with information. Tell me!"

He smiled. "Very well, my dear, very well. I have learned some of what our mutual acquaintance was up to on the Continent."

Emily toyed with a music box on the mantle over the fireplace, and it tinkled out the last notes of a mournful tune. "Besides bedding a very comely little actress?"

He liked the bite of jealousy in her voice. It boded well for his plans to reunite his friends in wedded bliss, a state to which he was convinced they both secretly longed to return. "Besides bedding la Gallant!"

"She's very pretty, isn't she," Emily mused, arrested in midmovement and staring out the window. "So lithe and thin . . . I was never so slender. She is as graceful as a little butterfly."

"Come, my dear," he said in a bracing tone, loathe to allow her to sink into maudlin jealousy. "Do you not want to hear what Del has been up to?"

"Of course," Emily said, returning from the fireplace to sit by her friend. "Tell me."

"He has been a courier! The last days of the war were very tense, and he carried papers, unofficially of course, for the Iron Duke! Castlereagh used him as well, and others."

"How thrilling! But why should that be such a danger? If his duties were concealed?"

"Perhaps someone found out. Or perhaps, and this is what I think, there is more to it than simply courier service."

"You think he was doing something else?"

"I am convinced of it. My contact refuses to divulge the information, but I shall wear away! I will be victorious, or my name is not Sylvester Lessington!"

Dodo came in that moment carrying a beautiful bowl filled with roses.

"Those are lovely, Dodo!"

"From one of your admirers," she said gruffly, handing Emily a note.

Her heart pounding, she remembered how Baxter had plied her with roses in the first years of their marriage, after he learned they were her favorite flower. Had he remembered? Was this a token of the truce they seemed to have made in his parlor the previous day?

She hurriedly opened the note.

My lady,

I have not yet dared confess my feelings for you, but they are of such a magnitude I can no longer keep them to myself.

Chérie, may I attend you in your chambers tonight, that I may give you tangible evidence of my worshipful love? Please say yes. I await your word to suspend my agony,

Yours always with hope in my heart,

Etienne

She paled. This was a request to move forward with lovemaking. He wanted to make love to her, and he wouldn't wait long before importuning her in person. She glanced up to see Less studying her face. She forced a smile. This was her own business, and no one else's, and her own decision to make. She had thought she had come to a decision, but found that it was still very tentative.

"What were we speaking of?" she said, brightly.

"Your husband," he said.

"My . . . my separated husband!" she corrected.

"You make him sound like he has fallen apart."

Emily laughed. "Oh, Less, I can always count on you for a smile."

"Do you go to the Enderby rout tonight?"

"No . . . I have, er, plans."

"Plans? Sounds exciting."

Trumble entered. "Vicomte Etienne Marchant."

The young Frenchman entered and his eyes sought Emily immediately. His quick gaze took in the roses as he bowed to Dodo, at the other end of the room, and Less.

"You received my roses . . . and my . . . my billet-doux?" he said, softly. He stood before Emily holding her hands in his after pressing a kiss to each one. His voice was caressing and his eyes traveled over her body with amorous heat glowing in them.

"I—I did." Emily felt herself color, and wished, for once, that she could be more sophisticated. Society lovers came across each other in ballrooms and parlors every day with no display of emotion. But she met the man she was thinking of making love with and turned a bright crimson. Very déclassé!

Marchant cast an irritated glance at Less and placed himself on the other side of Emily on the settee. He retained one hand in his.

Lessington felt his heart drop. There was no mistaking the body language of the very handsome young French viscount. He was desirous of making Emily his lover, which was probably what the note was about. If he wasn't mistaken, and he seldom was about women and their affairs, she was considering it . . . seriously! Del had left her alone for too long. While he was sating his sexual needs, Emily had been left to build up hers over the years, and now she was ripe for the plucking. And the eager Frenchman was not going to let this plump and tasty plum drop from the tree and wizen into a prune unsavored.

Grimly, he hoped he was not too late trying to reunite the husband and wife. Del was hurting, and Lessington had never had a friend who felt so much like a brother. He would just have to do whatever he could and hope that the two would find their way back to each other . . . with a little prodding from him, of course.

"I am Belle Gallant, and all the gentlemen are wild about me," she repeated to herself, turning in front of the mirror checking every angle of her lovely peignoir. It was peach, a very fetching color for her, she had been told, and if she moved just right one could catch glimpses of her body through the diaphanous fabric. She had sent her maid away and was waiting for Del to respond to her urgent summons.

All day she had not been able to obliterate the words his mother had said in the dining room. An heir. He needed an heir.

Del was a god, her savior, the only man she had ever known who had treated her with respect and kindness, even when she was a scratching, biting little spitfire being beaten by the manager of that mangy troupe of actors she had been traveling with. Del had rescued her, even though she had deserved that particular beating. After all, she had been caught stealing, and everyone knew that was wrong.

But Del had swooped down like one of them funny-looking fellows in the fairy books, all in metal, and saved her from the worst hiding of her life. And then he had taken her away and hired a gent to teach her how to talk, and then he had bought her clothes and sent her to Mr. Lessington—sometimes the weight of her debt to him felt like it was going to crush her. What could she ever give a rich, titled, perfect gentleman like Del?

A son. An heir.

She knew she was capable because there were those other two times . . . not that they had been born, exactly, but the old lady in the village she had been in when the last one was stillborn said it was just because she was so young. She had only been fourteen. Once she was more grown up, then she would be able to bring a life into the world. That was the same old woman who taught her how to prevent ending up with an unwanted child in her belly again.

But now she wanted a baby. Or rather, she wanted Del to have a baby. He would just take it away, wouldn't he? *She* wouldn't be expected to take care of it and raise it, would she? Because it sounded like too much work, and she frankly did not like children, ugly, noisy little brutes that they were. There had always been a ragtag crowd of little ones in the acting troupe, and sometimes she had been expected to take care of them. She would rather have done anything than that, and she had done a lot of unsavory things in those years.

Now, when she looked back, she thought of her life as being two parts—the time before Del and the time since Del. The time since Del had been a lovely dream, but now it was time for her to grow up and start repaying the debt she owed him. She paced the floor. Tonight she would start the attempt to have Del's child. It was the least she could do for him; she only wished there were more. It would be a fortunate child, to have a man like him to look up to.

She remembered her own father. He was the reason she had run away with the actors. As ignorant a little slut as she had been, she did know what a father wasn't supposed to do to his daughter, and he *wasn't* supposed to put his whatsit in her.

She heard a noise and looked up quickly. Was that Del's step on the stair?

Emily paced back and forth in her private parlor, not sure of what she was doing or what she was supposed to be doing. What did a woman wear who was having a rendezvous with the man who was going to become her lover? It wasn't the kind of thing she could discuss with anyone, either, even though Dodo, with a sparkle in her worldly eyes, seemed to know what was up. She had accepted an invitation to go out without Emily, a first since they had been in town.

And she couldn't ask her dresser, Sylvie, who was new. Agnes had left that morning to return to Yorkshire because the little dear was getting married to Emily's estate manager's son in April, and Sylvie was her replacement. But where Agnes was just a sweet English girl, Sylvie was terrifyingly French, with a wizard's ability with Emily's stubborn mass of dark hair and a ruthless fashion sense. But she was also dour in a way Emily had never thought a Frenchwoman could be, and therefore not one to confide in about a visit from a lover.

And so Emily had settled for her afternoon dress of rose-and-white-striped percale. It was pretty and flattering but suddenly seemed wildly inappropriate. Would Etienne stare to see her decked out as for an afternoon of visiting? Would he know her for the gauche, naïve country woman she was at heart?

But that was what she was, and she could not change it and would not pretend to a sophistication she did not own. For all her years as a society matron, she had never lost the feeling that she was an unsophisticated trout in a pond full of glittering goldfish. The brittle hauteur, the air of condescension—she had never mastered those arts. Baxter had it down to a science; he could freeze a mushroom at twenty paces with just a flick of his quizzing glass. She had teased him about that, but had never acquired the ability herself.

And now she was about to partake in that most sophisticated of society pastimes, taking a lover. And a French lover at that!

She had instructed Trumble to show the vicomte up to her private parlor, but when she heard his step on the stair, her stomach twisted. What was in store for her that night? Would the evening end in her bed, with a night of lovemaking? Would she awake in the morning a different woman for having broken the marriage vows she had sworn to so many years ago? Would she regret it for the rest of her life?

Etienne took the stairs two at a time. That she had agreed to see him alone could mean only one thing, and he felt his pulse quicken in anticipation. He had always sought out a certain type of woman since his first sexual experience with a friend of his mother's at the very tender age of thirteen; he liked softer, rounder women who cradled a man in warmth and security. Like a mother, but most definitely *not* like a mother. Large bosoms, gently rounded stomachs, wide hips—not a hard angle or bone jutting out anywhere.

He had hoped from the moment he saw Emily that she would acquiesce to his urging, but he had feared that being married would prevent her. She had, if he read her right, a streak of purity, of innocence, almost. He felt a moment's qualm when he thought of his purpose, his reason for being in London. Was he endangering it by bedding the foolish marquess's wife? But no, how could that be? They were separated, he had been assured by many who knew—separated for years, and the man had a mistress, so he was not likely to come back to his wife's bed. The fool! To leave a woman like Emily for that hard little trollop who fashioned herself an actress!

He tapped on the door the butler had indicated and heard a soft "Come in!" He slipped into the room. There she was by the fireplace, in a pretty rose-and-white day dress. It pleased him that she was not attired in some peignoir or other variety of *dishabille*. It spoke of her innocence in *les liaisons amoureuses*. It would be his pleasure to disrobe her, revealing her luscious bounty slowly. He felt himself harden at the thought and forced his mind away from racing ahead. Slowly, he must go slowly; that much he knew by instinct. Emily was younger and less experienced than his usual conquests—and incidentally, slimmer—and he must remember that though she was his senior by perhaps ten years, she would be his student in the art of love. He had been taught well by many women; now it would be his privilege to become the teacher.

"My lady, you enchant me!" His voice trembled with anticipation.

Her eyes, a delicious brown the color of melted chocolate, widened. "Monsieur, I . . . please, have a seat."

"Only if you will sit with me." He watched her and, with chagrin, understood that she was nervous and perhaps had not entirely made up her mind yet. He was confirmed in his belief that she had never taken a lover. All the better. All the more delicious to make love to a woman who had not been loved in a long time. He had all night.

Nine

"What is it, Belle? What is the urgent summons for?" Baxter stumped into her bedroom with the use of an elegant silver-knobbed cane and stared at his young paramour. He had expected to find her sick or in distress, but instead she stood in the middle of the room naked, a peachy peignoir in her hand and her blond curls ruffled as if she had just pulled it off over her head.

She tossed it onto the bed and threw her arms around him, throwing him a little off balance.

"Good God, Belle!" He staggered sideways and ended up sitting on the edge of the bed, her naked body across his knee. He had wrenched his ankle, and it started aching again, when it had just stopped.

"Yes, Delly?"

"What did you want?"

"You!" she giggled. She pushed him back and, kneeling on the floor in front of him, fumbled with the fall of his breeches.

He sat up and grasped her hand in an iron grip. "Belle, I thought there was something wrong! I left a rather important meeting to come here."

She made a face and got busy with her free hand.

"Belle!"

She sat back on her haunches.

At least he had gotten her attention. Now what? How to tell her that he was tired of her? That it was only his body that went through the motions? Did she love him?

Would she be hurt? He didn't know. He didn't even understand his own feelings in the whole affair. He only knew he did not want to hurt her.

It was bizarre, but he felt oddly paternal toward Belle, which made their lovemaking incestuous, which made him a dirty satyr of the worst sort. A wave of revulsion passed over him. At least he had successfully avoided her overtures since arriving back in England. But how to disengage himself from the affair without hurting a girl he felt an odd affection for? He couldn't seem to help himself from hurting Emily; he didn't want to start along that same path with Belle.

"Belle," he said, gently. "We don't have to engage in sexual relations every time I come to see you, you know. We can talk or . . ." He sighed in exasperation.

She gazed up at him, her small, heart-shaped face drawn with a puzzled expression. He reached out and smoothed a blond curl away from her forehead. She was so young. She was eighteen when he found her . . . or was she? She only looked that now.

"How old are you, Belle?"

"I'm . . ."

He watched her shrewd face calculating.

"How old are you *really?*"

She blinked and then shrugged. The candlelight flickered over her lithe, naked little body. Her skin was tawny, her small breasts high and firm.

"I think I'm nineteen. Or I could be twenty now. I can't remember when my birthday is. If I ever knew."

Del closed his eyes and shuddered. He had thought she was at least twenty-one, but it appeared he had been having sex with her since she was seventeen or eighteen. Most of his friends would not find that atrocious. After all, many prostitutes were that age or younger when they started plying their trade. But he had never frequented houses of prostitution, nor had he ever felt the need to have sex with girls young enough to be his own children. He felt her active little hands busy at his breeches again and seized them in his. He opened his eyes and gazed down into hers. Moisture was welling up.

"What is wrong, Belle?"

"You don't want me!" she wailed.

Oh, God, now the child was hurt. "It is not that I don't want you, my dear. Who could not want you? You are beautiful."

"Thanks to you, Del. I know what I was before I met you. I was a horrible, grubby little tart, but you made me into a lady!"

He sighed and pulled her up onto the bed beside him and put his arm around her shoulders, chafing her to warmth. "You were a pearl, my dear, just waiting for someone to rub the dirt off of you to see the luster. I hope you know that."

She snuggled against him. "So you *do* want me?"

Her voice trembled with hope and fear, and he hadn't the heart to say no. He felt cornered and manipulated and he hated himself for acquiescing, but he squeezed her and said, "Yes, of course, my dear. But not right now. I told you I had a meeting and only left it because I though you were in distress. I must now return to it." And find a way to say no to her without hurting her and let her go her own way, he thought. For her own good.

He was convinced, and had been for a long time, that she did not make love to him because she enjoyed it, and he had to find a way to break it off with her. They both deserved lovers who brought them passion and delight between the covers. Making love with Belle was very like his own first exploratory self-manipulations when he was young. It did the job efficiently, but was highly unsatisfactory other than that. They could not go on this way.

"Del! You seem much better, old man," Lessington said, clapping his friend on the back with a smile on his mobile and animated face.

"I am. I finally discarded the damned cane two days ago."

They stood together at the edge of the ballroom floor. The Harrises were always among the first to hold a large ball in the season, and it was among the best attended. There were twittering groups of girls in white gathered near them, prohibited from the dance floor because it was a waltz and they had not yet been sanctioned to perform that risqué dance by one of the patronesses of Almack's.

Many others circled the dance floor, though, among them Emily, in the arms of the host, Walter Harris. Del's eyes followed her progress.

"That dress is a little youthful for your wife, do you not think?"

Lessington's voice cut into his thoughts and he sent a dark glance his way. "I was just thinking that she looked quite lovely tonight! That shade of rose was always becoming, and there is something in her countenance . . . ." He caught his friend's laughing eyes. "You devil. You are saying things to provoke me, I believe. She looks lovely."

"I believe you said she was fat?"

Del shifted uncomfortably. "She *has* gained weight, Less. Two stone, maybe, but not more than that. It is not so very unbecoming. In fact, she looks as lovely as she ever did, and perhaps even more beautiful. When she went north to Yorkshire she was so pale and unhappy, but now she has regained that delightful glow she always had." He watched the dancers for a moment and then continued. "Why do you think she has gained weight?"

"Unhappiness?" Less said, quietly. "Seclusion, perhaps? Or just getting older. We all are, you know, even if some of us have darling little mistresses to keep us young."

The remark was rather more cutting than Less's usual toward him. Del glanced sideways. He knew that his friend often visited Emily and had always like her. But it was not his marriage, damn it, and he would stay out of it! "Less, I would not say any more, if I were you."

Less shivered theatrically. "My goodness, I believe I have been threatened by the Maudlin Marquess! Very well, my lord, I shall refrain from any more remarks like that. Shall I settle for gossip instead? Would it interest his lordship to know that a certain young, very French and *very* handsome vicomte was seen a few nights ago entering a certain society matron's private parlor—a marchioness, no less—who shall remain nameless but whose initials are E. D. And he didn't leave again for a very long time! I have it on the very best authority—servants, you know. They see everything."

Del was stung. Emily? With the Vicomte Marchant? Impossible. Why, the young man was ten years younger than she! He watched her circle the room, a healthy glow coming to her cheeks. Did she seem happier? Was the glow sexual fulfillment?

Emily had always been passionate in bed . . . and out of bed! Wildly so, at times. Was Marchant sampling those particular delights? His black eyes narrowed. Emily, in all the years they had lived together as man and wife, had never given him a single moment's worry that she had fallen prey to the immorality and sampling of illicit pleasures rife among the bored wives of the *ton*. So many of their friends accepted affairs as a way of life. But he and Emily were separated, and could he really expect her to go the rest of her life without physical release?

He remembered the last words he had said to her at Brockwith, that maybe she should go to bed with some other man to see if she got pregnant so she would stop blaming him. He couldn't believe he had said that—had never apologized in person or even in letter. What had gone wrong? How had they come to that?

Without thinking, he moved across the dance floor as the music ended. Harris had returned her to Dodo. Del approached them.

"Aunt Dianne. How well you look tonight." He bowed

before Dodo, taking in her lavender silk dress and white hair piled high. He turned to Emily. "May a husband beg a dance with his wife?"

Emily started and colored. Whatever she had expected of him, it wasn't that, and it gave him a moment of devilish pleasure to surprise her. Was that a guilty flush? Was she even now thinking of meeting her lover after the ball?

"I . . . I would be honored, my lord," she said, curtsying deeply.

Her rose silk was cut very low over her bosom, exposing creamy, plump mounds. He wondered how heavy they would feel weighed in his hand and whether the skin could possibly be as soft as it looked. The neckline was so low that an inch or even a scant half inch lower and her entire breasts would be exposed. And yet some other ladies in the room had dresses just as daring, or more so. She rose and put her hand in his. It was not a waltz, and he felt cheated that they must part time and time again in the figures of the country dance.

They did not speak. She was as graceful as she always had been. He watched her when he knew she wasn't looking and for the first time wondered what their life would have been like if they hadn't separated. Would he have taken on his current duties with the government?

Certainly not if they had been able to have children, but otherwise? He didn't know. Less had suggested that whatever he was mixed up in, it had a self-destructive edge to it, but he was not suicidal. If he was honest, however, he would have to admit that he didn't seem to care as much about self-preservation as he had when he was younger.

He joined with Emily again. Was she seeing the young Frenchman? Was he her lover? There had been admiration in the young man's eyes when they met, and it had surprised him at the time, especially with the young and lovely Belle Gallant in the same room. But the vicomte had not given the younger woman a second glance. His wife—how strange those words sounded in his head—his wife's deep brown eyes turned up to gaze into his and she missed the footing of the dance for once and stumbled into him. He righted her and they stood for one long minute, with the strains of the lively violin around them and other couples having to move to avoid them. The look in her eyes surprised and fascinated him. When they were together, he would have ordered the carriage immediately if he had seen that look.

"Are you spoken for in the next dance?" he asked, though he was not sure why.

"No," she replied. "I . . . I did not engage myself as I intended to leave early."

"Walk with me in the garden instead."

She nodded, wordlessly, breathlessly, and he took her arm and strolled out with her through the terrace doors. There would be a scandal, he knew. They were separated and everyone was aware of that. The gossips and tattlers would have a holiday when they learned that the Delafonts were seen strolling together out to the gardens.

She felt warm and comfortable at his side, and he led her across the flagstone terrace and down some steps to the garden, fragrant with spring blossoms. There was a gravel walkway, and he led her to a stone bench some distance from the house and a ways past the last flambeau. By London standards it was a large garden, and they were far enough from the house that they had a modicum of privacy. They sat together.

What was he doing in the garden with his wife? He had responded instinctively to the seductive softness in her large brown eyes and the throb of yearning in his loins. He had never before or since his marriage had a lover who could excite him as Emily always had in their years together, and a part of him longed for that fulfillment. Once experienced it was the measure by which all else was compared. Was it simply desire, then, that coursed through his veins? Could it be sated by possessing her body again or was there more than mere lust at work?

She shivered, and he realized that it was still a little

chilly to be taking a lady for a walk in the moonlight. He did not want to take her back just yet, though, so he peeled off his jacket, an awkward thing to do as his tailor made the fit so damned close, and put it around her shoulders.

"Thank you, Baxter," she murmured and huddled into it.

How many years had it been since they were alone together? Certainly not since that dreadful day at Brockwith. Uneasily he recalled the pain in her eyes as he spoke to her that day, until she had summoned up enough ire to strike back at him with angry words. It was as though he had slapped her, and she needed to hit back to maintain her dignity. Afterward he had been glad that she had shrieked at him like a fishwife. At least she had not given one of those martyred sighs or sad little shrugs. She had let him have it with all the angry fire in her.

"Emily, I . . ." This was not going to be easy. She looked at him, large brown eyes full of questions. "Emily, I owe you an apology. A long overdue apology."

"For what?"

She could ask that? Did she really not know?

"I wronged you in many ways, and I am sorry. Even if we had fallen out of love, I should never have treated you the way I did . . . making you leave Brockwith . . . saying the things I said in that last interview . . . ."

Emily flinched as if he had struck her. Fallen out of love. He spoke of falling out of love as if it were a mutual thing, but it wasn't. Only he had fallen out of love. Her heart ached with a queer, pulling pain. But he was still talking and she must attend and not lose the thread of what he wanted to say.

"I guess that is the penalty for a marriage such as ours," he continued. "In our parents' day, we would not have been allowed to marry for love. Maybe that is wiser after all."

He looked sad, she thought, longing to stroke his face and ease away the lines that time and trouble had placed on his brow. Still so handsome! Still the man who made her heart beat faster and her body ache with longing, even as pain coursed through her.

"I don't think so," she said. "I would rather have had those years of love to remember, even considering how it ended, than to have had the most cordial arranged marriage in the world."

"I'm glad you feel that way, my dear. It eases my burden of guilt."

A tiny spurt of anger flared in her bosom. Burden of guilt? Is that what she had become in his memory? She moved away from him a little on the bench and gazed off into the dark bushes. "You have no need to feel guilty, Baxter. Life goes on. So our marriage didn't work. I am sure we have both found happiness in other ways."

She heard his swift intake of breath and turned to gaze up at him in the dim, flickering light shed from the flambeaux on the terrace. His face was twisted in anger, which he mastered quickly. What was wrong that he reacted that way? He threw his leg over the bench and straddled it, moving closer to her. She felt the warmth from his body invading her own, but there was no room to move farther away from him. When they were together, he would sit like that and she would lean against him, cradled by his strength. Now she felt suffocated by clamoring need, racing through her body like an electrical shock.

His voice was stiff and hard when he spoke again. "I brought you out here to apologize, and I cannot rest until I have been specific. I am sorry for pushing you out of Brockwith Manor. It was your home and you had . . . *have* every right to be there."

"Your mother would never have been happy with me there, Baxter, you know that."

"I should have insisted she move to the dower house; that was my duty to you."

"I don't want to be anyone's duty! What an unpleasant word!" She hunched her shoulder toward him.

"I am also sorry for the things I said to you before

leaving. Specifically that maybe if you slept with another man and did not get pregnant you would stop blaming me." His voice was hard and determined, biting chunks out of the quiet night air.

"I have learned much since moving to Yorkshire," she replied quietly, resolved not to quarrel with him. There was no point in anger after all these years. "I have learned that no matter how much two people love each other, they cannot know each other's thoughts. Assumptions are made, feelings are hurt, mistakes are made. I never blamed you for not giving me a child. I thought *you* blamed *me*, though, as your mother did . . . as she still does."

"And that is another thing. I am sorry for not protecting you from my mother." His voice was softer, not as harsh. "She can be a bit much at times."

Emily chuckled into the darkness. "A bit much? Oh, Baxter! Understated as always. Wellington should have set your mother loose on the French. Napoleon would have had a mass rebellion in his ranks in a week and the war would have been over."

He was silent and she bit her lip. She had offended him, and after she had meant to maintain peace with him. She turned toward him and looked up into his dark, hooded eyes, glittering in the wavering light from the flambeaux. There was pain there, but not anger this time.

"I . . . I should apologize myself for a few things," she said. "I know it must have seemed like I blamed you that I could not conceive, but I never did. I did withdraw though, from you. I remember times when you offered me"—her voice broke, but she cleared her throat and continued, though she could no longer hold his gaze— "you offered me tenderness, and I could not return it. I was so unhappy . . . . I wanted a child so badly. Not just for the succession, but just to have *our* child. I felt less of a woman for not being able to conceive. I have always wanted . . ." She turned away from that unprofitable line of thought. Dwelling on the past and on what she would never have was a mistake; she had learned that in the years of their separation. She took a deep breath, and said, simply, "I was wrong to draw away from you. I apologize."

She risked a glance up into his eyes. There was turmoil in their dark depths.

"Emily, how could you ever think yourself less of a woman for not being able to bear a child? It is not that important in the larger scheme of things that I have an heir. I have a cousin William, a rather nice young fellow down in Shropshire, who will make a superb marquess. And he is even now married and his wife with child. The succession is secure."

"I told you it wasn't just the succ—"

"Shh, Em. I know. A child of our own . . ." He stopped and looked down into her brown eyes sparkling with unshed tears and a fissure cracked in his heart. She had not blamed him! It was her own feelings of inadequacy that caused her to pull away from him, to grow cold in their lovemaking! And he had reacted with harshness and fury. All of that turmoil over assumptions. He reached out and wrapped his arms around her. "Oh, Emily," he whispered in the echoey darkness of the garden.

Ten

She relaxed, her softness cradled against him. "Emily, I . . ." She was gazing up at him, her rosy lips parted, her warm breath fanning against his mouth like a gentle touch and it seemed the most natural thing in the world to kiss her. Her eyes fluttered closed as his head lowered and he tasted her lips with curiosity. What would it be like, after all these years?

She was pliant and unresisting in his arms, a warm, soft bundle of womanhood begging to be loved. He deepened the kiss, feeling heat bloom in his lower regions as arousal swelled against her rounded bottom, snug against his groin. She parted her lips more and he slipped his tongue in, groaning at the warm, sweet taste of her. He plunged deeply into her luscious mouth, relishing the satiny feel of her skin where his tongue probed, pushing deeper, demanding more. She quivered, and he heard her faint, stifled moan of suppressed excitement. He held her close and tight, her shivers of growing excitement vibrating through his body.

He could hardly think as the fog of sexual excitement closed in around his brain, but inevitably comparisons raced through his mind, the small part that was still working. He had kissed Belle, but she was impatient and demanding, forcing the lovemaking to move on to intercourse immediately. Emily surrendered herself to him and followed his lead, her arms going up around his neck as she moaned against his lips. Her awakening desire was a powerful aphrodisiac, and he knew he was already more aroused than ever he was with Belle.

It was startling, amazing! This was his wife in his arms. His wife of more than fifteen years! And yet he felt like he was stalking a new mistress, enjoying the eroticism of the hunt, the urgent thrill of pursuit and capture, and delectable ravishment.

Emily pulled away and started to stand, her eyes unfocused, her face a mask of confusion, but no! By God, he was not going to stop yet! He pulled her back to him, his body aching with desire, ferociously, *hungrily* aware that it felt good to be the pursuer, rather than the prey, as he was with Belle. He kissed Emily's lips again, plundering the delicious mouth, tasting faintly of wine, with his questing tongue as she shivered in his arms, quiescent now.

He moved his lips down to her throat, and she threw her head back in mindless pleasure, her hands on his shoulders kneading and massaging through his shirt fabric as he kissed the pulse point at the base of her throat. He nipped her skin and she gasped, a startled, faint moan of delight following. The inviting slope of her bosom and deep cleavage teased him, and he spread warm kisses down the silky skin, breathing in her delectable fragrance and nuzzling the full, rounded mounds that curved above the low neckline of her dress. He ached to dare more, to do more, and as he tongued the deep cleft of her exquisite bosom, he felt her body jolt with sensual awareness.

"Baxter," she sighed into the quiet night as he spanned his large hand over the fullness of one breast.

The garden was deserted. Did he dare? *Should* he dare? He longed to slip his hand under the fabric of her dress and stroke the milky white skin, kiss the pearly nubs and feel her breasts heave with mounting desire. Would she stop him? Or would she surrender herself to his needs and let him inflame hers? He moved, butting his arousal up against her bottom, eager to extend an invitation she had never refused in their years together.

"Baxter, no," she moaned. "Oh, Baxter, we mustn't . . ."

Her words died as he kissed his way down the plump mound, down to the very edge of her lacy neckline. He pushed his tongue under the snug neckline, and she grasped his shoulders, clutching at the fabric with hands tightened into claws, a low, inarticulate groan of raw need her only sound. He felt a surge of triumph and desperately tried to think—though his mind was remarkably uncooperative as far as coherent thought went—if he could convince her to go to his carriage with him. His arousal was almost painful now, throbbing against the tight confines of his breeches and the inviting roundness of her hip and bottom. If not the carriage, was there a gazebo or summerhouse? Somewhere! Anywhere he could lay her down or get under her skirts or . . . .

A footstep crunched on the gravel path just beyond the hedge. "Emily? *Chérie?*"

Emily pulled away from Baxter and with trembling, gloved fingers tried to restore order to her clothing. Her cheeks were flushing a deep crimson, and Baxter was seized overwhelmingly by the suspicion that it was guilt making her blush.

The young French vicomte turned the corner of the gravel path and came upon them. Baxter watched the slender young sprig with ill-concealed anger. Marchant paused.

"Do I come at a bad time? Emily?"

Emily forced a smile, though her breast was still heaving with passion. "Of course not, Etienne. We were just . . . uh, talking."

The young Frenchman approached closer and his darting eyes slid over her disarrayed dress and her blush. His eyes narrowed to slits and he cast an acrimonious glance on Baxter. He held out his hand and Emily took it, rising to stand beside him.

"Are you sure you are all right, *chérie?*" he asked, his voice tender and full of concern.

It was an absurd scene, Baxter thought, his passion blazing into anger. He felt like he had been caught groping another man's wife instead of his own! And with her full cooperation! What the hell was going on? If Marchant and his wife were having an affair, as it appeared from the young man's possessive demeanor, then what was she doing sitting in the garden allowing him to take liberties with her?

"We were just talking!" Baxter said, loudly, backing up his wife's assertion. Emily looked relieved. Marchant still had her rose-gloved hand in his own and was stroking it with the familiarity of a lover.

Marchant pointedly glared at Baxter's coat, which had fallen from Emily in the passion of the moment, and then his contemptuous gaze flicked over the evidence of Baxter's arousal. "Perhaps, my lord, you should achieve control over your person before rejoining the party."

With that, he tucked Emily's arm through his and walked her back to the ballroom.

Marchant was silent as he walked Emily up the gravel path and onto the terrace. Before entering the ballroom, he drew her aside and gazed into her eyes with blazing yearning.

"Emily, may I come to you tonight? After the ball?"

She pulled away from him. They had been through this, and she thought he understood. "No, Etienne, you know you cannot. I told you the other night; you are everything that is amiable and very handsome and very sweet, but I cannot do it. I cannot enter an affair. I am still married, and when I said the words *till death us do part,* I meant them. Forever."

"So, is that what you were doing in the garden with him? Mending your broken marriage?" The Frenchman's normally melodious voice came out in a harsh croak, and he gazed down at her with tortured eyes.

Had he fallen in love with her, Emily wondered. It was not possible. They had not known each other long enough, had they? But she had fallen in love with Baxter in a split second, or so it had seemed to her at the time, when she first met the man she would marry. She shivered in the night air, cold now that she did not have Baxter's arms around her and considered her next words.

"I don't know what that was about, Etienne," she told him truthfully. Honesty was all she could offer him. "He kissed me, and for a moment it felt like the old days, before we grew apart. Perhaps we can mend our marriage." A tiny bud of hope blossomed in her heart at the thought. He had apologized to her—perhaps not in the most eloquent way, but he had still apologized. And she had said to him what she had long hoped for the opportunity to say, that she had never blamed him for anything, or at least, if she had, she had long forgiven him.

"*Alors,* I wish you well," Marchant said, sadly, guiding her into the ballroom through open French doors. "I hope . . ."

His words were broken off when Lady Grishelda approached, glancing over her shoulder and then walking more swiftly. "Emily, there you are! Please come to the withdrawing room with me!" She grasped Emily's arm and darted another glance over her shoulder.

"Grishelda, what is wrong?"

"I can't explain here!"

Emily glanced around, but it didn't seem to her that there was any immediate threat in the large, crowded ballroom. Strangers surrounded them, the steady hum of conversation filling in while the orchestra paused between pieces. It would do the girl good to calm herself, and courtesy demanded an introduction. "Lady Grishelda van Hoffen, may I introduce you to Vicomte Etienne Marchant?"

"My lady," he said, bowing and taking her hand. He gallantly kissed it.

Grishelda pulled her hand away as if it had been stung and the young vicomte gazed at her with surprise. Then he smiled, a slow, seductive smile that lit his brown eyes with warmth.

"Please excuse me," Grishelda said, reddening unbecomingly as she curtseyed. "I . . . I am a trifle agitated at the moment." She turned away from the vicomte without ceremony and said, "Please, Emily, come with me!"

Emily threw Etienne an apologetic look and bid him a hasty good-bye, then followed Grishelda from the ballroom, threading, with difficulty, through the throng of people, some who wished to stop her to gossip. One even alluded, with an arch look, to the fact that she had disappeared from the ballroom with her husband and reappeared with the handsome Frenchman everyone was talking about. She made her excuses and followed Grishelda who, more slender and not as well known, had gotten through the crowd much more quickly.

The ladies' withdrawing room was a morning parlor with cheerful, butter-yellow walls and comfortable chairs, as well as a screened-off portion of the room for more intimate functions needed after too much wine or punch. There was a fire in the hearth, a tray of restoratives for any lady who might feel faint and a pert lady's maid ready to help with a torn flounce or other emergency.

Emily waved her away when she stood to approach them and joined Grishelda by the fire.

"What is wrong, my dear?"

The girl looked up at her with naked misery in her normally calm eyes. "I . . . I overheard my mother and Captain Dempster talking tonight to that miserable old goat Lord Saunders when they thought I was not around. He wants a young female to bear him a child, and that is to be me! I was right! They are going to marry me off to that filthy, old lecher." Her voice caught on a sob and she covered her face with her slender hands.

Emily sat down opposite her on a low stool in front of the sofa and pulled the young woman's hands away from her face. "Grishelda, you must not break down! You must be strong if you are to protect yourself." She stared into the leaping flames of the fire for a minute thinking. "Did you hear how they plan to marry you off without your consent?"

Grishelda shook her head. Her hair was back in its usual severe bun, and her dress was gray silk, elegant but austere. She was adorned with no jewelry, no bows or frills and not an inch of lace. "I can only assume," she said, her voice calmer, "that they intend the kidnap scheme. But how am I to guard against that?"

"And your mother is aware of all this?" It seemed incredible to Emily that any mother, even a sluttish tart like Lady van Hoffen, would countenance such treatment of her daughter!

"I don't think she knows the whole of it. Emily, there is more." Grishelda's voice was low, almost inaudible.

Emily leaned forward until their knees were touching. Grishelda's face was shadowed, but the misery was still visible. "What is it, my dear? I must know the whole if I am to help you."

"My mother does not know this part, I am almost certain. I . . . I cannot bear to speak of it!" Her voice choked off on another sob that shook her whole, slight frame.

Emily knelt down in front of her, hoping the inquisitive maid could not hear. The girl was watching from across the room, avid curiosity on her face.

"Tell me all, Grishelda. Tell me everything."

The young woman kept her face down as she spoke in low tones. "The captain was speaking to Lord Saunders separately, after my mother had left them. They did not know I was around a pillar and could hear every word. Lord Saunders said . . . he said he did not want to—he used an obscenity there, but it meant what is done on the marriage bed, I think—any skittish virgin, and that he t-t-trusted the captain to take care of things!"

Emily gasped.

"And the captain laughed," Grishelda moaned. "Such an evil laugh! He said he would make sure I was well b-b-broken in!" She broke down in sobs then, a heart-rending sound in the quiet parlor.

A roiling pit of bile in Emily's stomach threatened to rise. She quelled it and put her arms around Grishelda. She had never heard anything so evil in her whole life. "But surely if you told your mother . . . ."

Grishelda gave a sharp and bitter laugh. "She would believe that captain over me. She is totally in thrall to him! She has already sided with him in this matter of my marriage."

"But that is different! It might appear to her no different than her own marriage, to an elderly man who wanted an heir."

"But I have told her I do not wish to marry, and she still intends to go ahead."

"We shall not let this happen," Emily said decisively, sitting back on her heels and taking both Grishelda's gray-gloved hands in her own. "We shall find a way. Was any time mentioned when all of this takes place?"

"The captain has said they will do nothing until Lord Saunders comes across with the money he promised, and the old man said that would take at least a week to cash in funds. Captain Dempster will not take a banknote he says, because of all the forgeries. Until then I am safe."

Emily rose. Her knees creaked and she felt a trifle out of breath. "My dear, I must ask this. The simple way out of this predicament is if you were to marry before they can take action. You are old enough that you do not need permission. Is there anyone . . . any gentleman you prefer or who has made an offer?"

Grishelda gazed up at her with hopeless eyes. "No one. Even my money has not yet brought me an offer from anyone but a couple of broken-down gamblers, and I will not marry a man who would gamble my money away. I am too plain and have been condemned as a shrew because I speak my mind and do not flatter. And I do not wish to marry!" The last was said with some of her usual determination and resolution. "I will not spend my life shackled to some man because my mother would prostitute me!"

"Then, my dear, if you have the determination to avoid the marriage bed, you certainly have the determination to foil the plans of your mother and the captain. Come," Emily said, taking her young friend's hand and pulling her to her feet. "We will find a way out of this for you, and you will be able to go back to your estate and your village school and your way of life."

Grishelda sighed, her thin shoulders sagging in dejection. "That is all I want, truly! I am not formed for marriage. I have no need for love. I . . . I *hate* to be touched!" She shivered in revulsion. "And I do not know how to accede to stupidity or wheedle to get my way or flatter some man who has no brain in his head for other than gambling, drinking and whoring!"

Emily's eyes widened. "I do not know where you got your idea of marriage, my dear, but not all men are cut from the same cloth. There are many decent and good gentlemen, and lovemaking inside of marriage is a beautiful and sacred thing. But one must not drive good men away with talk of whoring and such!"

"You see," Grishelda said, miserably. "I have no idea how to go about it. I cannot rein in my mouth for any reason. It is just as well, because I truly do not desire marriage. But what shall we do about the captain?"

"Leave that to me. Is there someone in your household you can trust?"

"My maid Hannah. She has been with me my whole life and is devoted to me."

"Then we will arrange something through her, if anything should happen to you. You must send for me if you are in trouble or need to talk. In the meantime, I will try to learn what I can about the captain and Lord Saunders. If I can discredit either one, or . . . I will think of something. In the meantime, lock your door and keep your maid by you at all times."

The door opened and a couple of ladies came in fanning themselves from the heat of the ballroom and chattering in low tones. Grishelda seized Emily's hand and with a fervent tone, said, "Thank you, Emily. You do not know what your support means to me!"

"My dear, after this is all over, we shall laugh about it."

"I hope so. I hope we may."

"We will," Emily said with determination. "You shall marry of your own free will or not at all!"

Eleven

Dodo sat quietly stitching at a piece of embroidery by the window, where the light was best. Emily was restless, though, after the previous night's revelations and walked around the morning parlor touching this and that, adjusting the gorgeous bouquet of hot house orchids Etienne had sent her just that morning and touching the Dresden shepherdess Baxter had given her long ago. When she wasn't worrying over the problem of how to help Grishelda, her mind returned to Baxter and how her body had responded to him the instant he kissed her.

When she had turned Etienne away the night he came to her, she had made the decision the moment his lips had touched hers. He was sweet, and gentle and oh, so serious, but his kiss left her . . . not cold, exactly. What had been missing? He was a talented kisser. His lips had touched hers reverently and he had held her close, his lithe young body molded to her curves as though he wanted to get closer to her than even that, as though he wanted to be inside of her.

But she had felt nothing. It had been a mildly pleasant sensation, but her body remained untouched. Oh, perhaps he could have aroused her, given a chance, but she had no desire to give him that chance. Her only thought had been of Baxter and how she had stood before an elderly vicar with him and promised to love, honor and obey for the rest of her life, through any trouble, through any misfortune. And so, she had as gently as possible sent

Etienne away with a tactful apology for not having made
a decision earlier. He had accepted his dismissal with
good grace, but she had the feeling that he was not done
with his attempts at persuasion yet.

And then when Baxter had kissed her it was as if the
heavens had opened and poured out a pure white light,
bathing them in warmth and love and . . . passion. Her
heart had raced, her body had thrummed to life, and she
had felt a heat at the jointure of her thighs as he caressed
her in the pale moonlight. He had a power over her
senses that had not diminished during the years apart.

Closing her eyes against a wave of erotic hunger, she
remembered once or twice when they had made love and
she had come close to swooning, her craving for his love
and his powerful, lean body had left her so weak. So she
had felt last night—light-headed, drunk with desire.

She loved him deeply and completely for all the wonderful things he was, for his strength and his tenderness
and for the love he had shown her so many times. They
had become alienated from each other, but she now recognized that there had been two sides to their troubles,
two equal partners who had contributed to the separation.

What had never changed was the passion she felt for
him, and no one else could touch her that way. She had
the misfortune to be a one-man woman. What was she
going to do? Was there hope for them?

Trumble opened the door. "Mr. Sylvester Lessington."

"Less, how good to see you," Emily cried, approaching
him with her hands stretched out toward him.

"My dear, you are positively glowing this morning," he
said, holding her at arm's length. "You always look beautiful, but today you are radiant." He released her and
bowed before Dodo. "And Lady Dianne. If it is possible
for a beautiful woman to grow more beautiful, then that
is what is happening to you."

"Oh, pish-tush. Mr. Lessington, you are a flatterer!"
She put her embroidery aside and rose. "I have a letter

to write, and so I will leave you two children to gossip about last night, as you are no doubt panting to do, away from my elderly ears."

"Please do not feel you need to leave on my account, my lady," Less said, taking her hand and kissing it.

She squeezed his hand in return. He was a great favorite of hers. "Not at all. I do have a letter to write. I shall send in the tea tray on my way, Emily."

She closed the door behind her and Less turned to Emily with a roguish glint in his eye.

"And may I hazard a guess as to the reason behind your radiance this morning?"

"I don't know what you mean, Less." Emily felt herself coloring and damned her unruly physical responses. Would she never be so sophisticated that she would not show her feelings in her cheeks?

"Do you not think I noticed? And even if I hadn't, do you not think it was the subject of everyone's gossip all evening? Lady Emily Delafont disappears into the garden with her husband, from whom she is formally separated and comes back a half hour later on the arm of the ardent Frenchman, looking a little flustered and with the top of her gown disarranged. Did the handsome Frenchman challenge Del? Which of them was responsible for the disarranged dress? I do so love intrigue!"

Emily flushed more deeply. "Oh, Less!"

"You shall not fob me off, my dear. I want to know the truth."

Emily sat on the couch and Less sat beside her. "Baxter kissed me."

Less almost clapped, he felt the joy so vividly. He was pierced by it, and it puzzled him a bit that he could feel such joy for someone else's life. Was that, perhaps, because he had so little hope of love and fulfillment in his own? Was he living vicariously through his friends? He examined Emily's face for clues as to how she felt about the momentous occasion. "And?"

She shrugged, and sighed. "I am not going to tell you

everything that happened, Less. It's . . . it's private. But I understand some things now. He's the only man for me. The only man I will ever want. But I don't know how he feels."

"He kissed you, didn't he?"

Emily stood and paced to the window. "Yes, but . . ."

"It was his idea, wasn't it?"

"Yes. It was all his doing. I . . . just followed his lead. It was just the same as it always was." Her voice was low and vibrated with feeling as she stared out the window. "I felt utterly swept away. I love him so very much that it frightens me. What if he doesn't want me back? What if we never get together again? What will there be for me if I don't have Baxter?"

Less joined her at the window. The sparkling sunshine touched a silver thread or two in Emily's hair and sparked off the tears just forming in the corners of her large brown eyes. He put his arms around her shoulders and rested his head against hers. She was the one woman in the world he felt completely comfortable with, the woman he would want as a sister if he could choose. "He kissed you, my dear. It's a start. He wouldn't have done that if he didn't want to. Did he . . . I was going to ask if he went any further, but I know it is none of my business."

"I'll only say that yes, he went further. But we were interrupted by Etienne who came that moment looking for me."

"Hmm. Unfortunate."

"Perhaps not," she said with a rueful smile and lift to her elegant, arched brows. "I was in imminent danger of disgracing myself in a public place."

Less chuckled. They must have gone very far indeed if that was the case. But he had a far more serious reason for his visit that morning. He almost hated to bring it up, but it was important. He released Emily and went to sit down again. A handsome young footman brought in the tea tray, and Less smiled up at him as he set it down.

Returning to the sofa, Emily sighed and sat down to

pour a cup of Bohea for them both. "I can tell you now, my friend, that for the first time in my life I was thinking of taking a lover. Etienne. He . . . even came to me the other night, but I just could not go through with it. The sad thing was, I wasn't even that tempted. How do other women do it?"

Less felt a wave of relief wash over him. He had used the gossip of Etienne's visit to her chambers—which he had heard through servants' gossip that originated with her dresser, Sylvie—to spark a flame of jealousy in his best friend, but his one concern was that Emily had taken the young Frenchman's offer of passion. It appeared that he need not have worried. And if the gossip had pushed Del into making a move on his wife, then he didn't regret sharing it. But Emily must never know it was jealousy that had prompted his move. Women understood the efficacy of jealousy well enough, but he feared that someone like Emily would not appreciate its benefits. She must think that love alone motivated Del. And surely love and not just possessiveness was at the heart of his friend's jealousy.

He must get to the reason for his visit though and without more ado. They could be interrupted at any time, as it was one of Emily's at-home days, and she was invariably deluged with visitors. He sipped some tea and cleared his throat. "My dear, I have had some rather alarming news. My contact in the government has told me that the danger to Del is said to come from a young Frenchman."

Emily's teacup clacked against her saucer. "You don't think . . . Etienne?"

"Perhaps. Isn't it possible that it was no coincidence that he was close by when Del was last attacked? It could have been a plot to gain his confidence—as his savior, you know."

Emily pondered that. She supposed it was the most likely explanation, but there were problems, things that didn't make sense, if that was the case. "But then, why would he try to start an affair with me? And other than the first visit, I don't think Etienne has been to see Baxter. Wouldn't he follow up on his entrée into Baxter's house if his intention was to get closer to him?"

Less shrugged and shook his head. "I don't know, my dear. But isn't it too coincidental that the danger is said to come from a young Frenchman and poof! There is the vicomte. Can you find out anything more about him? Does he talk about himself?"

"He lost his family in the Terror. That is all he's said."

"I'll do some digging myself, I believe," Less said, putting down his empty cup. "I know somebody who knows everything there is to know about the French aristocracy."

"Not the dreaded Great-aunt Sybil!" Emily laughed, remembering from years gone by his terror of the grande dame, who lived holed up in her elegant and stuffy London town house.

"Yes, Great-aunt Sybil," Less said, with a shiver. He rose and flicked an imaginary dust mote from his rose-colored jacket. "You see me girding my loins for battle. I must go and beard the beast in its den!"

"Anything for a friend. That's why I love you, Less. You are so loyal." Emily rose and gave him a quick hug. "I missed you all those years in exile."

"And I missed you, my sweet." He kissed her cheek. "I miss you and Del being together. I miss being able to visit you both at the same time. We must see what we can do about that!"

"Oh, Less, please don't get me hoping. I am afraid to hope. And I'm afraid *not* to hope."

"Hope is never misplaced. I believe one should hope all the time, for the possible and the impossible. It is my motto in life."

"But Less, how do I know which one this is?"

"Which one?"

"The possible or the impossible."

"We shall see, my dear. We shall see."

* * *

The affair was a crowded musical evening. A famed operatic soprano was to perform, and Emily knew Etienne was going to be there. He had to be; he was staying with the owners of the house, Sir Francis Dutton and his wife and family. It was widely rumored that the knight was hoping the young vicomte would marry his eldest daughter, Cecile.

Dodo had begged off, so Emily was alone. Lord Fawley was supposed to accompany her, but he had been laid low with a grippe. She was glad, in a way, because she must get close to Etienne and find out more about him. What Less believed seemed impossible, but there was only one way to find out, and that was by examining every angle of the young man's life. What did he do with his days? What did he do before coming to London? Was he independently wealthy? That last part didn't seem possible, since the revolution had wiped out all of the French aristocracy's holdings. He was a bit of an enigma, this open, cheerful young Frenchman.

There he was, across the room, speaking to Cecile and her younger sister Mathilde. The knight had a penchant for French names when he christened his daughters, it seemed. When she caught Etienne's eye, she smiled an invitation, and he immediately detached himself from the girls and hurried to her side.

"Emily, *chérie!* I did not think you were going to be here. Indeed, you said you would not be!" His tone was low and caressing, and he stood very close to her and gazed at her with yearning in his eyes.

Was it all an act? Did he have other intentions? But that was impossible. If he was trying to get close to Baxter, the last place he would start was with his estranged wife. "I didn't mean to come, but . . . I wanted to see you . . . to explain about last night."

Slowly he shook his head. "There is no explanation necessary. It is clear that I 'ave little chance between a man and wife. I understood your marriage to be quite, quite broken, but it seems that I was mistaken."

"But you weren't. We . . . we have not . . ." Emily twisted her gloved hands together. This was impossible! She wanted to keep him close and question him about his life, but to do that, he must not think that she and her husband were on the brink of mending their marriage. And he must believe that she might be tempted into an affair with him.

Perhaps she had already said enough. His eyes were alight with a new fire. "So, per'aps last night did not convince you to return to *le lit de mariage?* Maybe your husband's kisses do not hold the fire you remember?"

She blushed at his mention of the marriage bed and looked down, hoping he would take that as a yes. It must have been a successful maneuver, for he moved closer to her.

"Per'aps, then, you will take a little walk with me later, in the conservatory? It is beautiful and very private." Desire trembled in his voice, and his words were pitched so low that in the babble of voices only she could hear them.

Her heart thudded. What did he expect of her in the conservatory? But she dare not say no. He must think her at least wavering on whether to take him as a lover, or he would probably attempt to stay away from her in future. She glanced up at him from beneath the thick fringe of her lashes and nodded. "Yes," she breathed.

Del entered Sir Dutton's opulent foyer and handed his hat and stick to the butler. He was late, even by fashionable standards, and he could hear that the soprano had already started. She wasn't the reason he was there, anyway. He wouldn't even have come if he hadn't been informed that Emily was attending.

His visit to her house that afternoon had been greeted with the information that she had already left to go shopping with his aunt. He needed to see her, and if he had not been tied up with government business all day, he would have gotten to her place sooner. But those damned

officials with their maundering questions and hypotheses!
Yes, there was someone still trying to kill him. And no,
he didn't know who it was. He could hazard a guess.
There were a few candidates and probably others he
didn't even know about who were connected with the
whole business but damn it! He would not roam about
his own city with a damned bodyguard as a shadow. It
was ridiculous.

He strolled into the drawing room where rows of chairs
were set up facing the fireplace and a large woman in
scarlet taffeta, who stood by the piano and sang an aria.
Where was Emily? He desperately needed to talk to her
about the previous night. He had slept little because of
her. Entering the ballroom in the condition she had left
him was unthinkable, so he had just gone home, knowing
that his problem was not going to desert him anytime
soon.

He had considered going to Belle. Wasn't that what a
mistress was for? To assuage the hungers of lust? But his
mind recoiled from that thought. He could not go to her
desiring Emily. And he had sworn to himself that he
would not begin again with Belle, no matter how much
he might need the physical relief of sex. She had pouted
and wheedled, but he was not interested. As far as he was
concerned, their affair was over. Now if he could just convince *her* of that."

Where was Emily? When he did finally sleep, he had
dreamt of her—dreamt of making love to her again in
the folly at Brockwith. As sweet as the dream was, the
reality was what he hungered for.

He searched the rows of men and women, looking for
the familiar coil of dusky hair. He knew most of the company, including the knight and his family. He stood with
a couple of gentlemen he knew, near the door and
scanned the crowd.

There she was in the second row! She wore lavender
silk with knots of purple ribbon at the neckline and . . .
and she sat with that damned Frenchman! The vicomte

had his arm casually and familiarly draped over the back of her chair, his bare fingers—the man didn't even wear gloves—lightly touching her skin above the neckline of her dress. It was a gesture elegantly indicating possessiveness, whispering to the polite world that he had the right to do this, that this woman was his to touch. Baxter's hands curled into fists at his side as he watched in impotent fury as the damned puppy caressed her neck and she turned to smile at him. A smile! A luminous, sweet smile of approval! What was she thinking? She was married!

The singing was over and the crowd moved, standing and heading for the door toward the refreshment tables. He would damned well nab her as they came through and demand that she go with him somewhere private so they could discuss things. She was short and disappeared among the taller people around her, but Del was taller than most in the crowd, and he kept an eye on the Frenchman. But it seemed that Etienne was going the opposite way, toward the other doors that led to . . . Del searched his memory for a plan of the Dutton house.

The hallway toward the conservatory?

But maybe she wasn't with him, then. He had best stay where he was, with the crowd surging past on the way to the refreshments, flattening him against the wall. He scanned the crowd, and kept his eye on the other door, too. There was the vicomte. And there, on his arm, was Emily, going with him out that door.

Del pushed through the crowd and followed them. He made his way into the hall just in time to see Etienne open the conservatory door for Emily. She glanced up to smile at her lover and caught sight of her husband. Her face reddened, and then drained of color and she gave an audible gasp. Etienne followed her gaze and saw Del. He smiled and nodded, and then guided the sagging Emily through the door and into the intimate privacy of the conservatory. Del watched them go, impotent fury twisting his gut into a painful knot.

But what could he do, call the man out? Beat him to a pulp and make a scene in Sir Francis's home? She went with him willingly, that was evident by her smile before she had seen her husband. With difficulty he quelled the violent urges that swept through him. Feeling more hollow and bereft than he ever had in his life, he turned and walked out, forgetting his cane, forgetting his hat, forgetting everything but the look of guilt on Emily's face and the expression of triumph on his young rival's. Youth had won. His Emily was lover to that damned smug French sprig. He rued the day that Marchant had come to his rescue.

Striding from the house, he looked back up at the brightly lit windows, finding the one that was, he believed, the conservatory. He wanted to howl in frustration. He felt savage and bestial, like he could tear something apart with his bare hands. He had finally realized what he had lost when he separated from his wife, only to find that it was too late. She was being loved by someone else.

He needed . . . he wanted . . . he shrugged in defeat. He would go to Belle. At least she wanted him, and he would not waste his time on a woman who did not.

Emily was shivering and Etienne was all solicitude. He put his arms around her and held her close, his touch becoming more amorous as he stroked her back and kissed her hair, nuzzling her ear.

But all Emily could think about was the look on Baxter's face. The shock. The anger. And something else. Hopelessness?

"Emily," Etienne whispered. "Please let me kiss you. I have longed to since the other night. Please allow this one caress."

She swallowed down her fear and dejection. It was possible that she had just destroyed any chance she had at a reconciliation with Baxter, but she could still do what she had intended. She must find out if Etienne was a danger to her husband, if he was the assassin who was trying to put a period to his existence. She closed her eyes and forced herself to relax in Etienne's embrace. She felt his lips cover hers in a soft kiss that deepened as his passion flared.

He wanted her! It seemed strange after all those years of self-hatred, all the times she had looked in the mirror and despised what she saw as she got older and softer and rounder. And yet this handsome young Frenchman, who even now was tightening his arms around her and caressing her as his heart pounded, wanted her, desired her.

She drew away from him. "Please, Etienne, I must breathe!"

"Pardon, *chérie*. I forget myself." He relaxed his hold but kept his arms around her.

The conservatory was dimly lit with wall sconces. The Duttons were known for their pride in their rare plants, and once in a while people wandered in. If she and Etienne were caught kissing, there would be a scandal. Or perhaps not. She was not a green girl, a virgin who must be chaperoned. Most people would just look the other way and pretend they hadn't seen them. They might whisper the gossip to each other, but no one would think the worse of her for taking a handsome young lover.

"What do you want from me?" Emily blurted.

If he was startled, the young man didn't show it. He smiled, a tender, lover's expression. "I want to love you. I will not lie; I wish to *make* love to you. I will not settle for stolen kisses forever. Ah, Emily, you would not regret it. I have been told I am a very good lover, and where I want to please . . . ." He kissed her again. Pulling away from her, his eyes still closed, he swallowed hard. "I want you!" His words were a whispered plea.

"Buy . . . why? Why me?"

His eyes flew open. There was understanding in the depths. "You ask this because you have not the fashionable figure, yes? You have learned to think yourself undesirable."

She nodded.

"Many men secretly prefer the roundness, the . . . how do you say it? The abundance, the opulence, the feminine body *volupteuse*. But fashion, it dictates that they must not. A woman should look still like a little girl even when she is no longer a girl, but a woman. But for men like myself, my love, you are considered the height of delectability: lovely breasts and rounded stomach and a woman's hips!" He stared into her eyes and ran his hands lightly over her body, pausing at her breasts, rubbing with light friction until her nipples firmed under the thin silk of her dress. His breathing became more labored and his eyes darkened.

"Such sweetness as you possess I wish to sample, to drink of your nectar, my love, to do things to you that perhaps no other man has thought to do . . . ."

Emily blushed and stood, pulling away from him. "Etienne!"

"I want to feel you shudder, *chérie*, as I kiss you in delicious places no man has thought to kiss you."

"Etienne!"

"I shock you?"

"A . . . a little."

"But you need to hear it—to know it. You need to hear that you are a ripe and succulent and lovely woman, and you should not deny yourself the pleasures of the flesh. And I can show you those pleasures. If I am not mistaken, it has been a long, long time since you have been made love to. Let me be the one! *Chérie*, I will make you happy."

His words were seductive. She felt a languor steal over her. Her body, dormant so long, had been aroused the previous night by Baxter's caresses and today every inch of her body longed for a lover's touch. Baxter's touch. Etienne was not Baxter, and, though her body responded with some sensation at the light brush of his fingers, her husband's touch would have affected her so much more. She would have been on fire, instead of just warmed.

But after tonight, Baxter might never want to see her or touch her again. The fragile bud of reconciliation had been crushed, and she knew how proud and stubborn her husband was. This might be her only chance to make love with someone that she cared for. And yes, she liked Etienne; she cared for him. He was sweet and tender toward her and treated her like a desirable woman. Perhaps, if she could just learn that he was not responsible for the attacks on Baxter . . . perhaps she would succumb. Or was that just the wine she had consumed speaking?

She would make herself mad with this indecision! If only she knew whether she had a chance with Baxter . . . but that should make no difference. She should make a decision based on her own desires and needs, not on the whim of her husband!

"Etienne, please, let us just talk for a while. This is difficult for me, and I need a little time, but I will . . . think about what you've said. I'll think about it seriously!"

"That is all I ask, *chérie.*" He bent his head to kiss her again.

Twelve

Going to Belle after seeing Emily retreating to the conservatory with Marchant had been a mistake, Del decided as he let himself out of her town house and strode down the quiet, damp street. He breathed deeply, aware of a change in the quality of the air around him. There had been rain, and the air, for once, smelled fresh, cleansed of the day to day odors of garbage and horses and human waste, all mixed with the ever-present smell of the Thames.

His boot heels struck the cobbles with a *thunk thunk* as he walked. He needed to think, and walked aimlessly at first, glad he had dismissed his carriage after arriving at Belle's. This was the same time of night as the night he was attacked, but that had been in a much nastier part of town, where his attacker would be more likely to escape notice. If he confined his walk to the better area, he should be all right. He strolled on and wondered, what was he going to do?

Belle had been, as always, pathetically glad to see him and eager to offer her sexual services to relieve his tension and disappointment. But he couldn't do it. God help him, he could not do it. And it was not just determination this time, not just keeping to his good intentions. He now knew that he wished he was with Emily, that he wished they had never separated. If they hadn't, there never would have been a Belle in his life, for he had been faithful to his wife until the moment the separation agreement was signed. And now even rage and humiliation had not been enough to make lovemaking with another woman palatable.

And it wasn't just Belle. He wanted no one else but Emily, his sweet, adored wife, the mate of his body and his mind and his soul. But it seemed that it was too late for him and Emily.

He walked through the quiet neighborhoods. In front of one stately manor, a carriage drew up and footmen emerged from the house, silently padding on soft-soled shoes down the steps and to the carriage. With the aid of the groom and tiger, the footmen pulled and tugged at a corpulent reveler, finally getting him out of the carriage and carrying him up the steps. There had not been a single word or command among the men as they worked, and their expressions were carefully blank, but Del found the scene ludicrous and walked away, shaking his head.

How many souls in the city of London would repeat that same scene tonight and every night of the season? How many men and women went about their usual routine, never wondering what they were doing or why or whether there was a better way?

Like him. He had reacted to his separation from Emily by throwing himself into much the same lifestyle—drinking, gaming, whoring—at least until his work took him to the Continent. But now there was no excuse. What did he want from life?

He frowned and pondered and kicked at an errant stone as he strolled the streets. He glanced at his pocket watch once. One A.M. The middle of the evening for some.

Life had taken some unpredictable turns lately, he thought. His work as a courier had become more, suddenly, and then there were the attempts on his life. No one had yet identified from whence the threat came, but they would track the culprit or culprits down eventually. Until they did the government had wanted to assign him a bodyguard or two, but he had steadfastly refused. There was no way he was going to be shadowed by a couple of hulking human shields. He could take care of himself, even if he was getting older and feeling it more every year. He would just be a little more careful, that was all.

Where had the time gone? He and Emily had been separated for five years out of their fifteen as man and wife. What a waste. Especially since he still loved and wanted her. Even five years away from her had not changed that, so why should he think it would ever be different? He stopped on the pavement and glanced up at the house before him. He was in front of Delafont House, which he had allowed Emily in the separation agreement for London excursions. How had he ended up here?

Was it just coincidence, merely a happenstance, that he should end up in front of his wife's house just as he realized that not only did he still love her, he likely always would? He did not especially believe in coincidence. It was more likely his unconscious desire that led him this far, to Emily's doorstep.

But his unconscious desire was doomed to disappointment because his lady-wife was at that moment in the arms of her paramour, no doubt. Perhaps she had even brought Etienne back here, and they were wrapped in each other's arms in her bed at this moment. A stab of pain rent his heart. The thought was vile and insidious, working into his brain like a parasitic worm. He should go, he thought, before he did something foolish, like beating on her door and demanding satisfaction from her French dandy. He turned, about to leave, and then, out of nowhere there was a rush of noise and pain thudded through his head and he felt himself falling forward.

It had been a long evening. Emily sighed and leaned back against the squabs in her carriage. They must be almost home! She was so tired, she only wanted to drag herself upstairs so Sylvie could undress her and she could fall into bed.

She and Etienne had talked for almost an hour, long enough for their absence to be noticed. And she had had to suffer the knowing looks of the men and the envious glances of the women. She was afraid her previous pure reputation had suffered. She was the cynosure of all eyes as she strolled back in to listen to the second half of the soprano's performance.

And she hadn't learned a bit that was useful! That was the frustrating thing. She had no more idea now of whether Etienne was the guilty party than she had when she started talking to him. Oh, he talked. He talked about his family's life in France before the Terror and how they had all been wiped out in one brutal attack, but his brave nanny—he was only a babe when it happened—had protected him and raised him as if he were her own.

But he had always known he was Vicomte Etienne Marchant; she had raised him with the knowledge that he was born to something better. He had left his country sickened by the bloodshed to come to England, about which he had always been curious.

And that was all she had been able to discover. It was slow going because he insisted on interspersing his story with kisses and caresses, some that came dangerously close to being indecent. Not as much so as Baxter's the previous night, but close enough.

The carriage turned onto her street. But suddenly the horses broke into a gallop and she started up as she heard her driver shout, "Hey, there, you leave 'im be!"

"What's going on, Gorse?" she called out. "What's . . ."

The carriage halted suddenly and rocked as Gorse, her driver, jumped down from his perch.

"You stay inside, my lady. Poor sot's bin set upon by thieves!"

Emily gasped in dismay and with trembling hands unfastened and threw down her window. They were almost directly in front of her own house, and Gorse had shouted for Trumble, who, minus his wig but still in livery even though the hour was late, threw open the doors and raced down the steps, all his dignity forgotten. She could hear, above the commotion, the sound of multiple footsteps running off into the distance, but Trumble, Gorse and one young footman were bending over a figure who lay on the ground, still as a corpse.

In a flash, Emily knew who it was. Later she wouldn't know how or why. He was just a still figure, prone on the pavement, but she recognized him even as she would recognize her own reflection.

"Baxter," she screamed and flung the door open and tumbled down to the ground, her skirts entangling her without the usual arm to aid her. She raced to the figure's side and threw herself down on her knees on the damp cobblestones. It was him. It was her husband, and he was as still as death, with a trickle of blood soaking the starched whiteness of his neckcloth.

She had him carried to her room and sent the housekeeper scurrying for a basin of warm water and cloths. She pulled his jacket off with the help of Trumble and sent the footman for a doctor.

It was a long and anxious couple of hours, but the groggy doctor pronounced that he was really in no danger and would likely come out of it with nothing more than a mighty headache. The wound was superficial, just a scrape that had bled quite a bit, as head wounds were wont to do, but was not deep. Emily sent the household to bed, insisting that she and no one else would sit by Baxter and bathe his head.

And so finally, they were alone.

Baxter's breathing was steady and even, assuring Emily that the doctor had not lied, nor been mistaken. The room was dark, with just a single candle guttering on the bedside table. She watched how the pale light flickered, sending shadows across her husband's grim and saturnine face, his expression stern and unrelenting even in repose.

But she loved him, despite the grimness of his aspect, his stubbornness, his dangerous, dark temper. He could be fierce when angry, but she knew his tender side, his gentle touch, his compassionate heart. She moved up onto the bed and stroked his face, the dark stubble of his beard raspy, as it always was at the end of the evening. He now wore just his shirt, and that open at the neck, and her fingers trailed down to his chest, the smooth, hard wall that she had lain against so many times after lovemaking. His heart thudded steady, even, thumping against her fingers in a powerful rhythm.

Desire threaded through her, winding down her spine and into her limbs and down to the secret recesses of her female core. Even now, with him so vulnerable, looking older than he used to, she thought—more troubled, more grim—she wanted him. She sighed and laid her head against his chest and kissed it gently, relishing the smell of his cologne and, underlying it, the faint scent that was Baxter. Her husband. Her love. The man someone wanted to kill.

Or did they? She sat up, her brow puckered in thought. Gorse said that it looked as though the two men were going to drag him away. Why not just kill him there if that was the intention? Was it an abduction attempt gone wrong? He was probably bigger and heavier than they had anticipated, and they were trying to figure out what to do.

Enough was enough, though. In the morning he was going to have some questions to answer, and she would not let him off the hook easily. He must know something about why someone would want him dead. Or would want to kidnap him. She lay her head back down on his chest and closed her eyes.

It was as dark as a tomb; that was the first thought. And then, pain—blinding, searing pain that got worse when he moved his head. He lay still and it receded a little.

The next sensation was more pleasant, and he sighed and nuzzled something soft and fragrant. A pillow? No, there was human warmth beneath the fabric and . . . something else. It was a woman, and she shifted a little, moving on the bed they shared. He was cradled in her arms and his face was against her breast, and as she moved, it brushed against his lips, the thin material covering it catching on his beard stubble and rasping.

Belle?

No, impossible. Belle's breasts were small and firm. He sighed, feeling the pain again, but also a curious awakening in his body, an enlivening as he tentatively darted his tongue out and felt her responsive flesh pebble to a taut peak through the now-wet fabric. Sensation shot through him at the woman's responsiveness. But whomever she was, she was not his woman, and he must move away from the comfort of her breast before he forgot himself

He shifted, and his head felt as if it were going to crack open. He groaned. Anything was preferable to this pain, and so he returned to the pillow of the woman's soft breast, forgetting his resolution of the moment before. A sleepy sigh, and her gentle hand cupped his head as she urged him closer, cradling him. It felt too good, and the erotic sensations darting through his body relieved the pain. He fumbled with clumsy fingers at the silky ties that held her shift closed and pushed the fabric aside, away from the full, curiously familiar roundness. He kissed soft skin, silky textured under his questing lips. The woman's warm breath quickened against his hair and her heart leaped, the steady beat throbbing to a faster pace.

A faint whiff of lilacs. Emily! It was Emily, his wife, and he was home in her arms, cradled by the love of his life. They must be at Brockwith, and she had stayed with him after they made love, as she always did. They liked to sleep together, the closeness of warm bodies cuddled against each other.

His wife. Why hadn't he known that right away, and why did his head hurt so abominably? No matter. Making love to Emily would cure it. Making love to Emily could cure any ill a man might have.

He slipped his arms around her and she shifted, holding him close with a sweet sigh.

"Baxter," she whispered, stroking his hair with gentle hands.

He answered with kisses rained on her fragrant skin until she was sighing and moaning as he nipped at her tender flesh, her skin slick and wet from his attentions. Then he moved up and covered her mouth, smothering her outcry of passion, darting his tongue into the wet recess, ignoring the sharp burst of pain in his head when he moved. Her hands roamed his back and moved down to his buttocks as she kneaded and massaged, sending every thought of pain away to a distance. It would come back, he knew, but not while he was loving Emily.

Emily! He was mad at her for some reason, wasn't he? And they couldn't be at Brockwith. Weren't they separated? And there was Belle, his mistress . . . .

Pieces of the puzzle fell into place, and he remembered visiting Belle, and then leaving, but he couldn't remember anything else. Emily's busy hands pulled up his shirt. He was coming close to remembering . . . ah! His wife's soft hands were stroking his stomach, making his muscles convulse as desire coursed through him and pulsed his arousal into throbbing awareness.

Touch me, he thought. Touch me, please touch me! But Emily was not Belle. She stroked his stomach in circles, widening the circles and lowering her hand gradually, tickling and teasing until he felt he would go mad if she didn't touch him. He claimed her mouth in a deep kiss, not letting go even as he caressed her, pulling at the dratted nightgown as he went. She froze for a moment as his hand stroked down, down to her stomach. It was slightly rounded and soft, so different from the flat plane it used to be. How curious. It was his wife but not his wife.

She had resumed her teasing stroking, and he thought he would burst if she didn't soon touch him. Belle would have grabbed him by now, but this was Emily, sensuous, arousing Emily.

Lost in a world of their own making, a fragrant, sensuous dreamworld of sweet love and delicious sensation, Baxter claimed her lips again and again as they clung to each other in the gray dimness of her chamber. How he got there, what he was doing in her bed, he cared nothing about that. The world could dissolve around him and nothing mattered but that he was holding his wife, the sweetest flower he had ever known.

Dawn's thin, pale light crept into the room, dove gray shadows falling across the bed, and Del, staring at his wife through dazed eyes, saw her brown eyes flutter open. She gazed at him with an expression of bewildered, wanton awareness and something else . . . something deeper and softer and more complex. Love, rich and pure, beamed from her and bathed him in warmth. Her expression cleared and lost the confusion. She smiled, then, and pulled herself up on her elbow and gazed down at him.

"Emily, I want you," he muttered and was startled to hear his voice as a hoarse whisper in the absolute quiet of the dawn. Soon the streets would be alive with delivery carts and hawkers, but for now, all that they could hear was the first *tap tap tap* of the rain beating softly on the window and their own heavy breathing.

"Soon," she whispered. She leaned over him, kissing him, her hair falling soft around him, closing out the light from the window.

"Now," he groaned. A deep growl emanated from the pit of his being, and he roughly grasped her by her shoulders. Her expression was bewildered, almost fearful, but he pulled her into his arms and kissed those plump, luscious lips and thrust his tongue, pushing her mouth open to receive him. He rolled on top of her, his need overwhelming every other thought in his head.

He kissed her eyelid and tasted salt. Crying? His Emily was crying? What had he done? He opened his eyes and stared down at her in the dim half-light of the rainy morn. Tears streamed from her closed eyes.

"Emily," he groaned. "Emily, my love, what have I done?"

She opened her eyes and smiled up at him, threading her fingers through his hair. "Oh, Baxter," she whispered. "I have dreamed about this so much, I'm afraid I'll wake up and you'll be gone!"

"Never," he whispered. "Never, my love, my heart, my life."

She was unbearably, unutterably beautiful, and his body sang with delicious desire as he enfolded her in his love. Pain was forgotten, and the world could go to hell for all he cared. All that was important was here, under him in this bed. He had come home—home to Emily's arms and Emily's body and Emily's love. Home.

Thirteen

Baxter lay peaceful in her arms, slumbering after murmuring a few sleepy words of love. His weight pressed her into the bed, but she wouldn't have had him move away for anything. She held him and caressed him and stroked his hair, kissing his forehead occasionally, the covers pulled up over them in the chill of the fireless room. She trembled still, shaken to the core by the full force of Baxter's wildly intense lovemaking. She felt very much that she had been loved thoroughly, deeply. It was what she wanted, to carry the memory of what they had done with her, every second of the day.

It had been the impulse of a moment that had urged her to shed her dress and climb under the covers with Baxter. She was exhausted, and, she admitted to herself, she wanted to be next to him. She had awoken to his lips at her breast, her body already singing with desire. The first time he touched her body, so changed since last they made love, she had recoiled from him. But that was soon forgotten as his desire for her, so potent and so evident, had carried her beyond self-consciousness. And it was glorious to touch him and stroke him and know she could arouse him still, even though he had a young and beautiful mistress.

She had forgotten. Had it always been like this? Had he always been able to make her tremble with desire with his merest whisper-soft touch? His kisses scorched like flame, searing her, branding her as his own. How could she ever have imagined making love with someone else?

She had no illusions that they had solved everything or that their marriage was whole again. They had to talk. There was a lot they still had to sort out. But he loved her; he had said so, and Baxter never lied. She closed her eyes and joined her husband in sleep.

Del stirred and opened his eyes to the unfamiliar bed, hung with curtains of a deep rose, and a slant of sunlight that told him it was midmorning. Emily! Where was she? He stretched and pulled the bellpull, touching his forehead and closing his eyes against the ache behind them.

A pert maid told him Lady Delafont had gone out in response to an urgent summons from a friend, but that she had ordered breakfast be ready for him if he so desired. She curtsied and left when he told her just coffee.

Trumble, efficient and competent, had already sent word around to his house, and his valet was waiting with a complete change of clothes and his shaving implements, and so, bathed, shaved and changed, he descended the stairs.

The butler bowed and without the barest hint of humor, said, "I trust you slept well, my lord?"

The headache had receded, and Del felt like a new man. "I did. I slept like a baby. However that is. Will you tell my wife that I will call on her this afternoon? I have some urgent business of my own to take care of, but I will attend her then."

He left the house whistling. His wife. It had felt so good to say that again, so right! His wife, the love of his life, the flower of womanhood, who bloomed only for him. He had waved away the offer of a carriage from a solicitous Trumble, and he walked home in a glorious frame of mind, feeling that something had been healed between him and Emily with their joyful union. He hoped she felt the same, but even if she hesitated he was willing and able to convince her that they should resume their marriage. He was convinced that when she disappeared into the conservatory with Etienne the previous night, there must have been some innocent explanation. He would ask her, or perhaps she would explain without being asked. She was his and only his.

His own butler, Cromby, was all solicitude and concern, but Del waved him off, too, handing him his stick and hat. It seemed a day for the family retainers to overreact. As for himself, he was getting used to failed attempts on his life. No doubt he would have to stop walking alone at night, but he still was not ready to concede to body-guards.

He paused in the hall and said to Cromby, "I will have coffee in the library and . . ."

A rap at the door interrupted him. Cromby, with the calm deliberation he always manifested, opened the door to an early visitor.

It was the vicomte, Marchant. Del could not very well deny himself, as he stood in his own entrance, so with bad grace he gestured the younger man in. "Come in, Marchant. Little early for a call, hmm?" He turned to his butler and said, "As I was saying, coffee in the library. For two."

It was as well, he thought, that the fellow was there now, for he had something to say to him. He was going to warn the upstart to stay away from his wife. And if the fellow did not listen, he would meet him on the field of honor. But surely the sprig would back off when he realized it was no use pursuing Emily.

The library was a dark room, much smaller than the one at Brockwith Manor. Fitted with ceiling-high book-cases and wood-paneling, its design was from the previous century, or maybe the one before that. He took a seat behind his desk and offered a cigar to Marchant. They both lit up and Del sat back, in an expansive mood. As the winner of Emily's affections he could afford to be gracious.

"What can I do for you, Marchant?" The lad must have had some reason for coming to his home, Del thought, so they would dispose of that business first, and then get down to the important matter of his bowing out and leaving Emily alone.

"I felt I should clear the air between us, milord."

"Call me Delafont," Del said easily, taking a puff on the cigar, relishing the mellow smoke that drifted up and dissipated. "Supposed to go by my title, Sedgely, but I never could stand that, so everyone calls me Delafont." A footman came in with the tray of coffee, poured at Del's indication and left on silent slippers.

Marchant waited only until the door was closed, and then said, "You saw me going, with your wife, into the *conservatoire* last evening."

"Yes. I did." Del waited. Etienne had, perhaps, come to tell him that it only looked bad, and that he and Emily had just gone in there to talk. Of course, that was what it must have been. Marchant was probably afraid of how it must have looked and wanted to ensure the wrong impression had not been received.

"I do not need your permission, of course, but I feel you should know." The young man's chin went up, and a martial light glowed in his light brown eyes. "Emily and I, we are having an *affaire de coeur.* We spent an hour in the *conservatoire* making love."

Del heard a buzzing noise in his ears. How curious, he thought. He would have sworn the young vicomte had just said he had made love to Emily. Impossible!

"I do not need to tell you, my lord, how passionate she is, how abandoned, and with what delicious fervor she makes love . . . ."

Del's hands fisted.

"She was afraid I would not find her attractive, but *mon dieu!* I ask you, who would not? She is lovely and soft . . ." The young man paused, and he smiled, baring his white, strong teeth. "But then, I do not need to tell you that, heh?"

A mist of red descended and Del thought he would lunge across the desk and strangle the popinjay or break his neck with one twist, like a farmer would snap a chicken's. He clutched the edge of the oak surface, clenching the cigar between his teeth. He would not give the little coxcomb the satisfaction of seeing his anger and jealousy. He had learned after years of effort how to master his violent impulses, but this was a test of gargantuan proportions.

So, Emily was playing them both! Perhaps she hoped for a romantic duel. Some women liked that kind of thing. It occurred to him that he must not know her very well anymore, for he would have sworn she had not been loved for a very long time, and here he was only burrowing into another man's tunnel. Shouldn't he have known? Wouldn't it have been evident . . . ah, but he had been dazed at first, from his head injury, and then eager with sexual excitement. She could have made love with a legion and he wouldn't have been aware. He wanted to throw back his head and howl—gnash his teeth and wail and rend his clothes—the pain was so terrible, but he would not give the sniveling bastard the satisfaction!

"Are you telling me that you and Emily have had . . . *are* having a physical affair? A sexual liaison? And that you did that in the Duttons' conservatory last night?"

Marchant looked wary. "Yes," he said, slowly. "We made love. I should not divulge the details to another man, but yes, we made love against one of the tables, hidden from view by the Duttons' *forêt des plantes,* and it was delicious, milord. The spice of the forbidden, you know, imminent discovery."

"And why did you feel you must tell me this?" Del said through gritted teeth, carefully guarding his tone. It all had too familiar a ring. He and Emily used to make love in unusual places, and yes, the danger of discovery had added to the thrill. He glanced once at the dueling pistols hanging in a case above the fireplace. He stabbed out the cigar in a dish and clutched his hands together on the desk in front of him.

"I felt it was just . . . civilized. She is your wife, even if you let her slip away from you. I will treat her well, you may be assured. Oh, yes, I will treat her well! I am like all the French, I have a talent for love!"

Damned little coxcomb. "I could call you out for this, you know," Del ground out, letting the dark anger surge to quell the pain.

"But you will not, I think, for that would expose you to ridicule, yes? I am willing to make my *affaire* with your wife very discreet, and you will suffer no loss of reputation as a result, I think. I will take care of her well." He stood and smiled, a triumphant gleam in his dark eyes.

Filthy little lecher! Pompous young ass! Del glared as the young man turned on his heel and left the room, pausing to bow at the door before exiting. Then from anger he was dropped into a pit of despair. He put his head down on the desk. Why had she made love to him? For comparison? For old times? For revenge? Did it matter? He felt desolation flood him, and a sob, wrenched from the deepest core of his being, echoed in the room. To have found her and lost her again so swiftly; it was more than he could stand.

"Less! I just this minute got home. Your timing is impeccable, as is everything else about you!" Emily almost sang with happiness. She had gone through the whole morning wanting to cry from happiness at every beautiful flower, every pretty child. She carried the awareness deep within her of what she and Baxter had done, and she pitied lesser mortals. Even as she had visited Grishelda—the unhappy young woman had summoned her with an urgent note that could not be ignored, even though she longed to stay in bed with her husband—and commiserated with her over her difficult position, she had clutched her secret delight to herself like an infinitely precious treat, to be savored later.

Her friend looked at her and cocked his head to one side. "You look . . . you look like a woman in love!"

Emily's eyes misted over and she hugged herself. But the secret was too priceless, too sacred. She could tell no one, not even her dear friend. "Silly. It is a glorious spring day. March is upon us, and daffodils and crocuses! What other reason does anyone need for feeling wonderful?"

They sat together on the sofa, while Emily carefully undid her bonnet and handed it to Sylvie, along with her gloves. The dresser curtseyed and disappeared with Emily's spring pelisse, bonnet and gloves.

Less had turned serious, and that was a side of him that few saw. Most knew him as a lighthearted, though rather mysterious, figure among the London fashionable. Born to a family of actors, he had proved to have a talent for management and money rather than acting, and he now owned two theaters. But he apparently had no love life and no mistresses, or at least none that he admitted to. Some whispered that he had a tragic secret, a love affair that had ended badly, but not a soul could name names or dates.

But it was known that where he professed friendship, he was steadfast. Emily gazed at him with affection. She knew that the scandalous verse purported to come from the pen of the Regent had actually been written by Less, but she didn't think that he *knew* that she knew. She didn't mind. She had known from the first that it was a gentle joke that had gotten out of hand. Even before they had met for the first time after the long interval of years, she had been aware he was still in London and had recognized his distinct style in the ribald, funny verse purported to come from the Regent's pen. Somehow a verse merchant had gotten a copy, printed it up and some low sketch artist had accompanied it with a bawdy cartoon. Now, though, the gossip about it was over; the *ton* had moved on to another scandal, and her brief notoriety was over.

How her life had changed since coming to London just a little more than a month before. She had been complaining to Dodo about the sameness of life, but she certainly could not make that same complaint now. She blessed the whim that had brought her to London, though, for it had brought her back to Baxter.

"Why so serious, Less?" She laid her hand on his.

His thin, clever face twisted into a wry smile. "Oh, I have any number of reasons for a somber outlook, my dear, among them a visit to my dreaded Great-aunt Sybil. She was in full raging vigor, and I had to listen to the story of her life—all her stage triumphs and the number of young bucks and beaux she bedded in her scandalous career as an actress and courtesan—before she got down to the business at hand. She would have me believe that Farmer George was an admirer, but I told her she was going too far."

"And what did you discover?" A bubble of laughter welled up in Emily, and her words were accompanied by a chuckle.

"Oh, you can laugh! You didn't suffer through it." His smile turned grim, and he turned his hand palm up and clasped her hand. He kissed it. "I am afraid that what I have to say may cause you pain."

A pinprick of presentiment prodded Emily. Last night she would have sworn that Etienne was exactly what he seemed, a harmless, flirtatious, sweet Gallic youth. But now . . . "Don't tease, Less. What have you learned?"

"Our young Frenchman is not the Vicomte Etienne Marchant."

"What?"

"Hugo Etienne Marchant, who, by the way, was not commonly called Etienne, but rather Hugo, the only male in his immediate family, the last child of his parents and scion of the Marchant line, before the Terror killed them, died with his family. They were victims of the mob's resentment, as were so many of the aristocracy."

"Isn't it . . ." Less, Etienne told me last night about his parents' deaths at the hands of the mob. He was just a baby, and his nurse saved him. She hid him and then passed him off as her own baby. Isn't that possible?"

"No, my dear. Hugo Etienne Marchant was a lad of twelve in the worst year of the Terror. That would make him . . ." He did some rapid calculation from 1793 to 1816. "Thirty-five. Do you believe the fellow is thirty-five?"

Emily's heart dipped, sliding down the slope of trust into the valley of disappointment. Etienne was twenty-four; he had told her so himself. He would have been just one year old in '93.

"And you are sure of this?"

"My great-aunt is many things, but she is never mistaken. The old crone is a veritable warehouse of accurate information on both the French and English aristocracy. It is a pastime of hers, to chart the rise and fall of families. The current vicomte, a cousin of the Marchant line who does not carry the Marchant name, lives in Italy, even though he could return to France. He is an 'artist,' it appears."

"So Etienne is at least a liar and probably an assassin."

"It appears so."

"Who do you think he works for?"

Less shrugged. "If Del wasn't being so reticent, I might know, but he hasn't said anything to me."

Emily flushed deeply, and sighed. "Do you think . . . would he have said anything to his mistress?"

"The little Belle?" He mused, eyebrows drawn down over his light, intelligent eyes. "You know," he said, slowly. "She traveled with him in Europe. If anyone has firsthand information, it would be she. Would you like me to speak with her? After all, she works for one of my acting troupes."

Stiffening her back, sitting up straight and smoothing

her dress over her stomach, Emily said, "No. Let me do it, Less. I . . . I would like to talk to the child anyway."

Less looked doubtful, but did not have time to protest. Trumble opened the doors and announced, "The Dowager Marchioness, Lady Marie Delafont."

Her mother-in-law swept in, swathed in furs that she refused to give up. She stood and glared at them. "Where is my son?"

"He . . . why do you think I would know, Mother?" Emily stood out of respect for the woman, although she couldn't abide her, and they both knew it.

"I wasn't speaking to you! I was speaking to him!" She pointed at Less.

Less sat back, one lean leg crossed elegantly over the other. He did not even make the courtesy gesture of standing as she entered the room. He raised a quizzing glass to his eye, making the orb enormous. "My lady, I have no idea where your son is."

The dowager sniffed and then turned to her daughter-in-law. "I wish to speak to Dianne," she commanded.

"Dodo is out visiting an old school friend," Emily said, trying not to giggle.

"Wouldn't think any of them would still be alive," the older woman said. She glared at Emily. "Have you started?"

"Started?" Emily wildly tried to imagine what the woman was talking about. Sometimes she thought that Baxter's mother was just the slightest bit mad.

"Started! Started losing weight! To get my son back!" She raised her lorgnette and studied Emily up and down, examining each rounded curve visible through the form-skimming fashion she wore. "Hmmph! You haven't. You'll never get him this way, my girl. He has a thin little mistress and you must compete. Must get yourself trim! Then after you have him back, you can get fat. After you get with child. The succession!" she trumpeted, one hand raised.

She turned on her heel and left.

Emily broke into laughter, joined by Less. She plunked down beside him on the sofa again.

"The woman is completely pulled about in the upper stories! Mad!" Less held his ribs and wiped his eyes with his free hand.

"I know! Attics to let!"

Less grew serious. "Well, I suppose that was the farce. We shall do things in reverse order and move to the drama. What are we going to do about Del?"

"Is there nothing else your contact in the government can find out?"

He sighed and stared out the window, at the park across the street. "He . . . my contact is very worried about compromising himself. He is in a precarious position, and I must not do anything to endanger him. He . . . I would not do that to him for the world."

Emily gazed at him. There was an odd note in his voice, one she had never heard before. It made her wonder if one of her suspicions about her friend was correct. It would explain so many things . . . . She abandoned that line of thought. That, after all, was Less's private business. "Then you must just do the best you can. And I . . . I shall visit Belle Gallant. She . . . well, she must love Baxter. Who could not?"

After Less departed, Emily restlessly moved from room to room. She picked at her luncheon, and then hovered near the front entrance, rearranging the flowers in the vase, and glancing at the door every few seconds. And the clock ticked, the sonorous gong marking the passing hours.

He must have gotten busy, she thought, over and over. He left a message saying he would come and her husband always kept his word. He must have just gotten busy. But he did not come, nor did a message arrive explaining his lateness or making a new appointment. Finally, she went up to dress for dinner and listened as Dodo chatted through that meal about her friend. Emily was unaware that all the while her aunt by marriage was darting wor-

ried little glances her way or that the woman some condemned as stiff and high in the instep would later grill
the butler about her niece's unhappiness.

Sick with worry and dread, Emily went up to bed, sending word that she would not be going out that evening
after all. There was no event in the world that could pull
her away from her own home and the hope that she
might receive a message or visit. But Baxter never came.

Fourteen

Baxter wasn't responding to her messages and even a bold visit to his home had gotten her only the cold and formal "not receiving visitors." Several days had passed. Emily had been assured that the latest attack, in front of the town house, had done him no lasting damage. This information had come from Dodo, who had seen her nephew in the park, escorting Belle in his new phaeton.

It hurt, she found—hurt deeply that he had evidently had a change of heart since his night with her. He couldn't even be man enough to tell her to her face, but had to hide and avoid her. What had happened? She would have sworn that the lovemaking had been as fulfilling for him as it had been for her. And not only that, it had seemed as if he loved her, really *loved* her, not just physically but with his whole heart. She ached inside with desolation, finding it was worse now that the memories of him were fresh and beautiful. It was like a particularly vivid dream, the memory of waking up to him and loving him in the dim and rainy morning hours.

And there wasn't a soul to whom she could complain. She had told no one about their night together and wouldn't now for the world. It might be the last memory she ever had of him, and she would tuck it away in her heart to cherish forever.

Damn the man, anyway! How could he do this to her? She had sworn to never again let mistaken assumptions come between them, but how else could one take this rejection?

In the meantime, Etienne had been importunate, visiting her house every afternoon and sending notes and flowers every morning, but she couldn't bear to see him alone and so did not go out herself, even in the evening. She stayed home most nights and read or did needlework, and after a while she stayed home so she would not meet Baxter, as well as to avoid Etienne. She even started talking about going back to Yorkshire early, assuring Dodo that she was welcome to stay at Delafont House as long as she wanted.

She went to church on Sunday and prayed, after the service, in the cool dimness near the altar. She prayed for Baxter's safety, and she prayed for herself, that she would find peace and that her heart would be healed. She found her appetite almost gone and wryly laughed to herself that her mother-in-law might get her wish after all, at least about the weight-loss part, if this tension and unhappiness kept up.

There was only one thing to do. It was time to tackle a task she was not looking forward to, but knew she must do. She had to go visit her husband's mistress. Maybe Belle Gallant could protect Baxter, could convince him to keep himself safe, where his wife could not.

Belle lay back on the silky sheets of her red velvet-draped bed. Another cramp razored a sharp pain through her lower belly and she waited for it to subside. Her little maid came in with a tray of tea and toast, setting it down on a table by her bed.

"Fanny," she moaned, pressing on her abdomen. "I will see no one today."

Fanny bobbed a curtsy and left the room.

Tears came to Belle's enormous blue eyes and she lay facedown on her bed clutching her pillow. What was she going to do? Her plans were made and she truly did not regret them, but they were not proceeding as quickly as she wanted. Del had been everything that was kind to her, and she must repay him before she could truly throw herself into the life she had planned for herself. Was a few months out of her life too much to give to the man who had given her everything? But how long was this going to take? And how could she manage it if he wouldn't sleep with her?

A sudden fit of terror overcame Belle and she started shivering. She clutched her pillow, bunching the silky fabric in her clenched fists. Was she doing the right thing? Mr. Lessington had been so kind to her, giving her a job, and she loved it! She loved everything about the theater.

Oh, she knew she was just an opera dancer right now, with only a few small parts thrown her way, mostly because Del was her protector, but she watched the actors and actresses, and she felt in her heart that she could do it. She had even been given a couple of lines and a part or two, once as a fairy in *A Midsummers Night's Dream,* and another time as a silly young girl in a light comedy.

Someday she would be a great actress, like the lead actress in their troupe, Madame DeMornay. She watched the woman move across the stage, confident and beautiful, and she memorized every tone in her voice and every delicate movement of her hands, to practice later in front of the glass.

Was she willing to endanger it all by bearing Del's heir? Would her position be still waiting for her when she was finished with the nasty business and was able to work again? She buried her face in her pillow, breathing in the rich scent of the hair lotion she used. The lacy pillow slip was redolent of it and she loved the different scents of the expensive creams, lotions and perfumes Del afforded her.

And that was why she would do it. He was so kind to her. He had saved her from a wretched existence and lifted her from her squalid life, teaching her how to walk and talk and live like a lady.

Well, maybe not exactly like a lady. Belle turned over on her back and stared up at the dark crimson that swathed the full-testered bed. Del's wife, Lady Delafont, even though she was fat and old, had moved as though she was on wheels, so smooth and graceful. And her voice!

"Hello, so lovely to meet you," Belle said out loud, trying the softer accents and rounded, plummy tones of her lover's wife.

It sounded barmy coming from her. For the first time, she wondered what had broken their marriage apart. Del didn't talk about it. He didn't talk about much of anything with her. Not that she was one for gabbing on and on when you could be doing something, but Del liked to talk. He spent endless hours talking to Mr. Lessington and some of his other friends, even ladies.

Belle touched her stomach and wondered what it would look like fully distended, like she had seen on some of the girls in the bawdy theater troupe she had traveled with, after the manager had gotten at them. The randy old fart had babies with at least three or four different women—it had made the so-called theater company like a damned nursery sometimes.

Would Del be excited when he found out she carried his child? Of course he would. And then, after it was born, he could take it away and . . . and what? Whatever you did with babies, she supposed.

In her experience all women did with them was change them and breast-feed them, endlessly. She shuddered and gazed down at her body. At least she would get lovely big jugs for a while. That ought to be some payment for all the ridiculous stuff a woman had to do. Take lovemaking, for instance. Lovemaking was a dead bore, but men seemed to like it and it didn't take much time if you did it right. And having babies! Well, if you asked her that was nature's biggest joke on a woman. First you had months of sickness, and then, just when that started to go away, came the big belly and the swelling—swollen feet, swollen hands, swollen everything!

Fanny crept into the room and close to the bed. "Miss?"

"Mmm?"

"There's a lady to see you!"

Belle was about to remind the girl she had said no visitors, since the last thing she wanted was to see one of the actors from the theater, but Fanny's wording stopped her. She sat up on the bed.

"A lady?"

"Yes, miss!" Fanny squeaked. "I told her you wasn't seeing anyone today, but she just said—ever so gently, mind—'Then I shall wait until she is able to see me.' And then she sat down in the parlor!"

"Did she give her name?"

"L-L-Lady Delafont, miss!"

Del's wife, come to see *her?* Mighty cheeky, visiting her husband's dollymop, wasn't it? What could she possibly want?

Belle straightened her spine. Well, if Lady High Muckety-muck Delafont could come to see her, then she could descend to the parlor to greet her. Summoning every ounce of dignity in her small frame, she patted down her morning dress and swept from the bedchamber, down the narrow stairs and into the first floor parlor.

Del's wife wasn't sitting. She was at the window, looking out over the scene on the narrow street of a small child being tugged along by a large dog on a rope. A slatternly nurse flirted with a groom, not minding her charge as she should.

Lady Delafont said without turning, "I would let that nurse go if I were that child's mother. He is likely to be tugged into the street by that monster of a dog, if she doesn't have a care."

Belle stood uncertainly by the door. Her loins had been girded to meet the righteous outrage of her lover's wife, and instead she was faced with a gentle voice worrying over a small child—a complete stranger's small child, at that. And her tone was almost wistful when she said, "If I were that child's mother," like she wished it was so.

Once Del had said in passing that he and his wife weren't able to have children. Belle had never heard of a woman being unable to have a child, and had passed it off as an example of a wife fooling her husband while she used some of the preventative measures Belle had learned. Now she knew that wasn't so. If ever there was a woman who longed for a child, this was her. Belle rested her hand on her stomach. If only them that wanted babies could have them, and them that didn't, couldn't! The world should be ordered that way. The woman by the window looked like she was made to be a mother, and if she truly wasn't able, it was a shame.

Lady Delafont turned and smiled, and Belle felt an answering smile tug at the corners of her lips. She wanted to hate her, this woman who had made Del sad, but she couldn't. Not yet anyhow. That might come after she had spoken her piece.

"You must be wondering why I have come to see you. It was rude of me to barge in and demand to be seen, but it is important."

"Not at all, my lady. Please sit down." It was easy to be gracious with this pretty, motherly woman. Belle watched her move across the room—glide, really, not walk—and take a seat, knees together, rose-gloved hands folded on her lap. She copied her, sitting just so, clasping her hands in her lap, too.

"Thank you. I must admit, I was a little nervous coming here. I . . . I didn't know what kind of welcome I would get. Or what kind I deserved!"

Belle stared at her. She sounded apologetic! She, Del's wife, was apologizing to his little piece on the side. "I—I—I . . ."

It was no good, she thought. There was no way to equal this woman's breeding and good manners. Belle relaxed back against the sofa cushions. She would just be herself.

It was all she could do, and somehow she didn't think this woman would hold it against her if she wasn't a perfect lady.

"I am curious, my lady. Del's told me about you, of course. And then we met that day at his town house. Whatever can you mean by coming here? Won't it wreck your reputation?"

The older woman chuckled. "I have begun not to worry about my reputation. People will think what they will think, and I can always go back to my home in Yorkshire if the censure becomes too great. But what about you, child? Do you not have parents who would be worried if they knew of your . . . um, situation?"

Somehow, after a few delicate questions from the marchioness, Belle found herself pouring out her story—the long sad tale of how she had ended up at thirteen traveling over the Continent with a disreputable band of players who pandered to the worst, most filthy tastes of gentlemen, performing lewd acts on stage nightly and serving the "manager's" needs in the meantime. Halfway through, as she stared down at her hands and recited the whole sorry tale, half of which she hadn't even told Del, she felt a hand take hers and pat it. At the end of it she looked up to see tears in Lady Delafont's great, brown eyes. The dark irises swam and glittered and a single drop overflowed and rolled down over her cheek.

"You poor child!"

No. She hadn't understood at all why Belle was telling her this! It wasn't to get her sympathy, but to show her why this life was so much better. "But you see, Del saved me from all that! Two years ago, or so, he happened to see me one night being beaten for . . . for doing something wrong, and he planted that old bastard a facer and carried me off. After that, I wouldn't leave him, even though he offered to give me enough to live on. I don't got . . . haven't any parents, not really."

"How sad," Lady Delafont murmured, quelling her emotion with difficulty.

Belle shrugged. "It doesn't matter. But you see why I don't want to be anywhere else but here? How could I leave a gent like that what done—who has done so much? He hired a tutor and a dresser and . . ." She gestured to herself. "And here I am! He sent me back to England ahead of him, with a letter for Mr. Lessington to give me a spot in his theater. And he set me up in this house and . . . and everything."

"My dear, how old are you?"

Belle sighed. "Age, age, *age!* You people think about it too much!"

"But you are very young to have been his . . . his mistress for two years! Why, you're a child!"

The first bite of resentment welled up in Belle, and she jerked her hand from the other woman's grasp. "I am old enough. I have seen sights, my lady . . . pardon me, but I think I have seen enough to know that being a rich man's mistress is the very top of the deck for someone like me. I was born the bastard of a drunken old poacher. I ran away from him when he couldn't keep 'is filthy paws off me, and became a squalid little whore in a third-rate acting troupe. Del . . . Del lifted me up and made me somebody!" Her voice trembled and she bit back bitter words. Nobody would disparage Del, not in her hearing!

She expected Lady Delafont to get up and leave after the unforgivable things she had just said, but the woman smiled, even though her eyes were still sad.

"My lady, you don't understand," Belle continued. The urge to make her see overwhelmed her with its power. There was no anger left, just this need to explain. "I *made* Del take me as a mistress. It . . . it was the only thing I could do for him. He's so rich, and there was nothing I could give him . . . nothing except me."

"Belle . . . may I call you that?" At Belle's nod, she continued. "I understand a lot more now than I did when I came in. My dear, may I say that you were somebody even before Del rescued you. You must have been very brave and very strong to have survived what you have lived through. I underestimated you and I apologize for that."

Dazed, Belle just murmured a pardon. At every turn Lady Delafont amazed her with graciousness and kindness. She had heard the upper crust disparaged as cold and bloodless and she had witnessed some of that in the months she had been in Mr. Lessington's troupe, but it was made up for in the people she met like Del and Mr. Lessington, who had been very kind, and now, Lady Delafont.

She wanted to cry. This was Del's wife, the woman he had left, and Belle thought he must have been all about in the head. She had the strangest urge to rest her head on the woman's bosom and sleep, cradled in safety and warmth, and she had never felt that way—never met a woman she liked that much or trusted. In her experience women were either cats, hating you for whatever you had that they didn't have, or whores with no more mind than a cow. So-called society women were just richer versions, she had thought.

But maybe there were other sorts, ones she hadn't met yet. Maybe there were other women in the world like Lady Delafont.

"I'm . . . I'm nineteen, my lady," she offered, timidly, as a gesture of reconciliation. "Or twenty. I'm not sure."

"You . . . you are young enough to be my own daughter, almost," she said and quickly turned her face away.

Belle watched the woman struggle for control. In a rare flash of insight, she understood that this woman before her still loved her husband. Whatever had separated them, for whatever reason they were not now together, Lady Delafont loved her husband with all her heart.

"What . . . what is it like?" she blurted, giving voice to her inner speculations.

Lady Delafont turned quickly, her eyes still moist with tears. "What is *what* like?"

"My lady, you love your husband. What is it like to be in love?"

"Aren't you . . . don't you love him? Baxter?"

"I don't know. I don't know what it feels like."

"It feels like . . . it feels like love. I don't know how else to describe it. When you love a man, your whole being is tied up in him." She hugged her arms around herself and gazed off into the distance, soft brown eyes dreamy. "You want everything for him—every happiness and everything good."

Belle nodded. So far, some of it sounded right. She did want everything good for Del.

"And at night, when the lights are low," the woman continued, gazing out the window, her voice quivering with a mixture of love and pain, "and he comes to your bed, you don't want the lovemaking to ever end; you want to stay joined to him forever. Sometimes you think that if you could just go away with him, to an island somewhere away from everyone—away from his friends, his *mother* . . . ."

Lady Delafont stopped, glanced over at Belle and blushed, and Belle watched her curiously, then shook her head. If that was love, maybe she wasn't in it. Lovemaking with Del wasn't unpleasant, but it certainly didn't do anything for her. It was best gotten over with, since men liked that kind of thing, and then they could talk about her career on the stage, or he could leave and she could dream about the future. "Stay joined to him forever"? Sounded like bloody hell, to her!

Despite her efforts to bring him back to her bed since his arrival back in England, she didn't really want to *do* anything. It was partly force of habit—as she had said, what else could you give the man who had everything?— but mostly to further her plan of presenting him with an heir. She couldn't remember what happened the night she had come to his home drunk—had they made love or had they not made love?—but whatever had happened, it had obviously not taken, or she wouldn't be getting her monthly courses right now. But then, Del didn't know that, did he? Hmmm. That was something to ponder.

"Was that what broke you two up?" Belle asked, and then remembered something the woman had just said. "Was it his mother?"

The marchioness drew herself up, until her back was ramrod straight. "Child, that is none of your affair, and if you know what is good for you, you will keep your nose out of business that does not concern you!"

Belle gasped, affronted at first, but then broke into laughter when she saw that the marchioness was copying her mother-in-law. Remembering the frigid dowager from the breakfast table the morning she had been at Del's she said, "She is an old fright, isn't she? Right proper old bag of wind."

Lady Delafont relaxed and chuckled. "I shouldn't say it, but yes! Yes, she is an old harpy and a harridan and she interfered in our marriage constantly. Blamed me for not . . ." The pleasant smile was gone, and the sad look was back.

"Never say she blamed you for not getting a baby? Anyone can see that you're mad to have your own . . . ." Belle trailed off.

Emily gazed at her curiously. The child had an arrested expression on her pinched little face. Everyone raved about what a beauty she was and she was pretty, but she looked wan and none too well to Emily. But the girl was unexpectedly engaging. She had expected a greedy little tramp, she supposed. Perhaps she had *wanted* to find that. But she couldn't dislike her. She could be jealous of what the girl and Baxter shared, but she could not hate her. Belle Gallant was ingenuous and artless, openhearted and guileless.

"You know," Belle said slowly. "I'm ever so grateful to Del. He has been nicer to me than any man, any *person* anywhere. But I don't really think I love him. Not if what you say about love is true."

"It's true from *my* experience. I don't know if everyone

experiences love the same way." How odd, Emily thought. She had come only to extract some information from the girl, and they ended up having a conversation about love. She glanced down at her folded hands. "You probably wonder why I've come to see you."

Belle shrugged.

"I have something important to ask. You traveled with him in Europe, didn't you?"

"Yes. For about a year and a half, and then he sent me on to London while he finished up some business."

"Did he ever tell you what his business was?"

"Just something for the government."

Emily framed her next question carefully. "Did you ever notice . . . anyone watching him? Or did anyone ever try to hurt him?"

"You mean when that bloke tried to kill him? That bandit?"

"Yes!" Emily nearly leaped from her seat. "Were you there? Did you see him? What did Baxter say about him?"

"Del didn't tell me much of anything ever, but his valet was worried about him. I saw him talking to some strange fellow, and he said something about Del having an accident. He was talking real low and fast, so I didn't catch it all, but I heard him say that, and the next day, Del got hit by the robber."

Emily stared out the window. There didn't seem to be anything in that. But why would the valet be talking about Baxter and an accident *before* anything happened? "What is the valet's name?"

"He were a Frenchie, not the one that he has here. He left him behind in Paris."

So that eliminated him as a suspect in the current attacks.

"Were there any other incidents?"

Belle considered that. "Well, there was the creeper."

"The creeper?"

"We—Del and I—were sleeping one night, and someone got into the room and was creeping around, looking for something to steal, I suppose. Del caught him and threw him out."

Emily resolutely ignored the tug of pain as Belle casually mentioned sleeping with Baxter. It was not the girl's fault that her husband was not home with her. "Was that before the valet said that about an accident?"

Belle nodded.

So perhaps the valet was speaking of that. Maybe he said "incident," rather than "accident." "Was there anything else odd that happened during that time?"

Belle shifted impatiently. "I don't know. Del was gone a lot. Sometimes he would travel somewhere else without me. Sometimes he would have very late meetings. And once someone sent a message for him to meet them someplace, but they never showed up. I know that because he came in raving about it. But the next day it turned out that the fellow had been set upon by bandits and killed. Del was very quiet that day, though I don't see why. It wasn't his fault the fellow was murdered."

Emily puzzled over all of this. Someone was trying very hard to kill Del and not succeeding. Was that because someone else was looking out for him, or was it plain dumb luck? She stared out the window, draped in heavy gold brocade. She didn't really know very much more than when she had arrived, except about Belle Gallant and her relationship with Del. She glanced over at the girl who shared the sofa with her. Belle looked a little green, her pale complexion blanched even whiter. She held one hand to her stomach.

"My dear, you don't look well," Emily said, taking her hand.

"Oh, but I am," she said, turning a radiant smile on her companion. "I am very well. Or I will be anyway, as soon as ever I can manage it. Have you ever planned something, and then wondered if you was doing the right thing, and then out of the blue something tells you that you got it right for once?"

"I can't say that that has ever happened to me."

"Well, it has to me. I was very worried about something before your visit, but now I know what to do. I know exactly what to do."

Emily, puzzled, rose to take her leave. "I am happy for you, my dear," she said, still retaining the girl's small hand in her own. She patted and squeezed it. "I must say I did not expect to like you, but I do. You are brave and resourceful and Baxter . . . B-Baxter is a lucky man."

"Yes, he is lucky, isn't he?" Belle looked up at her with a mysterious smile. "He's a very lucky man. More than he knows, I think."

Fifteen

Del ran his fingers through his silver-winged hair and sighed in exasperation. "I can't think of any other explanation," he said to the man across the desk.

Corpulent to an extreme degree, Sir Douglas Prong wheezed as he lit a cigar, and said, "My lord, we are concerned. We fear for your life. But the nest of spies you uncovered was completely eradicated; we are absolutely sure of that. How can any of them still be after you?"

"It is the only explanation," Del repeated, slamming the flat of his hand against the desk.

Sir Douglas's ancient pug, as asthmatic as his owner, grunted and snuffled under the desk in reaction to the interruption of his pleasant dreams. The knight leaned down and patted its head, coming dangerously close to bursting a blood vessel or two. His face was red and his breathing stentorian when he straightened. He puffed on the cigar, indulged in a fit of coughing as he blew the smoke out, and then settled back in his chair, which creaked as he sat back.

"I have not told anyone this," Del continued. "But that night in Calais, when I was coshed so inefficiently, I had had the feeling that I was being watched for some time. That is why I was on my guard. But even after my attacker was driven off, the feeling did not go away."

Sir Douglas sat absolutely still behind his desk. His huge, round face and indolent manner disguised a sharp intellect and the instincts of a very good gambler. He understood feelings and hunches. They were what had led him to a position of some prominence, though most in the government didn't even acknowledge his existence, in part because his bailiwick was spies. That is how Lord Delafont had first come to his attention; the marquess uncovered a nest of spies within the inner circle of British foreign diplomacy. Sir Douglas understood spies in a way that made him suspect to others in the diplomatic world. The British government had their own spies, but it was not "gentlemanly," nor quite acceptable.

"What do you make of that?" he grunted, referring to Delafont's "feeling."

"I am being followed, I think. I do not believe they, whoever 'they' are, want me dead. What I am not sure of is whether they wish to warn me, or whether the attacks have been kidnapping attempts."

"Warn you of what?"

Del shrugged. What did he believe? He had had a dangerous few weeks in Italy when he discovered that a trusted envoy for Lord Castlereagh was, in reality, gathering information for the French. The war might be over and Napoleon safe on Saint Helena, but there were still many who did not want a return to royalist reign in France. And there were many more willing to take *money* from those who did not want a return to royalist reign.

When he uncovered the spy, he had wisely not unmasked him the minute he knew, but rather waited until he could speak to someone he knew he could trust. Together they concocted a plan to draw the others into the open. Del posed as one vulnerable to bribery, and the circle was decimated with the knowledge he gained.

But there was another, a shadowy figure whose existence was not even acknowledged. Del was convinced that this was the mastermind who was plotting, for patriotism or money, to rescue Napoleon and defeat the Royalists. Sir Douglas Prong knew all about his beliefs on this subject; they had already canvassed it thoroughly. But he always had the feeling with the corpulent knight that there was something more that wasn't being discussed, some information he was not privy to.

"Have I been told everything?" he said suddenly, studying the man's face.

"My lord?"

"Everything! Is anything being held back from me for some reason or another?"

The man paused and puffed on his cigar. His dog grunted and wheezed, then lapsed back into snore. "My lord, you know everything that you need to know."

Not a very satisfying answer, Del thought. He sighed and kneaded his trick knee. Life currently seemed to be a confusion of problems that needed to be worked out—problems with Belle, with Emily, with that damned French upstart Marchant.

"What do you know about a young Frenchman, Vicomte Etienne Marchant?" he said, suddenly.

Sir Douglas coughed, exhaling a cloud of smoke. He hacked for a moment, then grunted, "Never heard of the man."

"Yes, you have! He is in my report. My purported savior!"

The older man did not answer, and Del felt a thread of suspicion wind through his entrails. Shadows behind shadows behind shadows. More was going on than he even knew about, and it was disturbing to think that he was only in some outer circle of trust. How could he protect himself if he only had half the information he needed? He got up, bowed and took his leave, exiting the smoky, stuffy office into the rain-washed freshness that even London dirt and smoke had not yet contaminated. He needed to think and the only way he could do that was to walk.

Emily lay curled up in her bed. There was too much to think about—too much to worry about! Was Baxter still in danger? Was Etienne involved? Why had Baxter not returned to her, not spoken to her, not . . . she covered her face with her hands, holding back the tears with difficulty. The answer to that last question was too easy to answer—because he had a beautiful little mistress who adored him, even if she didn't think she loved him. Because their night together had been just the result of his dazed unawareness. No doubt he had realized it was a mistake when his head cleared in the morning and could not think of a way to tell her.

She sniffed and wiped her eyes dry. There was no point in that unprofitable line of thought. Of primary importance at the moment was to find out if Etienne was involved and ensure Baxter's safety. It might be the last thing she could do for him, but she would not see him harmed for the world, even if the one who benefitted was Belle Gallant. She slipped off the bed and called out to her dresser. "Sylvie, *aide-moi, s'il vous plaît.* I am going out for the afternoon."

Del patted his pocket, hearing the crisp crinkle of paper as he strode up the steps to the small town house he had rented for Belle. The parlor maid let him in—Belle had not wanted a butler or footmen—and he waited in the downstairs salon. The faintest hint of lilacs on the breeze from the window teased his nostrils and he felt a sharp twinge of melancholy as it reminded him of Emily and what he had lost forever. He had not been able to bear to see her lying face after their beautiful night together, to know that he was a poor second, that he wasn't even her first lover that night! That knowledge tainted every day and haunted every night.

His stomach felt hollow and a sharp, acid taste flooded his mouth. He had not been eating or sleeping well for days. Food revolted him and sleep evaded him, so he pursued all of his activities in a fog of unreality. Decisive action was required though, and today he would take the first step to regaining his autonomy. He should have done this long ago. It was time he stopped letting the women in his life run it.

The door opened quietly behind him, and Belle's maid brought in a tray with brandy, which he gladly helped himself to as Belle floated into the room.

"You look extraordinarily happy, my dear." He sipped the brandy.

"And why should I not?" She drifted to a sofa and eased herself down into it.

He quirked an eyebrow, wondering why she was carrying herself as though she would break. Normally she whirled around like a top, moving like a cyclone through any room in a mad swirl of energy. She seemed . . . different somehow. Normally the first thing she thought of was taking his hand and leading him up the stairs to her boudoir for sex, after which she wanted to talk about her acting career or something like that. Instead she was gazing at him languidly through half-closed eyes.

"Del," she said, sitting up a little from her relaxed position. "You never talk to me about your life . . . I mean, your life besides me."

He took a seat beside her and she cuddled up against him, twining her arm through his. "My life besides . . . frankly, Belle, I had no idea you'd be interested."

She gazed up at him with reproachful eyes. "I'm interested in everything about you, Del. Really. What you do, who you see, what your life was like before I met you."

"Is that right?" He was bemused and nonplussed. This was a side of her he had never seen in the two years they had been together. This was what he had wanted, wasn't it? A mistress who wanted to talk as well as to make love? He felt a twinge of irritation, since he had come that day intending to cut the relationship off, and now this was going to make it more difficult. But he would not rush it. Disentangling oneself from an affair was a burdensome business, but with Belle it would be even more difficult. She did not have the sophistication to understand that love affairs were ephemeral or the philosophy to accept that all good things come to an end. And he did not want to hurt her, if he could avoid it. "What do you want to know?"

She stroked the sleeve of his jacket and then toyed with his wedding ring. He had been teased by friends when he married because he had wanted to wear a visible symbol of his commitment to Emily, unlike most of his married friends. The ring was a family heirloom of her father's, a band with a black onyx cabochon set in it. He had never taken it off even when they had formally separated, and Emily had never asked for it back. He had noticed that she still wore the ring he gave her, too.

"Why did you split up with Lady Delafont?"

The baldly stated question took him aback and he twisted to look down at her, but her head was rested against his arm. "What on earth makes you want to know that?"

Her blond curls trembled and she shrugged. "Curious, I guess. You don't talk much about all that."

"Not much to say."

She twisted and gazed up at him, the expression on her narrow face vividly expressing her disbelief. "What rot! Did you love her? *Do* you love her? Have you ever thought of going back to her? What broke you up in the first place?"

Del sighed. Women, but more specifically, *Belle!* She would not be put off lightly. Once she fastened on to something she was tenacious, like a terrier with a slipper. That quality had served her well when it came to the lessons her tutor had given her. She was not so much intelligent as she was clever and an excellent mimic. What could he say? What would satisfy her so that he could get on to the business at hand, which was the imminent end of their relationship?

And so in the cool placidness of her salon, gold drapes filtering the late day sun, he told her about meeting Emily and kissing her for the very first time. He told her about their marriage and even about their voracious sexual appetites through the first years of their marriage. Perhaps that part was none of her business, but he found himself saying it anyway, as though he were remembering out loud, holding on to every precious facet of their life together.

It soothed him to recall that once, Emily had loved him. He was not mistaken in that at least. What was hard to fathom was that making love to her again after all the intervening years had been like coming home. It had felt the same, the connectedness, the love, the feeling of joining two parts of a puzzle that fit so well no seams showed. How could it be that it felt the same and yet was so very different? *Had* to be different, if she had a lover!

At the end of his explication, Belle nodded, satisfied. "And she could never have a baby?"

"No. Though the fault may be entirely mine. In all my adult years, to my knowledge I have never impregnated a woman, and I have certainly had enough partners."

He felt her move as if startled, but then she settled again. She was silent for a moment, but then spoke again.

"Would it have made a difference, do you think? If you had been able to have a baby with her? Would you have stayed together?"

He stretched his long legs out over the worn Turkish rug and settled her against his chest, with his arm around her. For the first time he felt companionable with Belle, and it was an oddly heart-warming feeling. She felt, though, not so much like a lover as like . . . well, a niece or little sister, though he had had neither and could claim no real knowledge of those relationships. "I don't know," he answered truthfully. "I can see now that . . . we've talked, Emily and I, and I can see how she was blaming herself and I thought she was blaming me, and my mother constantly stirred up trouble between us, and I never defended Emily, never took her side out of some mistaken idea of loyalty toward my mother." And now it was too late for them, Del thought sadly, thinking of the lost opportunity for love, the changes that must have taken place in Emily for her to have taken a lover. He gritted his teeth, unwilling to let the black tide of anger sweep over him again. He controlled the surge of rage with an effort and said, "Is that enough? Do you know everything you need to know?"

"Would having a baby have made a difference? Would you have stayed together?"

Lord, but she was tenacious. He thought about her question. "I think we would have stayed together," he said finally. "We would still have had problems, but we would have been forced to work through them, with a child to consider. It was too easy to separate when it was just us. Now, is that enough? Is there anything else you want to pry into or stick your pert little nose into?"

"No," she said, sitting up and moving away from him. She faced him, her blue eyes challenging him. "Well, yes. Do you still love her?"

He blew out a long breath and straightened. He gazed down the room at the cold fireplace at the end, an ornate relic from the previous century. To his knowledge, Belle had not done a thing to this house that was leased in her name, except to gaudy up her boudoir with tarty red draperies. Emily had always stamped her imprint on any home they were living in, whether it was in the country or in London. She would have fresh flowers everywhere and would supervise the rearrangement of the furniture, moving it into comfortable conversation groups or . . . he realized that every thought he had began and ended with Emily.

"I . . . yes, to be honest, I think I do." He glanced over at Belle, hoping that admission had not hurt her. He didn't want to hurt her with his honesty. He was surprised by her smile, a mysterious expression like that of a cat with a mouthful of feathers. It was a mixture of smugness and satisfaction that he could not fathom.

His suspicion was aroused. "What are you up to, my dear?"

"Nothing."

She stretched and offered him more brandy, but he refused it, intending to get down to the business at hand. How to break off their affair. He was about to open his mouth to speak and draw the papers out of his pocket, but she forestalled him with another question.

"Why don't you go back to her now that you know you still love her?"

He gaped in astonishment, but a flare of anger made his answer easy. "I will not take another man's leavings!"

It was her turn to be astonished and she stared at him. "What . . ."

"She is having an affair with that French bastard, Etienne Marchant. He had the gall to come into my home and gloat."

"Are . . . are you sure, Del? That she is sleeping with him?"

"I've seen them together. She looked guilty, damn her eyes!" He covered his face with his long-fingered hands. "And I didn't know about it until after we had made love again."

"You . . . you made love to her?" Belle's voice was small.

He glanced over at her. "It . . . it was an accident." He explained to her about being coshed again and being taken into her house, into her bed. As he spoke he remembered the delicious sensation of waking up, finding her next to him, her body pressed against his, and making love to her. He didn't elaborate on the lovemaking, but Belle was ever forthright.

"Did you . . . did you like it better than with me?" She looked fragile and very, very young sitting on the sofa in her pale green gown, a vision of sylphlike and delicate beauty.

What could he say? What *should* he say? "It was different, Belle, it was . . ."

She held up one small, white hand. "Don't! You don't need to . . . it doesn't matter, Del."

She bit her lip, driving the blood from it until it was

white. He thought he could see tears in her eyes and he was deeply touched and sorry to be the instrument of pain in her young heart. Whatever she was feeling, she mastered it, took a deep breath and pulled herself up.

"I think, Del, before you judge her, you should think. Even if it is true, even if she had been with Veecompte Marchant, maybe she knew it was a mistake straight away, or maybe . . . maybe it made her realize how much she loves you. Maybe you should find out."

It had cost her a lot to know the truth, Belle thought. It was easier when it was all just in her mind, but now, to know that he still loved his wife and preferred her . . . . The one thing Belle had always been able to give him was sexual release, and now there was someone else he preferred. But wasn't that her plan? Didn't she want him to be happy, even if that happiness was to be found with Emily?

It was a struggle. Maybe she did love Del, she thought, looking at his harshly handsome face, the lines that grooved deeply to his mouth and the black eyes that looked so severe. She was one of the few people who knew that Del was as soft as blancmange inside, despite his dangerous looks and lofty, stubborn pride. But he loved his wife, and she loved him, and Belle was planning to have his baby, the one thing he and his wife hadn't been able to have together. It hurt more than she imagined it would when she made her plan, but it was still a good scheme, and she would go through with it. Maybe there was a way to make her baby the instrument of reconciliation for Del and his wife. Maybe she wouldn't even *need* to . . . .

She would think of something, and then the debt to Del would be paid, at long last. Then she could start living just for herself and planning her future.

Sixteen

". . . and I just don't know what I should do! He means to abduct and rape me!" Grishelda sat on the sofa wringing her thin hands together, almost vibrating with agitation.

Emily caught her hands in her own and chafed them. "Calm, my dear. Please do not give in to . . . ." She quickly dropped her young friend's hands as she heard a sound.

The door opened and a footman brought in the tea tray, setting it before Emily.

"As I was saying, I had a letter from Celestine. They are on their way home from Italy and have some sort of mysterious news that they do not want to relate in a letter." She gave Grishelda a significant look.

"R-really! I wonder what that could be."

Her voice stuttered a little, but she did fairly well, Emily thought.

"I am hoping to soon be a great-aunt. If that is the news it would explain why Justin and Celestine are returning when the Italian sun has proved so beneficial for her arthritis."

The footman moved to the window, twitched the curtains to the right to shield the ladies from the blaze of the spring sun.

"Justin has discovered an interest in antiquities and will be bringing back . . . there, he is gone," Emily said, keeping her voice low as the footman closed the door behind him. "It would not do to be indiscreet. Servants gossip. My dear, you must be strong. Do you really believe they will forcibly abduct you?"

Grishelda nodded. "I do. I have my reasons. You have not met Captain Dempster—he is not generally accepted in polite society, though my mother has managed to get him invitations to some balls as her escort—but I believe him capable of anything. He . . . he takes every opportunity to touch me." She shivered and swallowed, taking a great shuddering breath.

"Have you talked to your mother about this?"

"Her? She would think I was lying, or would accuse me of something worse. As hard as it is to believe, she is jealous; the captain has said something to her about me, accused me of impropriety toward him."

"Improp . . . what do you mean?" Emily was shocked and not a little diverted. Improper? Grishelda was the most proper of young ladies, to the point of prudery. It was that prudery that made her so vulnerable to this particular situation. Emily had always known Grishelda as a calm, intelligent young lady with a core of steel. But this affair had her as shaken and fearful as a child.

Grishelda, clearly distressed and embarrassed by her revelation, stared intently at a pretty vase with Etienne's latest offering of flowers. "Mama . . . my mother is besotted with Captain Dempster. He spends every night in her bed now; she has no shame when it comes to him and he takes full advantage of that. He takes liberties. I told you I have caught him in my room. Well, I think—I *know*—he has seen . . . seen a part of my body."

"My, God!" Emily cried. "How can that be?"

"One night we had no engagement, and so we sat and played whist together with a friend of the captain's. I became sleepy and groggy after evening coffee," Grishelda said. "I retired early, and fell into so deep a sleep, I cannot help but think that I was drugged. When I awoke, my nightrail was untied and open. My . . . my breasts and stomach were exposed."

"But that could easily happen, could it not? It could have come undone?"

For some reason, Grishelda blushed as she nodded. "It could, I suppose. But on the cover beside me were ashes. The captain smokes horrid, smelly cigars, and the ashes carried the same awful smell. They could only have gotten there one way."

Shocked and revolted, Emily exclaimed, "And you think the captain came into your room and . . . and what? He didn't . . . didn't violate . . ."

"No! Oh, no, not that! I would . . . I suppose I would know . . . ?" She cast a questioning glance Emily's way.

"Yes, my dear. You would most certainly know if you were no longer a virgin, and there would be tangible evidence on your sheets and . . . you would know."

Grishelda shivered and looked away. In the still quiet of the parlor, her voice hushed to little more than a whisper. "I . . . I think he looked at my b-breasts. I have a b-beauty mark—very identifiable—and C-captain Dempster . . . ." Her voice caught with a sob.

Emily moved to sit beside her and took her hand. It was much worse than she had thought. Grishelda was a very prim young woman, and Emily had considered the possibility that she was so afraid of marriage that she was becoming hysterical and imagining plots where they did not exist. But this . . .

"How did this come out?"

"Mother accused me of trying to lure the captain into my b-bed by exposing my b-body to him." She shivered again, her expression haunted and fearful. "At first she had not believed the captain, she said, but he had described my mark in intimate detail and only a man who had had a close view could do that."

Emily tipped the girl's plain face up and held it up, her fingers under her chin. "Do not be ashamed, Grishelda. This is nothing to do with you."

"That is the hold he has over me! I will never be able to convince my mother of his despicable plot, because she believes I want him for myself." She shuddered. "I can't stand it when he looks at me like he wants to . . . ." Grishelda's normally calm voice and serene manner cracked. "And to know he has seen me! And perhaps touched me! How can any woman allow a man to touch her: her body, her b-breasts . . . ."

"Grishelda!" Emily's voice held a commanding tone, and the young woman calmed. She would not allow the girl's exaggerated fears to become hysteria. As it was, Grishelda had some deeply held aversion to men that Emily did not understand; but that was a matter for another day, after the immediate danger was over. If that fear was all that was keeping her from marriage, then she needed to come to terms with it and make her life decisions based on reality, not some fiction that men were rabid beasts with only sexual hungers and needs. She needed to understand the tenderness that was a part of marital love.

And she could start to challenge Grishelda's beliefs now, in this situation. "Don't mistake how you feel when a man like Captain Dempster looks at you or touches you with the way it is and should be between a man and a woman."

Grishelda's pale blue eyes widened. "Do you mean you . . . you like it? Marital intimacy, I mean. I can't imagine . . . it just seems so foreign, surrendering your body to a man, allowing him to invade you in such an animal way."

Emily felt a surge of impatience. Perhaps young women were now being raised with an altogether too refined notion of relations between men and women. She had been raised in the country, with a country woman's ready understanding and acceptance of the physical nature of life. She had come to the marriage bed knowing what to expect after several very informative discussions with village women of her acquaintance. In fact she and Baxter, unable to wait another moment, had anticipated their marriage vows by several days in one ecstatic afternoon by a

stream in the countryside. That day he had gently and
sensually initiated her to the world of physical love, taking
her virginity, and then teaching her some of the ways they
would find to enhance the experience.

Grishelda was watching her curiously. Emily felt her
face flush hotly. Now was not the time to be daydreaming
about all she had lost. As it was, that knowledge followed
her every day, every moment and likely would for the rest
of her days.

"Surrender is a part of womanhood, a precious part.
It is the gift you give the man you love, and if you have
chosen to love wisely, he will treasure that gift and love
you all the more for it. But do not mistake it! Men give
up a part of themselves, too, and that is something not
too many women understand. I am going to tell you a
secret that not every woman knows. A woman can wield
considerable power over a man, and sex is the key. Some
women use this power indiscriminately and lose the efficacy of it. That is your mother.

"A wise women uses it sparingly, until it increases in
potency. At its full power, you can lure a man to your
side with just a look, just a glance. It is a heady feeling,
like the finest wine." Emily sighed, remembering her
marriage. Baxter never knew that the simmering looks
she would throw him across a crowded ballroom were
calculated, designed to entice him into a hasty departure.
She was not one much for balls and routs, and had found
a delicious and exciting way to cut an evening short whenever she had felt the need. Perhaps some would say that
it diminished a woman to use sexual power for her own
gain, but Emily believed it was a precious part of the
dance men and women engaged in, the parry and thrust
of everyday life and love. Men used the strength nature
gave them; why should women not use their own natural
endowment?

Looking uncomfortable, her guest shifted. "I . . . I
never thought that women had any power in marriage. I

always thought of them as losing all of their rights, all of their self-determination . . . ."

"We do give up some, but if you choose carefully and from the heart, you will gain more than you lose. Sex is not the only power in marriage, nor even the most effective; that of love is far stronger and more lasting. Look at my niece, Celestine."

Nodding, Grishelda smiled. "I have never seen anyone so happy as she was on her wedding day."

"Oh, but she was nervous about her wedding night!" Emily laughed. "I reassured her that it was only painful for a moment, and the reward is years of pleasure and happiness. I saw her the next day, and she was radiant. I think she discovered how right I was."

"I . . . I still cannot quite believe that. I have been taught that for a woman pleasure in marriage is not to be found in the marriage bed but out of it. I have always believed that my mother was one of the rare women for whom intimacy is enjoyable."

Emily snorted. "Your mother doesn't enjoy sex! She uses it as a weapon, thinking she is conquering a man, but she cheapens the nature of loving sensuality until she makes it into a farce."

"I never thought of it that way. I always thought that she craved it and could not help herself. I have long known that she is not in control and that she needs male admiration and seeks it the only way she can, but if you are right, she is attempting to take the upper hand in her dealing with men and failing."

Her pale blue eyes held a thoughtful gleam, and Emily hoped that she had given the girl something to think about. She now had a much better idea of what kept the girl from any intention of marrying and hoped that her rationality would win out eventually over irrational fears.

"But back to the business at hand. I think . . ." Hearing a commotion in the hall, Emily realized that more visitors must be arriving. "Do you go to the masquerade at the LaCoursiere's tonight? And is your mother going to be there?"

"Mother is going, but I had not thought to attend, though she has been most adamant that I go."

"Go then, and I will try to talk to your mother some time during the night, and see if we can resolve this nonsense of marrying you off to Lord Saunders. Perhaps she will see reason. More importantly, I will find out what I can about this plot to abduct you. I am not without influence, and Lord Saunders may not be aware of Dempster's despicable nature and nasty reputation."

The LaCoursiere masquerade ball was an annual affair that had started with the French émigré family's—the Duc de LaCoursiere, his *duchesse* and children—attempts to raise money for their impoverished brethren. Now that the war was over, the need had not disappeared and the event went on as planned, with money gathered to support the French who had been displaced and ruined during the revolution and long war.

Delafont, who had family in France, or at least distant relations, felt compelled to attend even though he had no intention of masquerading. A simple black domino and mask that he could shed as the evening wore on was all he would condescend to. As a generous supporter, Lessington was also there, dressed as an Elizabethan courtier.

"Haven't seen you lately, Del. Where have you been hiding?"

"Everybody has been trying to convince me to stay safe, and now you complain because I haven't been out and about enough? Come, Less, make up your mind."

Less held up his hands in mock surrender. "I shall leave it alone, then. Have you seen your wife? She is here, you know."

At that moment, Del saw her and his breath caught in his throat. She was dressed as a simple peasant girl, with a low-cut blue dress of deceptively simple line and a white apron over it. Her hair tumbled around her shoulders, a mass of dark curls. A throb pulsed through his body, and he felt his groin tighten at the first view of his wife since bedding her what seemed an eon ago.

Her attire might be simple, but to him it was provocative and arousing. It took him back to the first moment he saw her more than fifteen years before. Her eyes met his through the crowd, and, in one searing instant it was as if their marriage were alive again. She gave him that look, that wanton, sensual, burning gaze, and then the dropped eyelashes and sinuous movement that made her breasts strain the fabric and her hips sway.

His self-control crumbled and he was about to move across the room to her before he caught himself. He swallowed, took a deep breath and held himself rigidly, so overwhelming was his desire to sweep her away from the crowd to some private place. What game did she play? Why did she torture him?

Less stared at him, his gray eyes wide. "Like a moth to a candle."

"What?" Del, a hunger that had nothing to do with food gnawing at his insides, turned to Less. "What did you say?"

"Nothing. Ah, look! Her so-faithful Frenchman has caught sight of her as well."

Del was glad of the mask, then, because he felt his lips draw back from his teeth as rage surged through him. He was a sophisticated man, he would have said, civilized, intelligent, but something about this whole affair brought out his most primitive urges, the desire to rend and tear his rival limb from limb. All the control he had achieved over his temper in his adult years was perilously close to giving out. Emily greeted Marchant with a smile; he raised her ungloved hand to his lips and kissed it, holding it much longer than necessary and moving much too close to her. She looked across the room at Baxter again, but his heart had frozen to solid ice.

* * *

Emily cursed Etienne's timing. Instinct had driven her to use the sexual invitation she knew had always drawn her husband to her side. Their relationship was not purely sexual—they had loved each other from the start and she still loved him fiercely, tenderly—but there was a strong undercurrent of sensuality that had not waned, at least for her, with the intervening years apart. She had almost thought Baxter meant to come to her, but then he had paused. If Etienne had not joined her at that moment with fulsome compliments, she would have abandoned pride and gone to Baxter. They had to solve what was between them because their marriage was *not* over, no matter what they had agreed upon with a lawyer and papers. She was furious with him for his abandonment of her after making love to her again, but this time she had sworn not to let anger or misplaced pride destroy them. Perhaps she had no choice in this matter, though. If he chose to cut her off as he had obviously done, there was not a thing she could do about it.

Scanning the crowd for Grishelda and Lady van Hoffen, Emily merely nodded as Etienne spoke.

"I will bring for you some refreshment, then," he said and bowed over her hand, flinging back the cape of his Arab prince costume to reveal a very impressive saber sashed to his side.

"What? Oh, certainly," Emily said, just glad he intended to leave her alone for a while. His attentions, flattering at first, had now become irksome. She fervently wished he would find someone else to bestow his regard upon. She had not yet solved the puzzle of who he was and she longed to confront him with the fact that he was not the Vicomte Etienne Marchant, but until she knew if he was connected to the attempts against Baxter, she did not dare drive him from her side.

There was Grishelda! She was dressed in a simple white gown with the red ribbon around her neck that was a symbol of compassion and support for the men and women who had gone to the guillotine during the Reign of Terror. For a while the red ribbon had been the fashion among English girls, but that was long exploded. To Emily her attire seemed to say much more. Did she identify with martyrdom? Or did she feel she was being constrained and led to her slaughter?

She motioned to the young woman, and Grishelda floated over to her. She was not a beautiful girl, Emily thought, but she had presence. She was graceful and lissome, even more so in the simple scooped-neck dress, naked of any adornment save a silver cross that dangled in her modest décolletage.

Emily raised her eyebrows as the young woman joined her. "That costume is quite a statement, my dear. Do you see yourself as looking forward to a sacrifice on level with the French who died in the Terror?"

Grishelda flushed. The white silk mask she held did not hide her flaming cheeks or the sharpness of her light-blue gaze. "Of course not," she said, angrily.

"You must learn to take light teasing, my dear. I did not mean to be harsh."

"I'm sorry. I am just so . . . so worried!"

"What costume is your mother wearing?" Emily, mask-less, surveyed the crowd. She was sure whatever she chose, Lady van Hoffen would stand out. Once she had arrived at a masquerade in a dress that exposed her rouged nipples, as though she were at a Cyprian's ball. She had not stayed long and not everyone had seen her, but it had caused a stir and a scandal. Masquerades were a special opportunity for plain Maisie Taylor, as she had been before her marriage, a sluttish, third-rate opera dancer who had caught herself a European title. Now more than forty, she still dressed to attract the most prurient of notice and had become notorious for the transparency of her dresses and her aversion to undergarments.

"She has not arrived yet." Grishelda's voice was tight and controlled, but her eyes gave away her anguish.

"What is she wearing?" Emily asked with trepidation.

"She was planning . . . she heard that in some ancient cultures women exposed their bosom. I tried to tell her that she would mortally offend the LaCoursieres and probably everyone else, too, and that she was on the border of disgracing herself to the point that she would not be acceptable in polite society anymore. She would look the veriest whore! The LaCoursieres would have every right to have her physically removed from their presence, did she insult them that way. But Captain Dempster was encouraging her and she would do anything to keep his interest. I . . . I will die of mortification if she follows through with her threat."

"Your mother is not a complete fool, Grishelda. I—"

Agitated, the girl moved her hands, cutting off Emily's speech. "Will you call me May, Emily? It is the name I prefer, my second name. I *despise* my first name!"

Wishing that the girl would regain some of her usual calmness, Emily said in a soothing tone, "May, then. My dear, your mother is not a complete fool and always manages to just skirt banishment. Even she must know, deep down, that such a costume would see her barred from society forever."

"I hope so."

"Ah, here comes Etienne with some refreshments . . . ."

May's pale blue eyes widened, and she made an inarticulate noise of fear in her throat. "I will speak to you when my mother arrives," she said hurriedly and then glided away at a brisk pace.

May moved rapidly through the crowd, away from Emily and the encroaching Etienne Marchant. She could not bear to be near that man! She had met him just once, but the mocking light in his dark eyes and the warmth of his touch unnerved her. He had gazed at her with a keen and knowing look that had risen a blush in her cheek as no other ever had. He had seemed to delight in unnerving her, and she had schooled herself to be proof against any kind of seductiveness; she had been an heiress too long not to know what men really wanted.

But he pierced her well-guarded armor, and she felt as if he knew all of her secrets, all of her hidden wickedness and vice. She flitted through the crowd looking for a place to rest, away from the impertinent vicomte. This was not an event to enjoy, but to endure. Pray to God her mother did not disgrace herself this time.

The evening seemed interminable. She had arrived with some unacceptional friends who resided near her home. Sir Tolliver Gowan and Lady Gowan were a young and lively couple who persisted in trying to find her a husband even after her emphatic statement that she did not want one. As a result, she did not accept many of their invitations, since they invariably had some young Lord Something-or-other or Mr. Whosis they wanted to foist on her. But tonight it had suited her not to arrive with her mother. Their invitation had been timely.

So through the evening she stayed by Jenny, Lady Gowan, who was visibly with child and did not dance, while Sir Tolliver retired to the card room. She saw Emily, Lady Delafont, dance with the Vicomte Etienne Marchant. He had seemed possessive of her, from what May had observed. Whispers had been circulating that she and the young Frenchman were lovers, but May did not believe much in gossip.

Although . . . how could Emily resist him, if he bent his efforts on seducing her? He was the handsomest man May had ever seen—dark, expressive eyes, wavy, thick hair and a body that was powerful, and yet . . . and it was not her business to be looking at him that way. She flushed at her own thoughts.

A young footman in the LaCoursiere livery of blue and silver bowed before her. "Lady Grishelda May van Hoffen? I have for you the message." He proffered a silver tray.

May, her heart pounding, took the note. An unfamiliar

hand had written, "Meet me in the conservatory, and I will tell you something to your benefit."

Would Lady Delafont write such a note? She looked up and glanced around the large, glittering room. The orchestra played a cotillion dance, and she caught sight of Emily. She looked questioningly at the marchioness as she was whirled around on the arm of a new gentleman. Emily nodded and smiled.

That must be the sign.

May wondered what her mother had said. There must be some news if Emily wanted to meet her in the conservatory, somewhere so private and deserted. Maybe her mother had been made to understand Captain Dempster's machinations. She stood and looked anxiously around. The cotillion was almost over, and she did not want to be seen disappearing with Emily; it would look peculiar.

She murmured to Lady Gowan that she was going to the ladies withdrawing room to cool down from the heat of the ballroom and drifted away in that direction. Once out of sight, she moved through the crowd and tried to think where the conservatory was in this vast mausoleum of a mansion. By London standards it was very large. The LaCoursieres had always maintained a London residence and thus had had a place to go during the Terror. They had become vintners and distillers of extraordinary fruit-based wines and liqueurs in the more than twenty years since then, and had made their fortune many times over from the English starvation for French wine and brandy during the war.

And so they had a conservatory even in their London home. She had seen from the outside that a glassed-in room had been added on the south side of the house; that must be it. She had, luckily, an extraordinary sense of direction, and headed out and toward the right place.

She passed the card room, and another with other gambling opportunities, such as vingt-et-un and faro. As she moved through the majestic house, the hall became quieter and the people fewer. She felt a trembling in her stomach. Why couldn't Emily have named the ladies withdrawing room as the place for their coze? Her stomach turned as she caught sight of the Vicomte Etienne Marchant, but he was earnestly in conversation with another man and did not appear to notice her. Her heart throbbed in fear at the thought of being caught alone with that seductive scoundrel. Who knows what he could convince a woman to do with those warm caramel-brown eyes and beguiling voice? Not that she had anything to fear from a man like that. He would never look twice at a frozen spinster like herself.

She slipped down the dim hall. Fewer candles. Colder. Her feet, in sandals, were as cold as the marble floor, and she hoped the conservatory was warm and humid as most would be. There! That room at the end must surely be the conservatory. She passed a couple in a dim recess, the woman giggling and the man murmuring in her ear. They would be ruined if anyone saw them, she thought. She would *never* take a chance with her reputation like that!

Now, all she had to do was get into the conservatory and await Emily.

The heavy door squeaked as she opened it. Good. She would hear Emily when she arrived. There were a couple of flambeaux giving off a smoky smell, and the flickering light danced off the glass windows that arced in a semicircle. The high-ceilinged room was damp and earthy smelling with rows of tables. The Duchesse de LaCoursiere was a renowned grower of orchids and there were hundreds of examples of her ability.

May wandered along the rows for a few minutes, twirling her mask as she marveled at the variety of colors, happy to be away from the party so her stomach could settle. Serenity. That was all she wanted, and if Emily could help her settle with her mother once and for all time, then she would return to her home and never come back to London. Her mother loved London and would be glad to stay there all year long, but to May it was a stinking, dirty hole with hardly a soul to recommend it. She longed to go home, home to Lark House, where her horse, Cassiopeia, was still, home to her gardens and village school and long walks in the countryside. Home.

The door creaked.

Finally! Perhaps Emily would be able to tell her that the plot was over, her mother had been aghast and had called off her dangerous Captain Dempster. Maybe she could be packing the next morning to go home as spring woke the countryside.

"I'm over here, Emily!" she called out, feeling lighter of heart than she had in months. "What did she say? Did she believe you about that hideous plot to—augh!"

A horrible smell assailed her nostrils, and, as she began to fall, she felt a cloth sack being pulled over her head and a cord tightened around her throat, just before she lost consciousness. Her mask fluttered to the ground, unnoticed.

Seventeen

Etienne had not missed the side glance of the English miss as she slipped down the hall looking oh, so guilty. An assignation? That little one? He had imagined her as a frosty little thing, full of prudish English notions about men and sex. His curiosity was stirred, but the conversation he was having was a vital one, and very enlightening. He was afraid that he had been a fool of the first order, and that he would have to extricate himself from some very dirty business, business he had not liked from the beginning.

When he finally could get away from his informant, Lady Grishelda May van Hoffen, as she had been introduced to him, had been gone a full ten minutes or more. Only one room past him would be any good for an assignation and that was the *conservatoire*, that infamously dark choice for a *rendezvous d'amour*. He had seen no young man slip down the hall after her looking guilty and *excité*, but maybe there was another way into the *conservatoire*. Perhaps he should follow the miss, in case she got in a little more deeply than she knew.

She was, after all, a good friend of Emily, and any turn he could serve Emily that might bring her to his bed was worth doing. He still had hope of success, even though she had not been as encouraging as he would have hoped. He was patient, and he believed that she would be well worth the wait, though time was growing short. It might be necessary for him to disappear for a while very soon now, and he did so wish to bed his delectable heart's delight before he left.

The door creaked open as he pushed on it. He strolled in, intending to casually interrupt the English miss, who might not realize what danger lay in a secret rendezvous. She had not, he thought, the experience in such matters. He bent over and picked up from the floor a white satin mask on a beribboned handle. What was it doing there? A sharp chemical smell was in the air, and he heard a scuffle and the sound of an oath, in a brutish English voice. "Bitch" hissed through the air, and the sound of dragging, away from him, on the other side of the tables toward the high glass windows.

What was this? He followed the sounds, all of his senses alert. *Tiens*, there was something! A white figure was being dragged out a door that opened on to a terrace, and he knew that the young lady wore a white dress that evening. *"Arrêtez, vilain!"* he shouted, lapsing into French in his agitation.

"Shite, we bin caught, cap'n!"

Etienne tossed the mask aside, flung his cape over his shoulder and raced after the two men who dragged the English miss. It was execrable that a man would treat a woman that way, and he would stop it or he would die trying!

"Have you seen her, Less? She was wearing a plain white dress and a red ribbon around her throat. She had a white satin mask."

"I have not, my dear. I'll take a look around and ask some friends if they have seen her," Less said, turning to make his way through the crowd.

"Discreetly, though, discreetly! With a mother like hers people are always looking to attach scandal to the daughter."

Less glanced back at Emily, looking mildly offended.

"My dear, when have you known me to be anything but discreet?"

She smiled her apology, and he disappeared into the crowd. It was annoying in the extreme, Emily thought. The girl had clearly wanted to talk to her about something, had given her that expressive, questioning look, and Emily had denied her next dance partner, just so she could go to Grishelda, or rather May; she must think of her as May. And now she was nowhere to be found and Emily was hot and exhausted from searching.

There, finally, was Lady van Hoffen! Emily gazed at her with exasperation. She had been trying to corner the woman for an hour, but she was always surrounded, always busy. At least she hadn't worn the outrageous and indecent costume she had threatened to. She had dressed as a pre-Terror French aristocrat, with a gray powdered wig, heavily leaded face and bosom, and a multiplicity of patches, some low on her breasts. The irony of May's costume was complete.

She started toward her. Lady van Hoffen was gabbling about something, her blue eyes wide and her hands flailing. Emily moved closer.

"I told her he wasn't good enough for her, but she has defied me and run off. That old roué! She was determined to have him, said he wouldn't bother her much in bed and had pots of money. What does a mother know, after all! I've been keeping my eye on her, but the little harlot has slipped off and is likely on her way to Gretna by now with the old moneybags."

Emily drew back, an inarticulate sound of fear in her throat all she could make. What was the woman talking about? What had happened? A strong hand steadied her and she turned to find Delafont at her elbow.

"Baxter!" she gasped, grasping his strong arm as a prop. Her legs felt weak. "It's not true; its a lie! And if she's saying it now, it must mean—oh, God!—it means Grishelda . . . May . . . has been abducted!" Her voice had risen and hysteria threatened to overwhelm her, but

Baxter pulled her aside from the crowd gathered around Lady van Hoffen.

He shook her and stooped, gazing directly into her eyes. "What are you talking about, Em? What's going on?"

Mesmerized by his ebony gaze, she explained, falling over her words in her attempt to be quick and brief. She wanted to fly from the place and find May! It was all her fault; if she had taken her seriously earlier . . . .

Delafont's mind raced. The girl was in trouble; that was definite. If Lady van Hoffen felt secure enough to announce a runaway, then the trap had been sprung and the poor girl was caught. He glanced down at Emily. Her rosy cheeks had paled to white and her lips were tight with fear. She stared up at him, tears trembling in the corners of her huge, brown eyes. "Baxter, what shall we do?"

"Do not fear, my love, we will find her."

"But we must do something now! Maisie van Hoffen is ruining the girl's reputation with this story of her running away. If we speak up . . ."

"No! That will not serve. You know what people will say—even though the fault is not hers—if she has been abducted they will say that she is soiled goods now. Let us go carefully. We may be able to use our inside knowledge of this offense to force Lady van Hoffen to aid us. First we must try to find Lady May, and we must go immediately. I have my carriage here for once, so we will find out what we can and retrieve the poor girl."

Emily was so very grateful for Baxter's strength and determination over the next hour. Less had found a man who had seen a young woman who fit Lady Grishelda May van Hoffen's description strolling down the hall toward the conservatory. That same man claimed to have seen Etienne Marchant follow her a few minutes later. Baxter's face became darker and grimmer, and his eyes glittered obsidian in the dim light of the carriage house as a young stablehand confirmed that two men had had a carriage parked behind the conservatory. They left in a hurry, and then the Vicomte Etienne Marchant, whom the stablehand knew because he was an occasional visitor to the Duc de LaCoursiere's household, ordered his horse, a coal-black stallion, hurriedly and flew from the stable as if on wings.

"What does it mean?" Emily asked, as Baxter helped her into his carriage.

"I'm not sure," her husband said. "But I very much fear that he is mixed up in this somehow."

They left the city, the full of the moon lighting the way. Emily sat in silence, tears coursing down her cheeks. May had come to her for help, and she had not taken her seriously enough until it was too late. Dempster had her and intended to take her innocence in a hideous, violent way. How could she have failed her friend so?

She was ashamed, too, that she had fallen apart in the moment when action was needed. Thank God for Baxter's stolid presence and vigorous response to disaster. No wonder the country had been able to rely on him in its hour of need, just as she did. She was proud of her husband and humbled that he would still respond to her plea for help, though to be fair, Baxter was a gentleman, and no gentleman worthy of the appellation would have failed poor May at such a time. They had left Less to do what he did best, smooth over the social implications by making light of it and suggesting that it was likely nothing more than an error or lark.

He swore he would find a way to shut Lady van Hoffen's mouth, too, once he learned the truth of the affair.

They stopped at every inn on the most likely road out of town. Saunders had a hunting box near Chelmsford, and Baxter thought that would be the most likely place where they would take May, so they took Whitechapel Road out of London. It was slow going because they weren't sure they were on the right trail. Finally, after a couple of hours of riding and stopping at numerous inns, a stablehand at one of them confirmed that he had seen the carriage, which had only stopped for a few minutes, and after it a "Frenchie in fancy dress" as one man put it, on a large black stallion. That must be Etienne, Baxter and Emily agreed, and so they drove on.

Emily was puzzled. She could not believe that Etienne was mixed up in the abduction plot, but what other explanation was there for his having followed her into the conservatory, where she had been lured with a note, which questioning of the LaCoursiere staff had revealed?

"Oh, Baxter, I am so afraid for her," Emily said, as the carriage rumbled on its way again. In the dark, she felt herself pulled against her husband's side, his strong arm holding her firmly to him.

"We'll find her, Em, and we'll take care of things. Don't borrow trouble. The important thing is to find her before she is forced into marriage."

"But what if . . . what if that dreadful captain has—"

"Em, we will find her! With God's grace it will be in time. If not, then we will help her deal with the consequences, no matter what. I swear to you that we will handle this together and help the girl get past this dreadful night."

Etienne cursed the time it had taken him to go to the stable, make the sleepy stablehand know which horse was his and that he needed it *vite*. At least all of the Duc's staff was French, so his flurry of French phrases was comprehended and acted upon more rapidly than if he had spoken English, but still he had lost time. He could not gallop the whole way or it would be the death of Théron, his stallion, and he felt compelled to at least water his horse at the inn where he had learned that he was on the right road and that the carriage was still about fifteen minutes ahead of him. That meant that he had made up some time on his steed, and he hoped to overtake them still.

But he was experiencing some misgivings. He had in-

structed the stablehand to tell Lady Emily Delafont what
had happened, but the fellow was so slow and he had no
time to explain more correctly that he meant to catch up
to the bastards who had taken the English miss. Would
anyone know what had happened?

Ah, but he would enjoy catching the villains and shov-
ing their filthy teeth into the back of their throats! What
did they intend for that poor girl, one who was so shy
she could not meet his eyes when they had been introduced? *Dieu,* but he wished he was not wearing this foolish costume. But at the very least he had a saber, that
must be accounted a good thing when one was about to
face dirty English knaves. He would give them a taste of
his steel, and then the flavor of his boot. Indeed he would
and he would enjoy it.

Emily stood in the road shaking and crying. Baxter
held her tightly in his arms.

"Thank God you are not more than shaken up, my
love," he said, unconsciously falling into the form of address he had used through their marriage. It had been
a frightening few minutes when the carriage had been
run off the road by a passing mail coach. It now sat mired
in muck in the drainage ditch beside the road, up to the
axle in mud from the recent rains. He had lifted Emily
out and carried her up to the road, where she stood quivering from the ordeal.

He had cursed his groom soundly, but now there was
nothing to do but take one of the carriage horses and
ride to the nearest inn, which he thought was a couple
of miles up the road. As he mounted, he explained that
he would come back for Emily with the inn carriage.

"No!" she said, folding her arms under her bosom. "I
will not be left alone on this dreary road, Baxter, to await
your return!

She made an arresting sight on a dark road, the faint
moonlight touching her dark hair with gold, her simple

peasant dress enhancing her rounded, voluptuous figure.
He licked his dry lips. He had, of course, shrugged off
his domino long ago and was dressed as he always was,
and with her dressed in her peasant-girl garb, it reminded
him once again of his first meeting with the girl he had
assumed was a village wench.

"Then you will have to ride with me," he said, his eyes
glittering dangerously in the moonlight. "I will not leave
my driver without at least one horse, in case he runs into
trouble. Jarvis, help Lady Delafont up, will you?"

Settled sideways in front of him, her arms around his
waist, he started the short ride into the village just up the
road. Her hair, lightly perfumed with her lilac scent, tick-
led his nose, and the warmth of her soft bottom pressed
against his groin was delectably erotic. How could he be
thinking about sex when a girl's virtue, if not her life,
was at stake? But he was doing all he could for Lady
Grishelda. And he would be doing the same whether he
was thinking abut his wife's charms or not.

The ride was short, but with her bumping against him
as he concentrated on keeping his seat riding bareback
and her full breasts rubbing against his arm as he held
on to the reins, he found himself thoroughly aroused by
the time they arrived at the inn. Emily was drowsy, and
he kissed her ear before waking her to dismount. Maybe
now that she knew Etienne for the rotter that he was . . .
but no. He still would not take his wife back if she preferred another man; his pride would not let him.

The inn was a tiny one, not one that he would have
stopped at if he had had a choice. He tried to hire a
carriage, but there was not one available. He sent a stablehand back to help Jarvis, but even if they were successful
in getting the carriage out of the ditch and on the road
and there was miraculously no damage, it appeared that
they would not be able to go anywhere until the next
morning. They could not ride a carriage horse bareback
through the countryside.

"May we have two rooms, then," he said wearily. He

felt like a failure, but there really seemed no option.
Morning's light would see his carriage repaired, for there
was bound to be some damage from the precipitous lurch
into the ditch, and they could resume their search for
the unfortunate Lady Grishelda. With any luck her captors would not be in a rush. They would not think themselves followed because of Lady van Hoffen's story of her
daughter as a runaway bride.

"Sorry, milord, but there's only the one room left in
the ole inn." The innkeeper's wife, roused from her bed,
curtsied as she said this.

"We'll take it," he said.

Emily glanced up at him, tears forming in her eyes.
"May . . ."

"There is nothing we can do, my love. We must wait
until morning light and hope that her captors will do the
same." He pulled her to him and held her as she wept
against his chest. He saw the innkeeper's wife look over
Emily's attire with a skeptical eye. He would not explain.
If they wanted to think he was tumbling some village peasant girl, he would not argue. No one would think the
worse of him for doing what the nobility had done for
centuries.

"Wake us the moment my carriage is repaired! It is
vital that we be on the road again the second it is possible," Del said, then guided his wife as they followed a
chambermaid up the narrow, dark steps to their room.

The room was small and simple, with a bed about half
the size their bed at Brockwith had been. Emily gazed at
it with wide eyes, and then at Baxter.

"You may have the bed, my love, and I will take the
floor," he said, gallantly indicating the narrow bed.

The first hint of a mischievous smile glinted in her
eyes, through the moisture still there from her tears.

"Nonsense, Baxter. You, husband, are forty-two, not
twenty-two, and should not sleep on the cold, hard floor.
We will share the bed as we did for many years."

He gazed down at her sardonically. "Thank you for

reminding me of my advanced and decrepit age, my love. I am not a dainty fellow, though, and you are no sylphlike being. If we share that bed we will both be very aware that we are man and woman."

She smiled shyly. Her voice was saucy when she spoke. "Thank you for reminding me, my love, of my plumpness, but as for that, I have always rather liked being reminded that you are a man. Not that I need to be reminded when just the sight of you . . . ." She broke off, rather breathless. "I am sure we can muddle through the night." She sobered and sighed. "Oh, Baxter, I need you beside me tonight, because I am sure I will not sleep for thinking of poor May."

Gently, he folded her in his arms. "We will do the best we can, love. We will be off after her the minute it is possible, but we cannot ride a carriage horse down a dark road when we do not know the way. If anything has happened to your young friend, I will kill the bastard who has done it. I promise you that, though I know it to be poor consolation."

The bed was very narrow, but Emily realized that there was room enough that he did not *have* to hold her. He did that for her comfort. At first all she could think about was Grishelda, or rather May, as she preferred. But then the strong arms around her intruded on her consciousness, and she sighed, turning onto her side and wriggling until she was as close to him as she could get and his lean body was cupped around hers. His breath was warm in her ear, his lips so close she could move just an inch and they would be touching her.

An ache deep in her breast throbbed, but now it was not purely for her young friend, who was suffering such fear this very night. The pain was for the unrequited love she bore her husband. She wanted him back—*needed* him—but what did he feel for her? She ached with indecision. He had called her "love" as they raced to follow

May, but was that just habit? Or did he have a huge, painful void in his heart as she did in hers? She sighed, tremblingly close to tears that she had thought were cried out years before.

Del held his breath, concentrating fiercely on not breathing too hard as she wriggled closer to him, her bottom pressed to his groin, her breasts brushing his arms. It was going to be a long night. He ached to turn her onto her back and kiss her, pull her to him and awaken her body to the softness of womanly arousal as his was being awoken to the hardness of his own desire. It was all he could do not to move his hands slightly, enough to caress her bare skin. If he unleashed his pent-up passion, would she compare him to her youthful French lover?

The thought stung and dashed cold water on his lust. He did not fear the comparison, because he was confident in his own abilities, and he had not been mistaken in her arousal the night he had made love to her. But it came to him that that was just sex, and they had always had that between them. What of love? Did she care for Etienne Marchant, the villain? It did not bear thinking about. He settled himself to try to get some sleep.

Emily awoke with a start, her heart pounding with fear; she almost cried out. Where was she? What . . .

The awareness of Baxter's arm around her calmed her, and memory returned. May—oh, poor May! Where was she? What was happening to her? A silver blaze of moonlight touched her face, bathing the plain room in a surreal gilding. She shifted, a little uncomfortable. Something hard was pressed into her bottom. Something . . . Baxter! He was . . . oh, my! she thought.

A flush of desire spread through Emily. Making love with her husband the week before had awakened her long-suppressed carnal appetite, and with his arousal pressed so firmly to her bottom, her hunger pulsed in waves of heat through her. So close! He was so close and she wanted him so badly. Her unfulfilled hunger for him coursed through her, emptying her brain of any other thoughts. Carefully she rolled over until she was facing him. He had worn just his shirt to bed, open at the neck, and she stared at him in the stream of moonlight thinking that never had his face been so dear to her as it was this moment.

She reached out and touched his cheek and brushed back the silver wing of hair. She traced the deep groove from his nose to the corner of his mouth, then traced his chin and down his throat to his chest. He moved and murmured as she undid the rest of the buttons of his shirt and slid her hand down between them, to his flat, taut stomach muscles. She swallowed hard and stroked him, feeling the warm flood of throbbing desire stab through her, over and over again. Her eyes closed, she gloried in the feel of him, muscle and sinew, her handsome, masculine husband.

She opened her eyes and was impaled by his coal-black glare glinting in the moonlight, his mouth set in cruel, angry lines.

"I suppose you want another sample to compare by," he growled.

He lowered his mouth to kiss her, hard and without mercy. She could feel his puzzling anger, the lashing force of his fury, but as he took her in his arms and let his hands stray down her body, touching her skin, pushing her shift up and caressing her naked flesh, she felt his gentleness. Angry he might be, but his touch was not.

The world had shrunk to their bed, to that stream of moonlight and to his hands touching and stroking until she thought she would go mad with desire. She felt his bewildering anger but surrendered to the delirious joy of being caressed by the man she loved more than life itself. She whispered his name over and over, the word becoming a part of her ecstasy, a part of the waves of pleasure he could always bring her.

She abandoned herself to the joy, the tremulous sweetness, as they clung to each other in the small bed, bringing each other love and rapture.

Del thought himself delirious. She wanted him. She desired him. She welcomed him with loving passion, her sweet surrender filling his body with ecstasy and his mind and heart with confusion. He slowed his ardent lovemaking, pulling back from the point of no return. He would not take his wife like this, fast and hard as if her needs did not matter, nor would he abuse her with his pain and anger. He opened his eyes and gazed down at her, the dark spill of hair across the white pillow, the pale, perfect skin glowing in the moonlight.

Her eyes were closed, but her expression was one of profound tenderness. He freed one hand from under her bottom and undid the silk ties of her shift, pulling the fabric away and exposing her loveliness to the light. Swallowing hard as the sight of her flushed with his lovemaking, her rosy, soft lips slightly open as she whispered his name, threatened to send him over the edge, he began to really make love to her.

Irrationally he felt that she was his, when he knew that she had been with at least one other man. But he reclaimed her, body and soul, and when she surrendered herself fully to him, to his urgent need, he felt a knot loosen and a wave of love more powerful than he had ever felt in his life, more urgent than mere sexual desire, overcome him.

"Emily," he whispered. "Oh, my God, Emily!" The moon had moved on its nightly arc, and her face was now in darkness.

"Baxter." His name was a sigh on her lips, a soft whisper of satisfaction.

They lay together for a while afterwards, just holding each other. She made no move to push him away or off of her.

"Am I too heavy, my love?"

"Baxter, when did I ever want you to leave me after making love? We fell asleep like this many times."

He moved slightly and covered her mouth with his own, kissing her, parting her lips with his thrusting tongue. Her arms encircled him again, and she moved her bottom so that he was cradled between her legs. Incredibly, he felt his body respond to her again.

She moved her hands down, over his bottom and kneaded the muscles of his buttocks.

"You little minx," he groaned, feeling a surge of passion sweep through him. "Again?"

She giggled and pulled him closer. "Yes, again. And again, and again, and again. I want you."

Emily stretched and yawned as dawn's light filtered through the homely white curtains. For such an uncomfortable bed, she had had the most delicious night, as short as it had been! She turned over and stared at Baxter, willing him to awaken. He opened one dark eye and glared at her.

She laughed and touched his mouth, then leaned over and kissed him, taking the initiative this time.

Tease," he grunted. "Don't start anything unless you mean to finish."

"I am quite willing to finish, my lord."

"Saucy wench!" He pulled her to him.

"My lord," she said in mock astonishment. "Whatever is a poor maiden to do with a man like you?"

"I'll show you," he said, rolling onto his back, falling in immediately with her game. He pulled her on top of him and held her so close she could feel the muscles of his stomach and thighs tighten.

She shivered at the feel of his body and consciously relaxed. "Baxter, I want . . ."

"Hush, no words now. Only love," he said, moving sensuously.

Every thought fled from her mind, and she joined him in languorous lovemaking as the bed creaked and groaned beneath them. Every inch of her body was inflamed and sensitive, his wild, intense lovemaking and virile power intoxicating her as it always did.

"Say you want me," he grunted, kissing her throat and her throbbing pulse at the base of her neck.

"I want you!"

"Louder!"

"I want you!" Her cry echoed against the thin walls.

"Better, but still not loud enough. Say it very loud indeed, my love, if you want me." His vigorous ardor was almost more than she could take. It had been so long since she had made love, and every inch of her body was aware that her husband was a very demanding lover. But she wanted him. A wave of longing swept over her and she no longer could—nor did she want to—restrain herself. "I want you! Oh, Baxter, I love you. I *love* you," she cried out, eyes closed.

He stilled.

What had she done?

"Say that again."

She opened her eyes and gazed down at him in the dim light of very early morning.

"I love you," she said, softly, ardently. "I have always loved you and I always *will* love you."

"That's what I thought you said," he muttered, softly, running his hands down her back, touching her until she shivered.

He stared up into her eyes as he spoke, and she felt pierced by his searing gaze. His eyes questioned her, asking something of her that she didn't understand.

Guiltily, she was aware that they were wasting time; she should have been up at first light and finding out what they could about where May was taken. But surely a few more minutes, and the landlord had said he would tell them the moment the carriage was there and repaired . . . . She lowered her face, tracing the sensuous line of his lips with her tongue as he moved beneath her.

At that moment someone pounded on the door.

"Yes!" Baxter cried out, groaning at the interruption of what was proving to be a very interesting morning.

His carriage driver, on the other side of the closed door, babbled that the carriage was just then fixed. A wheel had been cracked in the accident, but after the wheelwright had worked through the night, it had been replaced and they could leave any time now.

"Okay, Jarvis, we'll be down in a minute," he said, pulling Emily to him. "Just one more minute."

Of course it was more than just one minute, but not very much more than that, before she collapsed on him, feeling the sweat from his chest drench her shift. She felt giddy with love, dizzy with ecstasy. But as their breathing and heart rates returned to normal, Emily sobered. With a last, lingering kiss to savor the sweetness of their love after an unforgettable night, she raised herself on one elbow and gazed down into her husband's piercing black eyes. "And now, husband, it is time to find poor May."

Eighteen

Dempster, no more a captain than he was really named Dempster, was sorely disappointed. His stupid cohort, a man with the appropriate name of Lug, had botched the whole thing. He was only to have used a drop of the knockout stuff on the kerchief they held to Lady Grishelda's nose, but instead his mistress's daughter had slept all of the journey away and was still sawing logs, now when it was almost morning!

He was to have had his bit of fun by now. It hadn't been his idea to break in that prudish little miss Grishelda, but Saunders didn't want to have to deal with a squeamish virgin, and he couldn't blame the old codger. All he wanted was a wife young enough to guarantee him an heir. Didn't even seem to mind if the kid wasn't his own, s'long as it was born once the vows were spoke.

He would take great pleasure in mastering Lady Grishelda after the disdainful way she had always treated him, like he wasn't good enough to lick her boots. It was what women secretly wanted, after all. Look at the bitchy little wench's mother. Maisie had tried her tricks on him, ordering him around and such, but he had soon showed her who was boss, and she had enjoyed the struggle. Now she did what he wanted, and gladly, too. Sometimes she was still naughty, but she took her punishment like a good girl, and greedily begged for more.

Grishelda—he refused to call her Lady May, like he knew she wanted—would be the same. When he was done she would understand women's rightful place in the world—underneath a man.

But it wouldn't be any fun if she was still sleeping. He wanted her awake and aware of what was about to happen to her. He wanted her to squirm underneath him and fight him every step of the way. He wanted to see the cold light of fear in her eyes. It had been a long while since he had had a virgin, or anything close to it, and he planned on enjoying this one.

The mother was much too easy now, and he lusted after new challenges. Maisie was a greedy bitch and enjoyed his imaginative punishments too much to make it any fun any more. Grishelda would be easy to frighten.

May had *not* been asleep the whole time, but she would feign it as long as she could. It had taken a supreme effort of will when Dempster came in and roughly turned her over, to still pretend she was unconscious. At first she had just wanted to buy enough time for the headache and lingering lassitude of the drug to wear off. Now she planned to wait until her captors, or at least one of them, had left the house so she could make her getaway.

She had no idea where she was. She had not dared to get up and look out the window; Dempster and his cohort were downstairs and would likely hear the floorboards squeak or something. It was still dark, though, with just a sputtering tallow candle lighting up the tiny room where she was captive, and it seemed to her that she had a better chance of evading recapture if she could get outside in the dark.

She heard a door slam downstairs, and outside someone started whistling, the sound getting fainter and fainter. One of them must have left. It was now or never.

She slipped from the bed, glad of the unfettered movement her simple white costume afforded her. She started to cross the room, but to her horror the door opened at that minute and Dempster, in his stocking feet, entered.

"Oho! Awake, I see."

He was a coarsely handsome man, strong and rugged, but with bad teeth and a foul odor about him. May always wondered how her mother could stand to be intimate with such a coarse, smelly man. A throb of fear pulsed through her at the lascivious look of anticipation she saw on his broad face, an expression that looked even more evil for the faint, flickering candlelight.

"I . . . I'm thirsty," she stuttered, her voice hoarse from a mixture of fear and the effects of the drug.

He moved relentlessly toward her. "Are you? Perhaps if you go along with what I want, I'll let you have a swallow of wine."

May backed away and eyed the doorway. But Dempster kept himself between her and the closed door. She would only have one chance to get away from him, and it had better be a good one.

"What do you want of me?" She would stall. If she could only find some weapon in the barren room. She cast her eyes around wildly, but there was nothing.

Dempster was relentless and moved still, even as he spoke. "I want to give you a little bit of fun before you settle down in the traces. Saunders intends to keep you busy at least until you give him an heir, but he's a wizened-up old sausage, ain't he? You might as well enjoy your first time—and maybe your second and third time if I've a mind—with a younger man what can pleasure you. Are you like your mother?"

He rubbed his hands together, his expression in the dim light one of greedy anticipation. "Will you squeal and need to be spanked when you're naughty? She likes that, you know. Gets 'er all hot when I lift 'er skirts and have at 'er. I'm surprised you haven't heard us goin' at it just down the hall from you at night. She likes 'er bottom smacked good and hard. Then she likes something else good and hard."

He took off his jacket and tossed it on the floor, then began to undo his shirt. May shivered all over in fear and yelped when she felt the bed behind her legs and could back up no further. Dempster, his thick-lipped mouth half open, undid the fall of his breeches and grabbed her arm. " 'Ere, girly, feel what you're gonna enjoy soon."

He took her wrist in his wrenching grip, forced her hand down his pants and laid it against him. Terror overwhelmed her when she felt him, large and hard against her hand. Instinctively she grabbed, squeezed and yanked with all her might, digging her nails in and pulling as hard as she could. Then she raised her knee quickly, stumbling a little but managing to get him somewhere between the legs. He cried out and crumbled to his knees.

May darted around him and raced to the door, flung it open and dashed down the steps. She glanced wildly around herself in the dimness of the small room. Which of the three doors was the way out?

Just at that moment her question was answered in a most unexpected way.

A door burst open and a man, holding a huge, thick sword leaped through it. "Die, villain!" he shouted.

May screamed. It was Etienne Marchant! He was in on this, too? She moved to run around him but he put out one hand and grabbed her wrist.

"Let go of me or I'll—I'll . . ."

"But I am 'ere to rescue you, mademoiselle!" He smiled broadly and bowed with a flourish.

"Then get on with it!" she cried, relief flooding her.

"Ah, but it appears I am too late. It looks, I think, that you have rescued yourself, mademoiselle," he said, glancing around questioningly.

"He's upstairs," May answered his unasked question curtly. He seemed to be almost enjoying himself, as if this were all some huge joke.

"Then the least I can do is offer you my mount to return to town."

A scraping sound from upstairs startled May. She

gasped and looked up. Dempster! He was coming after her.

"Where is his partner?" she asked the young Frenchman, panicked.

"He is, shall we say, in the arms of Morpheus?" Etienne grinned.

"Then let's get out of here," May said. She rushed past him and out the door he had burst through. "Where are we?" she said, glancing around at the dark wooded area that surrounded them on three sides. In the awakening light of dawn, she could see the figure of a man lying in the grass a few yards away. "Is he . . . ?"

"Caught with his pants down, one might say." Etienne laughed. "No, my lady, he is not dead, but he will wake up with a very sore head. I did want to even the odds just a little before I entered for my rescue. I had been waiting a while, wondering if they were armed, but finally I felt I could wait no longer, and when I saw the fellow come out to respond to nature's call, I entered. I had not counted on the intrepid nature of English women. I had thought that, like a proper French miss, you would need rescue."

"I still need to get out of here," she said through gritted teeth, pointedly looking around for his mount.

Etienne grinned once more, his white teeth flashing. He whistled through his teeth and a coal-black stallion erupted from the misty shadows at a trot, came up behind him and nuzzled his shoulder. "Your mount, my lady."

"But how will *you* get back to town?" May asked, eyeing the stallion with some trepidation. Cassiopeia, her own little mare at home, was a much different horse from this big male.

"I will be riding with you, of course."

"With . . . ? I don't think so, monsieur . . ."

"No? Then I will go to the nearest town, secure a carriage and come back for you in a few hours. Of a certainty you will not ride Théron alone."

"But . . ."

The door of the cottage opened just then, and Dempster stumbled out with pistol in his hand. He was bent over and raised his arm shakily. "You bitch! I'll show ya what women are made for!"

Etienne leaped up on his mount and leaned over, offering his arm to May. She paused only a moment, then took it and felt herself swept up in front of Etienne. Expertly he wheeled Théron around and they galloped off, the sound of a pistol shot causing the horse to snort and put on a burst of speed.

"This is becoming very uncomfortable," May complained. Morning had come, and birds chirped and sang in the hedgerow. The thick morning mist had burned off to the promise of a glorious spring day.

"Mille pardons, mademoiselle. In the haste of the night while you were being forcibly abducted I did not think to go to my host's home, rouse my groom and 'ave him hitch my carriage, so to provide you with more comfortable passage."

May flushed and wriggled, then gazed up into his face. He was extremely handsome, she thought, trying to be dispassionate. His eyes were the brown of caramel, with flecks of amber and mahogany. "I am sorry," she said. "I'm very grateful that you happened to see what was happening and came after me."

He smiled down at her, and she had the feeling he was being indulgent, as one might be toward a fractious but adorable child. She felt a spark of anger. He couldn't be much older than herself, who was he to assume airs?

"Why did you do it? Why didn't you just go get help?"

"There was not the time. It would have taken too long to go back, explain and get help," he said. "Besides . . ."

He paused.

"Besides what?" Conversation was better than silence, she thought. When they were silent she was all too aware of how close she was to him and how good he smelled

and looked and how hard and lean his body was where
they inevitably touched. He roused feelings she thought
she had stifled long ago, and it worried her.

He shrugged. "I am hoping I have done a certain lady
a good turn and that she will look more favorably on my
suit."

May swallowed a lump of disappointment. So he had
an ulterior motive, so what? It didn't change that what
he had done and was prepared to do was very brave. "You
mean Emily, don't you? You . . . you want her."

He frowned. "I had not thought you to be so perspi-
cacious, little miss. I would not have said anything if I
thought you could guess the lady in question."

"I have heard the gossip. And I have seen with my own
eyes how you dance attendance on her." She held herself
up straighter, trying to keep from touching his body, but
it was impossible. There was barely enough room in front
of him on his saddle, and he held her firmly to him. "So
that means you have not been successful so far." She
could not keep the hint of satisfaction out of her voice.

"No," he said grimly. "She vacillates. She is undecided.
She is driving me out of my *mind!*"

"Do you . . . are you very much in love with her,
then?"

He chuckled. "How little you know of men, little miss.
And how very English you are."

"What do you mean?"

"I mean that romance 'as little to do with love. You
English, you pretend to be so pragmatic, so unemotional.
You claim that the French are irrational, explosive, emotional. It is true that we excel at romance, and that is
what I want from my *chére* Emily, but love? No. I do not
believe in love."

"Well, I think she is in love with her husband," May
said, wanting for some unfathomable reason to hurt him,
to erase the smugness from his voice.

"Did she say that?" he asked, sharply, glancing down
at her.

"No, not exactly, but she talked to me about . . . about *making* love, and she was talking about her and her husband. It was . . . I'm not quite sure I understood what she said, but she sounded . . . well, wistful." May leaned wearily against Etienne's chest.

They cantered in silence along the country road. It had been a horrible ordeal and she was so very tired.

Etienne, lost in thought, rode on. He had much to ponder, if what the little one had said was true. When next he looked down, it was to find that the English miss had fallen asleep. As uncomfortable as she must be and wrapped in his Arab prince cape, she slept against his chest. An unexpected wave of tenderness passed through him. How unusual she was, but a good girl, and he was glad she had not suffered at the hands of that monstrous villain. She had told him the whole story when they first started out to head back to London, and he was horrified at her unnatural mother. He would deliver the little miss to Emily. Emily would protect her, he felt certain.

What he would do after that, he was not certain. Things had changed, and so his plans must change too. It was a stupid man who did not know when to bow out gracefully. Perhaps it was all for the best, for his other plans had gone awry, and he was beginning to believe it was as God intended. He had never been committed to a certain course of action anyway, had backed out on the point of success, even, and must now find a way to put an end to it. It would not be easy, for he was involved in a scheme *diabolique*, a scheme that he should have known to stay away from. He must leave London immediately, after depositing the little miss on Emily's doorstep.

Wearily Emily climbed the steps to Delafont House, with Baxter behind her. "Where can she be?" A sob choked her voice. It was late afternoon, and they had been traveling since before dawn.

"I don't know. I was sure she would be at Saunders's

hunting box, but she wasn't. We were so far behind them, and there are hundreds of tiny backroads and lanes. We couldn't explore them all." Baxter, too, sounded exhausted, but more than that, he was deeply mortified that he had not been able to help the girl after all. What had become of her? How would they find her?

Trumble flung open the door. "Oh, my lady, I am so glad to see you! Mr. Lessington is here and has been worried . . ."

"Your mistress is very tired, Trumble," Baxter said, guiding Emily past the unusually garrulous butler. "I want her maid called and she should be put to bed immediately with a hot tisane and—"

"It's all right, my love," Emily murmured. "I would really love a good cup of tea, though, Trumble."

She headed for the drawing room, the first room off the main hall. Baxter was close behind her as they entered.

Two people glanced around at them from a sofa by the window.

Emily cried out, "May!" She rushed to her friend, who was wearing one of Dodo's day dresses.

"Less," Baxter said to the man on the sofa with her. "How did this come about?"

"In a most miraculous way. You must hear her story and judge for yourself if this is not the most amazing turn of events you have ever heard of."

The foursome settled in. Dodo joined them when the tea tray arrived. She had been the one to welcome first May, late in the morning, and then a worried witless Less, just a half hour ago, into Delafont House and insist that they stay until Emily got home.

May assured Emily that nothing had happened to her, other than a bad headache from the knockout drug and being frightened out of her wits and being a little sore from riding awkwardly sideways on a saddle for hours. Reassured on that point, Emily finally relaxed enough to allow her to tell her story.

At the end of it, and after several cups of tea for the ladies, sherry for Less and brandy for Baxter, she looked around at the four gathered near her. Emily and Baxter exchanged glances.

"And so Etienne Marchant was your savior? Pardon me, but I find it very odd that he seems to be there whenever someone is in trouble," Baxter Delafont drawled, his dark, sardonic eyes on May.

"Nevertheless," she said, smoothing down the cream muslin of her skirts. "He took me away from there and I am grateful. I didn't know where I was, I had no money for food or a place on a mail carriage and I was in my costume. Captain Dempster was just stunned and was on his way out with a pistol. He actually fired it! He would have killed me if Etienne hadn't swept me up on his horse and ridden off."

"I don't know what to make of this; I really don't," Emily said. She glanced over at her husband. They had gone all the way to Saunders's hunting box just ten miles south of Chelmsford, and indeed he was there, but May was not. The elderly rake disavowed any knowledge of an abduction or worse, and appeared shocked by the idea. Neither Emily nor Baxter believed him, and Baxter, speaking to him privately, told him that if any rumor reached his ear ever again having to do with Lady Grishelda May van Hoffen or any other young lady, he would expose Saunders for the dirty lecher he was. Right before he killed him.

Baxter and Emily had returned to London exhausted and worried, not knowing what to do and only hoping Less had found out something about where she could have been taken. To find her safe and in Emily's home, watched over by Dodo and Less, had been overwhelming, but then to hear that Etienne, whom Emily had begun to think the villain of the piece, had rescued her, was past belief.

Less pardoned himself to attend to theater business, and shortly after he left they heard a commotion in the hall. Trumble raised his voice, something he was not wont to do. "My lady is not at home!"

Baxter left the ladies to find out what was going on. They heard his voice saying, "No, Trumble, we must deal with her sooner or later. It might as well be now."

He ushered in Lady van Hoffen.

"Ah, the Queen of Tarts," Dodo said acidly. She had no patience for women who pretended to gentility and acted like whores.

"What is going on?" Lady van Hoffen said, her common accent more pronounced in her anger. Her face was unbecomingly flushed and her dress a little less immaculate than usual. "Grishelda, what are you doing here?"

May stood. Emily caught her hand in her own and felt the young woman tremble.

"Not Grishelda, Mother—May. My name is May! There is no need for pretense. Lord and Lady Delafont know all about your plot to have me abducted, raped and forcibly married to that doddering old fool. Thanks to them, and . . . and others, I am safe."

Maisie van Hoffen had paled at May's bold speech, especially at the word *rape*.

"Whatever do you mean, May? I have been worried sick about you all night, running away like a naughty girl . . . ."

"Don't touch me," she said, evading her mother's outstretched hands. "I overheard your plans to sell me off to Lord Saunders. And I overheard that old villain ask your Captain Dempster to break me in! Break me in, as if I am some kind of wild animal to be tamed." She shuddered.

"That's not what . . . he wasn't going to . . . ." Lady van Hoffen's legs gave out and she plopped herself down uninvited on a convenient chair. "He was going to do that to you? Take you to bed?" There was trembling hurt in her voice.

May's expression hardened into something worse than distaste. "That's what really bothers you, isn't it? Not that he was going to rape me, but that he would have had me despite being your . . . whatever that disgusting animal is to you."

Dodo had discreetly left the room, and Emily and Baxter had drifted away and stood together, their arms around each other, at a convenient distance. This was May's fight, unless she needed or asked for their help.

May felt stronger than she had ever been in her life. Etienne had been right. She had fought off Dempster herself; she had saved herself from him. She glared at her mother, and there was pain in her heart that the woman who had borne her could have done such a thing, but there was a growing peace, too. Nothing after this could shock her. Her mother would never change, but she didn't have to be her victim anymore.

"I could have you arrested for conspiring to have me kidnapped. You would be transported, at the very least, sent to live in the wild with criminals."

Lady van Hoffen stirred. She looked older and very tired, the red of her hair glaringly fake in the bright spring light that filled the room. "But, my darling daughter, it was only because you will marry no one! A woman needs to be married, *should* be married! I . . . I thought it was for the best. I really did."

"I don't believe that, and you know my feelings on the subject. But you are still my mother." May tried hard to keep her voice stern, but it softened just a little. "I am steadfast in my determination. I do not want to marry ever! I am going to return home to Lark House, and I never want to come back to this stinking hole again in my life. So I will give you the London house to live in and a small allowance on two conditions."

Maisie stared down at her hands and said nothing.

"You will never come home to Lark House, and you will never, *ever* see Captain Dempster again. I don't know where he is or if he will dare show his face in London again, but you are not to see him."

"But . . . ."

"Never!"

Maisie glanced up at her daughter's implacable expression. "I . . . May, I did not know he intended to . . . to do that to you. I was in love with him or . . . or in thrall to him. I . . ." She buried her face in her hands and sobbed.

"It is over, Mother. He is evil, and this is for your own good as much as it is for me. I cannot stand to think of him with you! It makes me sick, the things he said about you, the way he talked . . . . " She was perilously close to tears, but she sniffed them back and straightened her backbone. Never again would she face that kind of fear. She would have the life she had always wanted, free from her mother's interference, free of demands and free forever from men. She would go home—home to Lark House and peace.

Nineteen

The last few weeks had been the most confusing period of his life, Del thought. Sir Douglas Prong had ferreted out the information that the one man Del had thought was still alive and who was the one trying to kill him was dead, ostensibly killed in an accident two months before. As the ancient knight had said, all the spies Del turned in were either dead or incarcerated. He also confirmed that there was no Etienne Marchant. The current Vicomte Marchant was an artist living in Italy. No one had seen the faux vicomte since he had deposited Lady May van Hoffen on Emily's doorstep the morning after her ordeal.

Del had traveled the countryside, to the house in the woods that Lady May had described, to find that Dempster and his cohort had deserted the residence. It had taken him days to confirm that the "captain" had left the country and was now, presumably, on the Continent. From there he had traveled to Brockwith, and then returned to London.

Del finished up some paperwork at his desk in the library of his London home and thought about what he was going to do with his tangled personal life, other than avoid it, which is what he had been doing. What was wrong with him? Why could he not come to terms with his pain and confront his dilemmas?

Making love with Emily three times in one night had been . . . there was no other way to say it. It had been like coming home, a joyful blend of sensual fulfillment and blissful love. She had told him she loved him. She had shown him she wanted him over and over, but fool that he was he could *not* get over her having been with someone else. Could she truly love him and yet have slept with Etienne Whoever-he-was? It was a question that haunted him day and night.

Was he an idiot? He should be banging down her door, demanding to see her, but instead he had filled his days with business. After gallivanting around the countryside looking for Dempster he had stayed at Brockwith for more than a week to straighten out some problems his steward could just as easily have attended to when he returned from a trip to the north to buy some sheep. Del was deeply troubled and confused, and that did not sit well with him. He was a decisive man, one who took action to solve problems, but this time he feared the truth and was avoiding it at all costs. He couldn't do that forever.

Cromby came to the door of his library, his sanctum, and cleared his throat.

"What is it, man? I told you I didn't want to be disturbed."

A gloved hand pushed the butler aside and Lady Marie Delafont, the Dowager Marchioness, erupted into the room. "Since when will you not see your mother?"

Inwardly groaning he stood politely and said, "Mother, if you intend to visit, let us retire to the parlor, where Cromby can see that we have some tea." He nodded to the long-suffering butler.

In the parlor, seated in front of the tea tray, his mother fixed him with her gimlet stare. "So, Delafont, do you mean to breed with your wife or not? Don't think I will forget about this. Do you want the Sedgely estate and title going to some Frenchie if you die tomorrow?"

"Stop talking nonsense, Mother. William in Shropshire is my heir. He is perfectly capable of carrying on the estate in a respectable manner and already has a child on the way." Del settled back in his chair and closed his eyes. He had not slept in two days and he was too weary to deal with his mother at that moment.

There was silence.

It was unusual to be in the same room with his mother and for there to be silence.

He opened his eyes and stared across at her. She shifted uncomfortably and fiddled with the teapot. She stripped her gloves off and tossed them aside.

He sat up straight and glared across the tea tray at her. "What is going on, Mother?"

She eyed the plate of cakes with a stern eye and poked one. "Dry. I thought as much. You need a wife to keep a close eye on the cook. He and the staff are probably living high and feeding you dry biscuits and—"

"I have a wife, if you remember." His voice was ominously quiet and hard and his mother glanced at him.

There was a trace of a wistful smile on her grim face, but it was gone so quickly Del could not swear to having seen it.

"So like your father," she muttered.

"Mother, out with it. What is this about a French heir to the Sedgely title?"

"Your Aunt Ophelia—you know she is the keeper of the family history—tells me that your great-grandfather's brother moved to France, where the line originated back in the mists of time, you know, and married a French woman and bore two or three sons. They in turn had sons, who had sons, who had sons."

"Yes."

"You are the last direct male descendant on the English side; your cousin William is removed from the direct line."

"Yes, Mother, we know all of this. It is well documented."

"Well, now that the war is over, if you should die it is the French side who would inherit because they are several degrees closer than is dear William."

"But we are not in contact with the French . . . you know something!" He gazed sternly at his mother who had taken one of the stale tea cakes and crumbled it into crumbs on the tray. This nervous action was so unlike her that it gave him pause.

"The direct descendant has been traced, Baxter. We know who he is; now the lawyers are just trying to find him to confirm this and to do the paperwork. He is your legitimate heir, and his name is Etienne Roulant Delafont."

"Understandably, Del is livid. Positively in shock." Less sat with Dodo, May and Emily in Emily's cheerful morning parlor.

Dodo chuckled. "I would give up my next quarter's allowance to have seen his face when Marie told him the news."

"But is it known definitely that Etienne Marchant, or at least the Etienne we knew, was Etienne Delafont?" Emily could not take it in. It seemed absurd to think that the man who had been romancing her for so long had been her husband's legal heir.

"The dowager says so, and she is never wrong. And not only that, my dear," Less continued, leaning forward. "But it appears that he may have been trying to hurry his inheritance along a little. It is rumored that the young man was in the soup and owed a great deal of money. He may have promised things based on his expectations. It has been suggested that he was behind the attempts on Del's life."

"No! I will not believe that," May said, speaking up for the first time.

Emily frowned and glanced over at her. "May, we suspected he was up to something, we just didn't know what it was. This is logical, though I hate to think it of him as much as you do."

"Especially after the intimate nature of your relationship," the girl sniped.

Emily, her dark eyes wide, gravely stared into the younger woman's blue eyes until the girl flushed and looked away. Grishelda May van Hoffen was staying with her until she could finalize the paperwork for her mother's possession of the London house and organize the move back to Lark House. Inevitably she had suffered nightmares after her ordeal and had never recovered the equanimity of disposition she had always seemed to have. Perhaps this hinted at a reason. Had the girl fallen in love with, or at least become infatuated with, Etienne during their ride to London? She did not speak of that part of her ordeal. How to tell her the next truth if that was so? She exchanged a look with Dodo, who shrugged.

"My dear," Emily said, taking her hand. "You were not here when Less first arrived. I must tell you something rather bad, considering that you seem to have some affection for the young man we knew as Etienne Marchant."

May started. "What is it?"

Emily glanced worriedly over at Less, who picked up the story.

"My dear," he said, clearing his throat. "You must understand that since this ordeal, people have been looking for Etienne. If he could just have explained himself . . ."

"You speak as if . . . as if . . . ."

Dodo moved to the other side of the girl and took her other hand.

"I'm sorry," Less said, his voice gentle. "He was traced to the coast and to a boat that set sail to cross the channel. It never made it. It went down in a storm, and everyone on board is presumed drowned."

Emily watched worriedly as May took in the news. She was affected, it was clear, but she held together. Tears started in her light-blue eyes, but she blinked them back.

It was anguish, May thought, dispassionately, trying to identify the pain that stabbed through her at the knowledge that Etienne had died a lonely, cold death in the dark water off England. How could she feel such a sharp pain for a young man she barely knew? And one who, if reports were right, was attempting to murder Lord Delafont. She would not believe it of him. Perhaps that is what he intended originally, but he hadn't done it after all, and he had the opportunity. She would think of him always as he had last appeared to her. He had brought her to Delafont House and left her on the doorstep that morning after her abduction ordeal. She had been so sleepy, but before knocking at the Delafont House door, she had turned and watched him ride away.

At the last moment he had stopped in the middle of the quiet square, turned his magnificent horse and swept her an imaginary bow, and then he blew her a kiss. She would always remember him like that—young and handsome and vibrantly alive.

She had never thought to be here again, Emily reflected, glancing around at the dimly lit gold salon in Belle Gallant's town house. But Belle's summons had been urgent, and she had liked the girl, despite everything. If she was in trouble or needed her, she would be there.

She paced back and forth in the small room. Life had taken some strange turns of late, she thought. Engraved in her memory was the precious night she had spent with Baxter in that tiny inn on that uncomfortable, narrow bed, making love virtually all night. Once more she had thought of it as the dawn of a new era in their relationship, a step toward reanimating their marriage. She had had hope, especially since he had been so tender toward her as they parted the morning at Delafont House. He was the husband she remembered from the early days of their marriage, gallant and compassionate, her chivalrous knight.

True he had made no plan to see her again. When he

left, it was to see if he could track down any information on Dempster's whereabouts. He had sent a note later saying the man seemed to have disappeared, presumably for the Continent, but it was a note meant for May as well and she had expected no endearments in it. But surely he could have said something, done something . . . ?

And she still had no explanation for the strange anger with which he had loved her at first, that night in the inn, anger glinting in his obsidian eyes. What had he meant when he asked if she was looking for another sample to compare by? She had ignored that strange remark, considering the teasing tone they had fallen back into as they made love in the morning. One could not refine on every comment, every moment as if it held some secret meaning.

But then he had disappeared for almost three weeks! She was furious and hurt and . . . wounded. That was the only word for it. He was unaccountable. When he had made no attempt to visit her, she had broken down and gone to his house, only to be told by Cromby that the marquess was "unavailable." Unavailable! Even to his wife?

Cromby had looked uncomfortable, but had said that he had no instructions when the master was going to be home again.

She felt humiliated and used. How could he treat her that way, make love to her all night and then abandon her like that? She dreaded seeing Belle again. In some strange way it felt as though their roles were reversed, as if Belle were the wife and Baxter had gone back to her. Clearly he preferred her to Emily, and that hurt so deeply that the pain was a throb in her belly, a queer twisting feeling in her gut. And seeing Belle again would remind her of everything she was not, everything that made her husband prefer the girl to his wife. She was young and slim and . . .

The door to the salon opened and she steeled herself

to see her husband's young mistress again, only to be faced by her husband! Baxter, here!

"Emily?"

He was thunderstruck, she noted with satisfaction. She hardened her heart, trying not to notice that he looked weary, trying to ignore the lurch in her stomach, the nausea that threatened to overwhelm her. If only she could rip her love for him out of her heart and start over. She straightened.

He strode across the room and roughly took her arm. "What are you doing here? You must leave; this is not right! You . . . you . . ."

She had yanked her arm from his grasp and rubbed it where his strong fingers had bruised her. *"Don't* touch me! Don't ever touch me again!"

"You should not be here! I will escort you back to Delafont House." His voice was a commanding growl, and he moved to take her arm again.

She moved swiftly to evade him. Chin up, she swore that he would not see the pain he had caused her or how her heart leaped the instant he came near. "I will go where I want and see whomever I wish. We are married in name only, sir, *if* you remember!"

"I remember," he said, grimly. "You have made it plain, madam. It does not change the fact that this is not a fit place for a lady to be. Good God, Em, this is my mistress!"

"And well I know it! But I have been here before, so what is so different about now?"

"You have . . ." His dark eyes burned and he glared at her. "What game are you playing, Em? I will not be made a fool of by my mistress and my wife. Is that what that night at the inn was about? Comparing notes with my harlot?"

"You bastard!" Emily quickly crossed the short space between them and slapped him as hard as she could. She had the satisfaction of seeing a red imprint on his cheek, though he did not flinch or move or in any other way indicate that she had hurt him. He was like a wall of rock.

He smiled, but it was a frigid expression. "You can take some consolation, Emily. Not many wives could say this, but Belle is jealous of you, I think. My mistress is jealous of my wife." He laughed, a swift, brutal bark. "And never have I taken her three times in one night; I did not think I was capable of that kind of sexual feat any more. Are you going to tell her about that? Have you already?"

"You bastard," Emily said again, in a low, choked voice, close to tears, her throat closing convulsively. "Was that what that was about? Proving to me that you could still perform? Or were you just trying to give me a taste of what I have been missing?"

"Ah, but have you been missing it, my lady? *Have* you?"

She moved to slap him again, but he grabbed her wrist in his iron grip and yanked her toward him. Expressions flitted across his face, but she understood none of them. She would almost think he was gripped in some deep pain, some inner turmoil that equaled her own. And then his mouth closed over hers in a demanding kiss, and, despite her fury, she felt the familiar swell of love and desire well up, bubbling from a seemingly inexhaustible spring within her heart. Rage warred with passion, but ultimately she knew passion would win. Passion and love would always win where Baxter was concerned; she could not hate him as he deserved. She would have him that instant if she could, though the knowledge of her own weakness diminished her ire not one whit.

He released her and she stumbled back, putting one shaking hand to her mouth. He opened his mouth to speak, but the door swung open just then and Belle entered.

"Good, you're both here," she said. "Won't you sit down?"

She seemed oblivious to the tension in the room and took a chair, sinking into it with a tired sigh.

"You mean you summoned us both here at the same time?" Baxter said, his words choked with anger.

"Yes," she said, looking up at him crossly. "Sit down, Del, you tower so! What I have to say concerns you both."

"Pardon me, my dear," Baxter replied, lapsing back into his familiar sardonic coldness, all of the passion dissipating from his face. Once again his face had the carved appearance of a stern idol, deep-grooved slash for a mouth, furrowed lines from nose to mouth. "But there is nothing you would have to say that could possibly concern us both."

"I think you should let her be the judge of that," Emily said, gracefully assuming a spot on the lumpy sofa. She would match his coolness if she could.

Belle shot her a grateful glance, then looked back at her lover. "Sit!"

"I am not a lap dog," Baxter said in an ominous tone.

"Please, Del." She pouted. "Considering you haven't been to see me in over three weeks I think I have a right to summon you here."

Three weeks! He hadn't been to see her in more than three weeks. Since *they* had made love. Emily digested this news. She had been picturing Baxter laughing with his sweet little mistress about poor Emily, who probably thought that she had her husband back, but Baxter had not been to see Belle either. Did that mean he had a new mistress? What had he been doing for three weeks? Where had he been? Damn the man, anyway!

Baxter sat down at the opposite end of the sofa from Emily.

"That's better. Now, we'll have some tea and talk."

"Belle," started Baxter.

She held up one tiny hand as the maid came in with a tray of refreshments. "I could order chocolate, if you prefer?"

"No. Tea is good. I have been suffering a bout of indigestion the last couple of days, and tea is the only thing that settles me." She glared at Baxter. "I haven't been sleeping at all well!"

"Well." Belle glanced from one of her guests to the other. "Well."

There was an awkward pause.

"Emily, will you pour some tea?" Belle asked. "Nothing in mine, thank you."

Emily presided over the tea tray and dispensed a cup to them each, even though she knew that Baxter did not enjoy tea. She purposely added cream and sugar as well, because when he did drink it, he drank it black.

"Thank you, Emily," he said, black eyes narrowed into slits. "How sweet of you to remember how I take it."

"I remember everything about you, Baxter, every detail, large and small." She met his eyes and glared.

Again Belle glanced from one to the other, finally sensing the antagonism in the air. Well, what she had to tell them would solve things. She hoped. She was taking a dreadful chance, but if it worked out, then they could all be happy.

"I have called you both here with a proposition."

They gazed at her expectantly, and she shifted, patting down the pretty, conservative morning gown she wore, self-consciously smoothing it over her flat stomach.

"I have learned a lot in the last couple of months," she continued. She raised her chin and summoned her courage, hoping she could pull this off. She glanced over at Emily. "You still love your husband. If it hadn't of bin . . . if it hadn't been for your mother-in-law, you probably would never have separated from him."

She ignored Emily's choked swallowing of tea.

"And you! You didn't even have to say it," she continued, sadly, staring into Del's eyes. "I knew that you felt the same about your wife, especially when you told me you'd made love to her again. You two belong together, and I can give you the only thing you were missing during your marriage, the only thing that tore you apart.

"I am pregnant with your baby, Del, and I will give

him to you to raise as your heir on one condition. You two must get back together and raise him in a proper family, as his mother and father."

Twenty

Emily felt a wave of nausea pass over her and blackness threatened to engulf her. In a moment Baxter was beside her and she sagged against him.

"Damnation, Belle, did you have to be so blunt?" He held Emily close, pulling her onto his lap, cradling her to his chest. "And what the hell are you talking about? How . . . ? It's not possible . . . ."

Emily felt her husband's arms close around her in the black void, and she felt smothered. What was she going to do? Belle was with child, Baxter's child! She had been able to do what Emily in nearly ten years of trying had never been able to accomplish, and it hurt more than she had ever thought anything could, ever again. The sting pierced deep, deep into her womb where no life would ever grow. Belle—young, pretty, slender, fertile—everything she was not and never would be . . . .

Emily struggled to free herself from Baxter's grasp and stumbled to her feet in an uncharacteristically inelegant movement. "I have . . . I have to go, I have to . . ." She raced from the town house, hearing the voice of the maid floating after her, asking if she wanted her carriage. She needed to get away, to walk. She escaped down an alleyway, determined to evade Baxter. He would follow her—somehow she knew it—but she needed to be alone, and so she tripped down unfamiliar backstreets, behind houses, through odorous lanes.

And then she walked. She walked through parks and

streets, ignoring sound and sight and smell. She walked through Hyde Park, ignoring the stares of passers-by, their shock at seeing a woman of quality unaccompanied writ on their faces, and to the Serpentine, where she sat on a bench, staring with sightless eyes at the calm gray surface of the water. But her mind seemed to race in circles, with agony and a ripping sensation of betrayal at the base of every thought.

Belle, with Baxter's child in her womb. It was too much to bear.

Hours later, with no more idea what to do than she had when she left Belle's parlor, Emily approached Delafont House. Dodo must have been on the watch, because she bolted out of the front door and down the steps, her speed belying her age.

"Emily, my dear! I have been worried sick about you! Your groom came back hours ago after trying to find you, and Del has been here three times! He wouldn't tell me a thing! Where have you been? What . . ."

"Dodo, please," Emily said, holding out one hand. Her aunt by marriage grasped it and helped her up the steps. "I'm so tired. I just need to go to bed and get some sleep and then I'll tell you everything. I promise. All I need is some sleep, and then to come to terms with what has happened. I will be going back to Yorkshire very soon now. Tell the servants, please."

But when was life ever so simple, she thought, two days later, pacing in her room. She had thought a good sleep and some time to think were all she needed, that she would be able to ingest the changes in her life and deal with them, but she still felt as sick and anxious and nauseous as she had two days before. Dodo, appalled when Emily told her the truth of what had happened, had recommended sending her nephew "to the devil," as she put it. Of course that sage advice did not help her one bit. What should she be feeling? What should she be thinking?

She was reconciled to the notion that Belle could give Baxter what he needed, and she acquitted the girl of any underhanded motives. Baxter should indeed take the baby, since it was his and he did need an heir, especially with the revelations about the French branch of the family. Etienne was dead, but who else was there and where would they spring from? The best insurance against that kind of insecurity was a direct heir to the Sedgely title. It was unconventional but not unheard of for a man to take his illegitimate child as his heir. He *could* make it legal.

But Belle had very firmly stated that she wanted Emily and Baxter to raise the baby together, and she didn't think she could do that. Every day she would be faced by the image of Belle in her child, and her and Baxter's reunion would be in name only, for the sake of the child, because he clearly did not love her, not if he could so easily stay away from her for so long after they had enjoyed such an ecstatic physical reunion. She had thought it signaled some new beginning in their relationship, but it must not have meant as much to him as it had to her. What was she going to do?

"*Merci,* Sylvie," Baxter said, placing a coin in the Frenchwoman's outstretched hand. "I will take it from here." He watched her slip back down the hallway and gazed at the door.

Emily was in there, he could hear the rustle of her skirts. It sounded like she was pacing. He had said some terrible things to her and could not really blame her for refusing to see him, with this mess that Belle had created hanging over them. He had come to Delafont House every few hours for the last two days, but still she wouldn't see him. Dodo had frostily told him that Emily was making herself sick with worry and pacing, and that seeing him would only make matters worse. It was clear that Emily had told her some part of what had happened from her grim expression and cold eyes. She had never thought much of him since he was a lad, but now he was irrevocably sunk in her estimation, he feared.

But he didn't give a damn what his aunt thought of him. He would not explain himself to her. How to make things right with Emily—that was of paramount importance in his mind and heart.

He pushed open the door and gazed at Emily, who leaned against the window gazing out on the cloudy spring day. Her rounded figure, a little slimmer than she had been a month or so ago when he had first caught sight of her, was clad in a rose-and-white-striped day gown, and she clutched her stomach as though she was in pain. She held a little bisque figurine, stroking it with her fingers, rubbing her thumb over it. She hadn't heard him yet.

How many times lately had he thought to himself, if only she hadn't had that affair with the damned Frenchman . . . . He could not forget it, though he didn't know if his worst feeling was jealousy or hurt pride. But he still loved her. In the week or so he had spent at Brockwith, with every memory around him of places they had talked, walked, made love, it had come to him that he had never stopped loving her, he had just been in turns angry, alienated, unhappy and resentful. But never had he actually fallen out of love with her. The time they had wasted! Years spent away from each other when they should have been solving their problems, problems that seemed so petty in retrospect but had loomed so large at the time.

If only they had turned to each other instead of away from each other. If only . . .

But all the "if onlys" in the world would not change things now. What could he do? He had said some terrible things to her, had been unbelievably brutal. Why was it that it was only with the woman he loved more than life itself that he could become so angry? Was it because only her love mattered, only what she thought about him, felt for him, that could affect him so deeply?

She might never forgive him, but perhaps it was time to put all of the complications aside and decide once and for all—did they love one another enough to get past all of that? Did she love him enough to forgive him for things he had said and done, like abandoning her after making love to her? Did he love her enough to forget about her affair with Etienne? It wouldn't be easy, but he rather thought that he was killing himself slowly with jealousy, when he should be putting what must have been a brief affair into perspective, given his own long history of mistresses since their separation.

She turned and started. "Baxter! What are you doing here?" She clutched the tiny figurine to her bosom.

He launched into speech, not sure how long she would allow him before having him thrown out. "We have to settle things between us, Emily. I've behaved badly, brutally, and I want to apologize. I said things and did things . . . . But it's just that I've never stopped loving you, and when I found out you were having an affair with that damnably young and handsome Frenchman, it almost killed me. It hurt so very deeply, I wanted to murder him, and I wanted to wound you in return for the pain I was feeling."

There. It was out, all his jealousy and vulnerability, what amounted to an admission of weakness.

"Affair? You love me? Baxter, what are you talking about?" Her lovely face was puckered into a puzzled frown.

He moved into the room and stood staring at her, drinking in her brown eyes, shadowed with pain right now, and the lips he loved kissing so much. He badly wanted to touch her, to hold her, to take her to bed even, but there was much to sort out. The merely physical must wait this time. Lovemaking could ease the pain, but right now he must feel the anguish and deal with it and put it behind them. He glanced down, recognizing finally, as she set it on the table near her, the figurine she had been stroking. It was the tiny Dresden shepherdess he had given her years ago, for some forgotten anniversary or birthday.

"Your affair with Etienne," he said. He couldn't even say the name without pain. "I . . . I have never considered murder before, but I did when he told me about it. I have been consumed with the most bitter jealousy! A black mist descended, and I felt like my insides were being wrenched from my gut while I watched and felt every awful tear! I wanted to kill him, and I would have challenged him—considered it, even—but it would have destroyed your reputation, and even in my anger I loved you too much for that."

"He told you we were having an affair?" Emily's tone was incredulous.

"He did, the arrogant pup! And I saw you disappear with him to the conservatory, and you looked as guilty as hell, madam!" Consciously he relaxed his balled fists and stifled his anger, tamping it down with an enormous effort. He must learn to get past it, no matter how difficult that was, if he was ever to have her back, and he knew now that he wanted that, needed it. And after all, Etienne was dead and could never come between them now. "I did not come here today to accost you about that, though. I . . . I still love you, and I will try my damndest to forget the image of you making love with that . . . . Oh, God, Em, I haven't known what to do. I . . ." He drove his long fingers through his immaculately styled hair and strode across the room to her, but in the end he just stood in front of her, not touching her, not holding her as he longed to.

She faced him and put her hands on his shoulders, gazing up at him with an unexpectedly mischievous glint in eyes the color of brown pansies after spring rain. "Oh, my darling, beloved, *maddening* husband, that poor young man used the oldest trick in the book to rid himself of the man he must have known was his only competition. He lied to you. Told you an enormous bouncer, probably thinking it would be true before long."

"He . . ." Baxter gazed down into her eyes, searching for the truth. "He wasn't your lover?"

"No! Oh, he tried, and I thought about it."

His eyes glinted dangerously and she hastily added, "Not very seriously! He never did more than kiss me, Baxter, and after being loved by you, it seemed dreadfully pallid and tame. How could a mere child compare to the man I married?"

It never occurred to him not to believe her. Emily had always been honest to a fault; it was part of her as much as the color of her eyes or shape of her face. She valued honesty above almost everything else. He caught her to him then and kissed her until she was breathless. When he released her she was quivering and touched her lips with a trembling hand.

"See what I mean?" she said, laughing shakily. "How could anyone affect me after you?"

He pulled her back and lowered his head, touching her lips with his tenderly, reverently. He kissed her deeply, savoring her passionate response. When he released her, he said, "I was so angry and jealous! I just couldn't get over the image of you sneaking off to that conservatory with that damned Frenchman. I put all my fury into making love to you at that inn; I wanted to teach you the difference between a man and a boy."

"And you did," she murmured, clinging to him. "Magnificently and repeatedly, if memory serves. If there had ever been any doubt, it would have been erased that night. But there was never any doubt in my mind and in my heart. You are still, Baxter, the only man who has ever touched me. That night in the conservatory, I was trying to find out who Etienne really was. I was afraid he was the one trying to harm you, and I was so worried about—"

"My love, you do not have to explain anything. I believe you. Nothing happened."

"I can't believe the trouble he caused just because he wanted to take me to bed!"

"I can understand his motives," Del said, smiling down

at her. His expression became more serious, though, and he said, "What are we going to do, my love? What do you want? I was breaking things off with Belle, you know, before this occurred. I have bought and deeded her the house she is living in as a farewell but . . . ."

Emily drew away from Baxter and looked up into his eyes.

He launched into speech again, afraid of what she would say next. "I sent my mother back to Bath, too, with the threat that if she ever interferes in our lives again, I will disown her."

Emily chuckled, then sobered. She hadn't known what she would say before this second, but she knew now and with her whole heart. She leaned back and looked up into his eyes. "Baxter Eggleton Godfrey Delafont, fifth Marquess of Sedgely, I love you. I have always loved you and only you. I don't think I understood it until this moment, but I could never turn away any child of yours. It may be hard, and I can't say I will always be successful, but if you would like to try and if it is what Belle really wants, I will raise the child with you and love it as if it were my own."

Staring down at her, Baxter's dark eyes cleared and all the pain drained from his lean, saturnine face. "Oh, Emily, brave Emily! My love . . ." He nestled her back in his arms, close to his heart. "My love, there *is* no baby."

"There . . . there is no baby? Did she lose it? Oh, poor girl, I must go to her, I must—"

"No!" He held her fast against his heart, his love for the woman in his arms a wave of deep devotion that welled and surged like a tide. "No, my love. There never was a baby. It was all a charade. Belle was trying to force us to reconcile, and she took the only means she could imagine. She intended to get pregnant, thinking to give me an heir, but I have not been with her since returning to England. Never once have I made love to her. I only wanted to end things, but I did not want to hurt her. She *thought* she had made love with me one night, though, when she was . . . well, she was drunk, so she pretended to be pregnant. Belle wanted me to be happy, and she came to understand, after meeting you, that the only way I would ever be truly happy again was if I could have you back. She thought if she could force us to agree to get back together again for the sake of a baby, we would . . . we would love each other again. She was crushed by your reaction, poor girl, but she is beginning to understand, I think."

She had listened in absolute stillness, but a lump choked Emily's throat. Her world, so wrong a scant few minutes before, had revolved and become right. "That dear, sweet girl! Oh, Baxter, I . . ."

She stopped, her face an interesting shade of pale green.

"Emily? Em, my love, what is wrong?"

She broke away from her husband and, clutching her stomach, raced to the basin on the washstand. The only other sound from her was a deep moan as she quite thoroughly cast up her accounts.

Epilogue

A glorious summer had adorned the English country-side with a rainbow array of flowers and the tender green of leaves, golden sun and a brilliant blue sky. At Brockwith in Surrey crops were planted, grown and harvested, and as the grain ripened and the fruit grew full and plump on the vine, so Emily blossomed with the life she and her husband had started with love and passion.

And yet Baxter and Emily's anxious time was not quite over. Her doctor, concerned with her paleness and her inability to keep down anything but the most bland of foods, had ordered her to bed, for her sake and for the life in her womb. And so her world had shrunk to her pretty rose bedchamber, where she lay in bed, wistfully gazing out at the wide world beyond the window, the countryside where she loved to wander but now could not.

"I wish I could go into the garden," Emily said, glancing slyly over to her husband who sat at her side reading from *Mansfield Park*, a novel by her favorite author.

Baxter sighed and gave her a stern look. He set the book aside and took her hand in his. "My love, you know that is not possible. The doctor said . . ."

"The doctor said, the doctor said! Oh, Baxter, I am so restless!" She lay back and stared at the ceiling. "I have been in bed two weeks, and I already think I shall go mad. I want to walk in the garden. I want to go down to the stream where we used to go fishing and make love all afternoon. I want . . ." Her voice choked off and tears oozed from under her sealed lids.

Moving up to sit on the bed beside her, Baxter gazed down at his wife. The doctor had explained that mood changes, sometimes rather abrupt, were quite normal in a woman who was with child, but it stabbed a pain deep through his heart to see her unhappy. He rested one hand on her swollen belly, still holding her hand in the other. "My sweet, this is just a precaution. You know the doctor said he sees no trouble with you giving birth, if you are just cautious for these last months. T'will only be a few more months before the babe—or babies—is born."

Emily's eyes flew open. "Oh, Baxter! Do you think we might have twins, as the doctor says?" Her face was wreathed in smiles even as the tears dribbled down her cheeks. "Just the thought of that gives me patience, my dear. I would bring our little ones into the world in lusty health if I can, at my advanced age!" She laughed.

He leaned over and planted a kiss on her rosy lips, letting it deepen into as passionate a sign of his devotion as he dared, given that there would be no easing of desire—not with her less than three months from birth and in such delicate health.

"Ehem, I hope we do not interrupt?"

Baxter turned on the bed. "Less! As I live and breathe! And you have brought Belle with you! Welcome to you both." He moved so Emily could see their visitors, standing hesitantly in the doorway.

Struggling to sit up, Emily motioned them into the room. "Come, both of you! Oh, how good to see you both! You must tell me all the news from London, and how your new play goes on, and who has taken who as lover, and . . . and everything!"

"My lady is bored to tears," Baxter said dryly, taking Less's hand and shaking it, then kissing Belle's proffered hand. He slipped from the bed. "I shall return in a moment, but I think I will have tea brought in, and see that rooms are readied for you both."

Emily looked up at her guests and then blushed, glancing ruefully at her swollen belly and the bed. "I would get up and receive you properly, but my husband would be most upset. I have been ordered to bed. How are you both?" She examined them anxiously. Less, she thought, looked a little sad behind his smile, but Belle was more serene and self-possessed than she had ever seen her. The girl was dressed modishly in a pale-gold traveling gown with brown velvet trim; much better taste governed her attire now than in the past. It seemed that Less, an infallible arbiter of refinement where women's apparel was concerned, had been advising her. From his recent letters it was apparent that he was quickly revising his previous low opinion of her. They had become friends as well as employer and actress.

Less smiled down at Emily and took her hand. "I am well. And Belle is blooming." He put his free arm around the girl's shoulders and gave her an affectionate, brotherly hug.

Emily smiled, remembering when he had disparaged her as a little tart with no conversation.

"How are you, my lady?" Belle asked, her piquant, narrow face lit with a sweet smile.

"Emily. Call me Emily, Belle. I will be fine, once I have this child or children." She moved restlessly. "You will stay, won't you? You will visit us for a while? Please?"

Less and Belle exchanged glances.

"We'll stay a while, my dear," Less said. "For we have much to discuss. A new show, a touring theater group with Belle as the star performer. We are going to the Continent for the winter."

"How exciting!"

"Our new production will not be half as exciting as this one," Less said, laying a gentle hand on her stomach, covered in a soft rose coverlet. He sighed. "This is the one thing I will miss about never getting married. I will have to visit often and become your brood's favorite bachelor uncle."

"Godfather, Less, you are to be the babies' godfather!" Her heart broke at the sadness in his eyes, but he was who he was, and she could not condemn any person for whom or how they loved. He was the gentlest of souls, and she loved him like the brother she had never had. "I am selfish enough to be glad for my babies' sake that you will concentrate all your love on our children. They will be quite spoiled."

"I hope you have girls," Belle said, softly. She glanced around the room. "They will be so lucky to grow up here, and with . . . with you as their mother. I . . . I never knew my mother."

Emily put out her hand and took hers, pulling her closer to the bed. The girl seemed almost shy today, a little dazzled by Brockwith, perhaps, or by what could be a very awkward situation. Baxter had told her much about Belle since coming back to Brockwith—how he found her, how hard she had worked to better herself given the opportunity—and everything he had said just confirmed that she must be a very strong young woman to have survived what she had, and be, at the core of her, so loyal and giving.

"I don't think I ever had the opportunity to thank you for what you did for us," Emily said, gazing into the girl's cornflower blue eyes. "If it hadn't been for you, we might never have come together again."

"But I wouldn't even have thought about it if you hadn't come to me out of your concern for Del! And I was so awkward . . . caused you so much pain . . . ." She trailed off and looked away.

She had long since apologized for shocking Emily so with her offer, almost in tears that she could have been the cause of Emily losing the life that was just starting within her. She had only done what she thought was best, but she admitted that it had been a strange scheme at best.

"I wish I could repay Del for everything he has done for me, mostly for introducing me to Sylvester," she said, taking Less's arm in her own.

Emily smiled up at the two of them. What an odd pair! Bound only by their love of the theater, she had originally thought, but she began to think that they were learning to genuinely like each other. If circumstances were different, she would be hoping for wedding bells, but . . . well, best not to wish for the impossible. She would be happy that they both seemed to be finding peace at last.

"Enough of that. We have all been exceedingly lucky. Now tell me about this traveling troupe," she said, indicating the chairs that were nearby. They sat, and Belle became most animated talking about her part as Kate in *Shrew* and how she was to reprise that role as they traveled through France and Italy.

Baxter came back, followed quickly by footmen with tea trays and they had a merry half hour over tea. But finally Baxter, glancing over at Emily, saw that her eyes were becoming heavy with fatigue.

He leaped to his feet and said, "We must let our guests have a chance to settle in, my love. I will show them to their rooms while the footmen clear away the tea things."

Drowsily, Emily waved good-bye. "I insist on at least a week or two's visit," she said. "You have quite lifted me out of my doldrums already."

She turned on her side as the door closed quietly behind the last of the servants and gazed out the window at the verdant countryside, starting to tinge ochre and umber with fall. In the distance she could see oxen pulling a cart through a field as workmen loaded sun-ripened grain. She rested her hand on her stomach and thought about the miracle of her life. Why, she had asked the elderly Brockwith doctor, had she suddenly conceived when she and her husband had tried for almost ten years to have children and had not been able to?

There was no real explanation, the old man had said, shrugging and closing his bag. Perhaps a condition that had prevented conception had corrected itself in the interim, or mayhap it was just chance. To herself Emily had giggled and thought maybe it had more to do with three energetic bouts of lovemaking in one night, for that was the night she conceived. The doctor had interrupted her naughty musings, going on to say that he had seen many cases where a couple, longing for a child for years, had finally given up, and *then* conceived.

In any case it was a miracle and she would cherish this time, even if she was restless and impatient from being confined to bed. She had teased her husband that if they wanted more children he would have to store up his energy to repeat his feat of the night at the inn. With a shiver of desire she remembered his answer. A smoldering look in his coal-black eyes, he had said that he didn't think that would be a problem. Maybe they would do that a few times, just to ensure a repeat of this experiment.

She glanced up to find that he stood in the doorway gazing at her, the harsh lines and angry look of past months gone permanently, to be replaced by contentment and a tranquillity she had never known him to have. He had released his anger and found peace. Her heart swelled with love, and she felt like she would burst with the joy that had come to them since making a pact to never let doubt or distrust separate them again. She felt equal to the task, because she would always remember the years without him and the time before that, filled with doubt and anger and pain. She never wanted to go back to that, and she would fight to hold together a marriage all the more precious for the years wasted.

He came to her and sat up beside her on the bed. He placed one hand on her swollen belly, and threaded the fingers of his other hand through her loose hair, down in waves around her shoulders. They sat in silence as Emily drowsed, their union perfect in silence.

The long months since they had reunited had not been without struggle. Baxter, with the new responsibilities of fatherhood impending, had had to extricate himself from his dangerous job with the government. He had reassured her that there was no connection now and no further danger to him; his duty was done and now others could carry on.

Though the full story was hazy at best, it was concluded that Etienne had intended to kill Baxter for the title and the inheritance. It was known that he was aware of his position and had deliberately concealed his identity, so it seemed the only logical answer, even though one puzzling aspect remained unsolved—he had *not* killed Baxter when he had had the chance.

While Baxter was busy in London, tying up loose ends, Emily and Dodo had gone with May in late spring and seen her settled at Lark House near the Dover coast. She was now, from her letters, happily engaged in setting up a school for the village children, to start after harvest, and planning new gardens and new vistas for her home. Dodo had volunteered to stay with her a while, until May felt secure again. In her last letter, Dodo had said that she thought May would do just fine, that in fact she seemed to have new interests and spent a great deal of every day away from Lark House and that it was time she, Dodo, returned to Brockwith so she could be with Emily during her confinement.

Celestine and Justin had returned from the Continent, as their letter had intimated, and had just welcomed into the world Colin Joshua St. Claire, heir to their estate of Questmere in Cumbria. Celestine must have become pregnant immediately, almost on their wedding night. If Emily hadn't been so heavily gravid herself, she would have gone to her niece, but Baxter convinced her that her job right now was to rest, and take care of their baby or babies.

She opened her eyes to find Baxter's steady gaze still on her. Her heart throbbed as it always did when he looked at her with that love shining from his eyes, bathing her in warmth. She was so lucky, and she knew it. She had even made a tentative move toward peace with her mother-in-law. Marie would ever be an interfering, tactless harpy, but now, secure in her husband's love and with the knowledge that she was first in his heart and mind, Emily disregarded the woman's waspishness. It had come to her one day that Marie had never learned how to be happy, and that was a sad thing. She was so fortunate to have rediscovered, before it was too late, that happiness came with love and compromise and hope for the future. She felt sorry for Marie.

"I love you," Emily whispered, sleepily.

"You are my life," he whispered back, and bent down and kissed her tenderly.

ABOUT THE AUTHOR

Donna Simpson lives with her family in Canada. She is currently working on her next Zebra regency romance *Lady May's Folly,* which will be published in February 2001. Donna loves to hear from her readers, and you may write to her c/o Zebra Books. Please include a self-addressed stamped envelope if you wish a reply.

Put a Little Romance in Your Life With
Constance O'Day-Flannery

__**Bewitched**	**$5.99**US/**$7.50**CAN
0-8217-6126-9	
__**The Gift**	**$5.99**US/**$7.50**CAN
0-8217-5916-7	
__**Once in a Lifetime**	**$5.99**US/**$7.50**CAN
0-8217-5918-3	
__**Second Chances**	**$5.99**US/**$7.50**CAN
0-8217-5917-5	
—**This Time Forever**	**$5.99**US/**$7.50**CAN
0-8217-5964-7	
__**Time-Kept Promises**	**$5.99**US/**$7.50**CAN
0-8217-5963-9	
__**Time-Kissed Destiny**	**$5.99**US/**$7.50**CAN
0-8217-5962-0	
__**Timeless Passion**	**$5.99**US/**$7.50**CAN
0-8217-5959-0	

Call toll free **1-888-345-BOOK** to order by phone, use this coupon to order by mail, or order online at **www.kensingtonbooks.com**.

Name _____

Address _____

City_____ State _____ Zip _____

Please send me the books I have checked above.

I am enclosing $_____

Plus postage and handling* $_____

Sales tax (in New York and Tennessee only) $_____

Total amount enclosed $_____

*Add $2.50 for the first book and $.50 for each additional book.

Send check or money order (no cash or CODs) to:

Kensington Publishing Corp., Dept C.O., 850 Third Avenue, 16th Floor, New York, NY 10022

Prices and numbers subject to change without notice.

All orders subject to availability.

Visit our website at **www.kensingtonbooks.com**.

Put a Little Romance in Your Life With
Betina Krahn

More Zebra Regency Romances

DO YOU HAVE THE HOHL COLLECTION?